Playing by the Rules

BEVERLY BIRD

Silhouette®

SPECIAL EDITION™

Published by Silhouette Books

America's Publisher of Contemporary Romance

SILHOUETTE BOOKS

ISBN 0-373-24529-7

PLAYING BY THE RULES

Copyright © 2003 by Beverly Bird

This edition published by arrangement with Harlequin Books S.A.

® and TM are trademarks of Harlequin Books S.A., used under license.
Trademarks indicated with ® are registered in the United States Patent
and Trademark Office, the Canadian Trade Marks Office and in other
countries.

Visit Silhouette at www.eHarlequin.com

Printed in U.S.A.

Chapter One

The last time things were normal between Sam and me, we were fighting in Judge Larson's courtroom.

We're lawyers. At least, *I'm* a lawyer. Sam Case is more like a world-class actor with a law degree. He lulls the opposition into a false sense of security by coming off as overly polite and just a little slow-witted. He's transplanted from south Texas, land of drawling cowboys and good tequila, so he can get away with it. He cultivates an impression of bemused confusion at our East Coast aggression, and it always seems to work.

Judge Larson should have been wise to his tricks by now because he'd been appearing before her for the better part of six months. But she was a pretty blonde on her third marriage—having sacrificed her first two husbands in the interest of her career, or so rumor had it—and Sam likes blondes. Ergo, Larson likes Sam. It's virtually impossible not to like Sam once he decides that you're on his list of favorite people.

The judge gave him a dopey smile. It's my firm opinion that no one ought to be allowed to simper while seated on the bench, but she did it, anyway.

"You have a point to make, Counselor?" she asked him.

"Well, something sort of occurred to me, Your Honor." He swiveled on his heels to languidly look my way. Languid was part of the whole performance. "I believe my adversary's chief argument is that a full-time mother is preferable to a half-time father. Is that about right, Ms. Hillman?"

I stood. "A full-time mother is preferable to a *twenty-five*-percent father. *That's* my premise."

"Hey, where did my other twenty-five percent go?" He sounded genuinely injured.

I stepped around the defense table and moved closer to him, then I spoke in a hiss meant for his ears alone. "My guess would be down your client's throat." I turned my attention back to the judge with a polite smile. "Mr. Woodsen has a drinking problem, Your Honor. This has been established. Until he gets treatment, the children are better off with their mother as the custodial parent. We're willing to grant ample visitation, provided it's supervised, but Mrs. Woodsen simply isn't comfortable with her children spending overnights with Mr. Woodsen when no other responsible adult is present."

"No *other* responsible adult?" Sam grabbed that one quickly. "Your Honor, I do believe she just called my client responsible."

"No, I did not."

"Yes, you did."

I rolled over him before he could finish turning everything around on me, shoving a shoulder in front of him so

I stood between him and the judge. "Lyle Woodsen is anything *but* responsible, Judge. There's every possibility that he wouldn't be coherent or capable during his parenting time."

"Pshaw," I heard Sam say in an undertone.

I wheeled on him in disbelief. "What?"

His eyes widened innocently. "I didn't say anything."

"You said *pshaw*. Is that a Deep-South word or something?"

"I don't know," Sam protested. "They sure don't say it in Texas."

"People, please," Larson interrupted. "This is a courtroom."

This time Sam stepped around me to speak earnestly to the judge. "Mr. Woodsen isn't comfortable with his children spending unsupervised overnights with their mother, either. She has that—how can I put this delicately?—rather complex sense of self."

A rather *what?* I felt tension wrap around my spine. "Be more specific," I snarled, nudging him aside again so I could see the judge, too.

"It's my understanding that Lisa Woodsen has spent a good part of the last several years undergoing vigorous psychiatric treatment," he said.

Drugs, I thought. It had to be drugs. He'd need something worse than Lyle's alcoholism, and that would do it.

I went back to my table and sat again, feeling a headache coming on. I glared at him, trying to figure out what he had up his sleeve and why I hadn't been aware that there was *anything* there until just this moment. Sam crossed his arms over his chest and watched me right back. If he smirked, I would have to wipe the floor with his face, I decided.

"I have no idea what he's talking about, Your Honor," I said finally. And, oh, how it rankled to have to admit it.

Judge Larson sighed gustily. "Mr. Case, I like you. I genuinely do." There's a revelation, I thought. "But I don't like you well enough to overlook your generous use of evidentiary loopholes. Even in divorce court, we have such a thing as discovery."

Hallelujah.

Then Sam turned a soulful gaze on the judge. The man had blue eyes that could charm Satan, and a crooked smile that could melt that same black soul. He'd just broken the most basic court rule in the book, and I was pretty sure he'd done it intentionally, yet he managed to look abashed and a bit confused. "Gosh, Your Honor. I'm sorry."

Gosh? I choked, and—predictably—Larson forgave him.

"Very well," she said, "but I'm still going to adjourn these proceedings until Friday to give the defense a chance to catch up."

As slaps on the wrist went, it was relatively minor, but I consoled myself with the fact that at least it was something. The judge banged her gavel and rose neatly from the bench. I waited. It took Sam no more than a minute to clear his client out of the courtroom.

I shifted in my seat to look at Lisa Woodsen. "So how right is he?" I asked her.

"A little."

I felt my headache pop behind my eyes, gaining life. "This isn't one of those gray areas in life, Lisa. Either you've had psychiatric treatment or you haven't."

"Well, then, yes. I did. Do. But I'm staying on my medication this time."

Medication. Oh, glory, I thought. "What's your problem exactly?"

"It's complicated."

"I can probably grasp it," I assured her.

"It's…well, a form of schizophrenia."

I folded my arms on the defense table and lowered my now-throbbing forehead against them. A complex sense of self, indeed! It wasn't drugs after all, but this was definitely worse than Lyle Woodsen's nightly twelve-pack-and-shooters habit.

Lisa Woodsen began to cry, so I lifted my head and dug a tissue out of my briefcase. In family law, tissues—along with candy, coloring books and trading cards—are crucial accessories. I raided my daughter's supplies with some regularity. So far Chloe hadn't caught on.

I spent another five minutes comforting the woman before we left the courtroom. When she'd passed through the heavy oak doors of the lobby into the blinding sunlight outside—for some reason the sun always shines brightly on the rotten moments of my life—I looked around for Sam.

I knew he would have waited for me, and he had. The sad truth was that he was my upstairs neighbor and my very best friend—platonically-speaking—to boot. All in all, that made it very hard for me to hate him on any kind of regular basis.

He stood beside the water fountain, leaning one nicely broad shoulder against the wall there. I bore down on him.

"You just talked your way right out of tonight's linguine and scampi, pal," I said.

He straightened from the wall and his eyes went as soft and hopeful as a puppy's. "You were going to make me scampi?"

"No. I was going to make Chloe and me scampi. I was going to let you have the leftovers. But now I've changed my mind."

"You're a hard woman, Amanda Hillman."

"Only when I've just been played for a fool."

"I thought Lisa had told you. I thought you were just holding it close to your vest and hoping I didn't find out."

"*You* were holding it close to *your* vest and hoping that *I* didn't find out." No wonder he hadn't wanted to bother with exchanging interrogatories, I thought. He'd said it would just run up the Woodsens' respective bills, and we both knew the couple couldn't afford that. But the simple act of having my client answer all those detailed questions would have revealed all sorts of vermin in the woodpile.

I rubbed my forehead.

"Another headache?" Sam asked.

"You gave it to me," I muttered.

"Lisa Woodsen gave it to you. She should have confided in you. And I keep telling you that your forehead isn't the root of the problem. It's the way your neck gets all knotted up. Turn around."

I wanted to be obstinate, but it would have been a little like cutting off my nose to spite my face. Sam has hands to die for.

I turned and gave him my back. His strong fingers flexed at the base of my skull and found all the tight spots down the line of my vertebrae. My headache waned even as something coiled in the pit of my stomach. This was a normal reaction to Sam's neck rubs that I had learned to ignore over the months. But this time I think I might have groaned aloud.

"Better?" he asked.

"Much. I'm still mad at you, though."

He laughed and his hands fell away. My loss. I turned to face him again.

His dark hair had fallen over his brow sometime during our long afternoon in court. Together with his just-slightly crooked, bad-boy grin, it gave him a rakish look. It was something else I'd noticed before and that I tried to disregard. As a general rule, it's not good to get all quivery inside over your best—platonic—friend.

"Our first priority should be those kids," I said finally, pulling myself back to business.

"Agreed. So share your scampi with me and we'll talk about it over dinner."

"No." I pivoted sharply and headed for the big oak doors and all that sunshine outside.

"I have a date, anyway!" he called after me.

I swung back to him. "That's two already this week, Sam. You've got an obsession going on here. Want me to ask Lisa Woodsen for the name of her shrink?"

"Hey, I'm busy looking for the wrong woman."

Which I knew he had found many, many times. More accurately, Sam didn't seem to want to find the *right* one. I put my back against the door and pushed it open.

"Good luck," I called back to him. "Maybe *she* can make you shrimp and linguine." I was all the way down the big stone steps outside before I shook my head and let myself laugh aloud.

"Sam again?" asked a voice from behind me.

I turned to find Grace Simkanian on my heels. Grace was also my neighbor. She lived one floor up from Sam in a one-bedroom unit she shared with Jenny Tower. They had to buddy-up to afford the place. Jenny was a waitress and Grace clerked for one of the criminal court judges. Law clerks are paid worse than volunteers, but they have very bright futures.

"Sam again," I agreed. I matched Grace's stride and we headed for the municipal lot. I always gave her a ride home when I was in court in the afternoon.

"When are you two going to stop fighting and start clawing each other's clothes off?" she asked.

My stomach lurched hard and suddenly. "There's a ridiculous notion."

"Ah. Clawing is beneath you."

That stopped me in my tracks. Grace headed on to my car without me.

"I claw," I protested finally, shouting after her.

Grace stopped at the trunk of my Mitsubishi and looked back at me. "When? Tell me the last time you even considered it."

I caught up with her and unlocked the trunk, and we tossed our briefcases inside. "Let me think."

"This will take a while."

The hell of it was, she was right. I was coming up empty. I hadn't had a date in six weeks and even then, Frank Ethan—the last guy—had definitely not been the clawing type.

"Well," I said finally, "I could claw if I wanted to." Then I frowned. "Why are we even discussing this?" I asked.

"Because I think you should be clawing with Sam. He's got the look of a man who'd be good at it."

There was that action with my stomach again. I was starting not to like this conversation. "Sam isn't interested in me that way." I wondered who he was seeing tonight, if it was the same voluptuous blonde from Monday.

"You're touching your hair again," Grace said. "What's that all about?"

I dropped my hand fast. "What?"

"Whenever you talk about him, you touch your hair."

"I do not." Then I thought about it. As I've mentioned, Sam has a strong preference for blondes. Specifically, he likes blondes with a lot of hair. Mine is short and black. I have that kind of face, with small features. Anything more would overpower me. I have that kind of life. I'm a single parent. I don't have time to fuss with voluminous layers.

My headache chose that moment to come back with an extra punch. "If you're that impressed with Sam, then why don't *you* claw with him?" I asked her.

Grace shrugged. "I scare him." She's sleek, sophisticated and sharp as a tack. She says what's on her mind and she makes no apologies for it. She's a stunning woman with reams of dark hair, a flawless dusky complexion, and the kind of figure that stops men dead in their tracks. Then they get to her mind, and that usually backs them off. At least it does if they have any sense.

"He tried to snuggle up to Jenny once, though," Grace said.

I frowned. This was the first I'd heard of it. Jenny is a sunny blonde transplanted from Kansas.

"What happened?" I asked.

"Nothing. *He* scares *her.*"

I nodded, understanding that, too. Jenny is waiting for Mr. Right. The last time I checked, her list of prerequisites had not included good-hearted wolves like Sam.

I opened my car door. "I want to go home now. I've had a long day."

"Let's go to McGlinchey's, instead," Grace suggested. Jenny worked at the bar there and would be getting off at five-thirty.

I looked at my watch and decided that I really didn't want to cook shrimp for two tonight after all. I took my cell phone out of my purse. "If Mrs. Casamento can keep Chloe an extra hour, then I'll go."

Grace settled into the passenger seat. Grace doesn't sit, she settles. It's a kind of gentle floating-down with her. Men tend to be very appreciative of the phenomenon.

I made the call to the baby-sitter as I got in the car with

a little less finesse. Sylvie Casamento keeps me on a short leash even as she laps up the money I pay her. Sam says it's her express purpose in life to ensure that no one she knows enjoys anything. No one except Sam, that is. Most women adore Sam, and Mrs. C. is no exception.

I got the okay from the baby-sitter, but not without a lot of aggrieved and chastening sighs over the fact that I might—heaven forbid—have a good time. I started the car. When I turned out of the parking lot, Sam was just stepping into the street. I stomped on the gas to pass him before I was tempted to run him over.

McGlinchey's was mobbed, as it usually is at that hour. The bar was crammed with enough bodies to rival a New York subway at rush hour. I was still trying to explain my feelings about clawing to Grace as we squeezed past a knot of people in animated conversation. They, too, were lawyers.

Philadelphia's legal community is incestuous. Don't get me wrong—we all know how to draw lines in the dirt and keep to our own side of them. Favors are owed, calculated and warily exchanged, but that occurs during regular business hours. The rest of the time, it's sort of a family affair. Many of us have, at some point in time, been married to a handful of the others. For example, Chloe's father is an attorney here in the city, though I pride myself on the fact that I had the good sense not to go tying any knots with him. But the bottom line is that everyone seems to know everyone else's personal business, and they talk about it.

As I shoved my way through the crowd, I saw too many considering expressions on faces I recognized. Here's Mandy, those expressions said, and she's with a female friend again.

I never considered myself exempt from the storytelling, but I *did* think I knew what they said about me: She's more interested in her career than in men. Chloe's father started that one. His name is Millson—Millson Kramer III. If he were going to be honest, he'd tell you that he was actually relieved when I refused to marry him. He was just ''doing the right thing'' by asking me in the first place. Right after Chloe was born, he suffered a hiccup of conscience and tried to make things neat and legal and tidy for all of us. I declined his offer, and that, of course, looked bad for him, so he saved face by informing Philadelphia's legal community that he had tried his best but that I was a cold and brittle workaholic.

I'm pretty sure that Frank Ethan—the last date I'd had six weeks ago—contributed to Mill's version of Mandy Hillman when I declined to go out with him a second time. There have been a few others like Frank over the years who've failed to excite me, so no doubt they've all tossed their two cents into the pot, as well. But I'm not cold. I just like my own company. And your perspective on these things changes when you pass that milestone of turning thirty-five, which I had just done. You don't need to claw quite as much.

''When you're in your twenties, you're just seized by all the possibilities,'' I tried to explain to Grace as we waded through McGlinchey's clientele. For all her jaded world-wisdom, Grace is only twenty-six.

Someone nearly spilled a drink on her, and she curled a lip in the man's direction. He apologized profusely. ''What possibilities are those?'' she asked me.

''Sexual. Life advancement. Societal compliance.'' We finally reached the bar. I had to raise my voice to order. Then we began trolling for a table, each of us armed with a glass of Chardonnay.

At McGlinchey's, this is a game not unlike musical chairs. The trick is to be near a table when the inhabitants stand to go. It took us twenty minutes, but we managed it. Grace slipped into one of the vacated seats. Her stockings whispered as she crossed her legs. The noise level in McGlinchey's was at full throttle, but every male within a six-foot radius heard the sound. Heads ratcheted in Grace's direction.

"That," I said, looking around at their faces, "was the sexual part of it."

Grace shrugged. "It's the Pavlov syndrome, an automatic response to stimuli. It means nothing."

I pursued my point. "Anyway, when you're young, you're more inclined to settle into a relationship just because the sex is fantastic."

"That's a very good reason at any age, Mandy. Assuming one was the settling type."

"Over thirty-five, you're less likely to be satisfied by the sex alone," I insisted, sipping wine. "And you're less likely to hook up with someone for the express purpose of having children and raising a family. Most people take care of that issue in their twenties."

"Not so much in this day and age. Women are having their children later and later in life."

"I said *most,* not all." I held up a three fingers. "Third, you're also not likely to settle down in your thirties just because it makes it easier to get a mortgage. You've probably already done that, too."

"*You* haven't."

"I live in Philadelphia. Real estate is ridiculously expensive."

"So move out of the city."

"I love the city. What number was I up to?"

"Four."

I nodded. "Last but not least, you're also less likely to

take a mate just because society is geared almost exclusively toward couples.''

''That's the compliance part?''

''Yes. So you see, if you hook up with someone once you get past thirty-five, I think you do it for the purest of reasons. Compatibility. Comfort. Conversation. Then throw in a little lust for fun and games. The whole situation becomes easy and noncombative. You don't fall into a relationship for what the guy can give you, because you've probably already gotten it for yourself. You don't have the need to demand anymore. You can just accept.''

Grace swallowed wine. ''Oh, joy. I can hardly wait. Does this come hand in hand with crow's feet?''

I ignored that. ''It's why I don't date…much,'' I explained. ''And why I don't have an overriding need to claw.''

''Because you've already got a child, you don't want a mortgage and you don't care what people think anymore?''

''In a nutshell, yes. I can afford to be selective now, so I am.''

Grace put her wineglass on the table and leaned forward. ''Mandy. You haven't dated lately because you spend all your free time with Sam. Let's not lie to each other here.''

My spine jerked straight, hard enough and suddenly enough to hurt a little. ''That's not true.''

''What's not?'' Jenny Tower asked, flopping into one of the chairs. By the way she shifted her weight in her seat, I knew she was toeing her shoes off under the table. She looked tired.

''Mandy doesn't date because she's too busy hanging out with Sam,'' Grace said.

''It's my choice!'' I was going to get that through to her if it killed me. ''I can afford to wait for compatibility, comfort and conversation because I'm thirty-five!''

Jenny took her apron off and laid it on her lap, pulling a wad of tips from the pocket. She started sorting the ones from the fives. "I don't ever want to be that old."

"It's better than dying young," Grace said, "but barely." Then she grabbed the money from Jenny's hand. "Honey, you're not in Kansas anymore."

Jenny looked around the bar and blinked as though coming out of a dream. If there's anyone in the world more trusting than Jenny is, then it would have to be Toto himself—and even Toto had the good sense to bark at that goofy wizard. "You think someone's going to snatch it right out of my hand?" she asked disbelievingly.

Grace took the hand in question and pressed the money back into it, folding Jenny's fingers over it. "Call me mercenary, but our rent is due in two weeks."

Jenny sighed and pushed the money into her jeans pocket. "Okay. I'll count it later. Let's get back to why Mandy doesn't date."

I launched into my theory again. "I haven't met anyone recently who particularly inspires me, and I don't need all those other things I was mentioning—the mortgage and whatnot—so I won't tolerate someone who *doesn't* inspire me."

"Which brings us back to Sam," Grace said. She cut a look at Jenny. "We were talking about clawing his clothes off, at which point Mandy went off into this business about relationships at a certain age. Compatibility. Comfort. Conversation. Wait, what was the other thing you mentioned?" She glanced at me again and tapped a finger against her cheek exaggeratedly. "Ah. Now I remember. Lust."

"Lust is good," Jenny contributed. "But I agree, the other things matter a whole lot, too."

"You and Sam are compatible," Grace continued, still aiming her words at me. "You're comfortable with each other. The conversation between you is great—just ask any of us who've ever tried to horn in on it. Therefore, according to everything you just told me, the progression is obvious. You two ought to be having sex.''

I opened my mouth to argue and realized that I had just been boxed in by my own theory. Grace was going to make one hell of a lawyer when she finished clerking for the criminal court judge.

Then she sat up a little straighter and looked over my shoulder. I turned in my chair and followed her gaze and my pulse hiccuped.

Sam had just arrived. He was standing at the bar.

Chapter Two

"Who's that with him?" Jenny asked, leaning forward at our table to check out the situation.

My gaze hitched to Sam's left. It was the woman he'd taken out Monday night. Surprise—she had a *lot* of hair and all of it was blond. "I think he said she works for Fox, Murray and Myers," I said. "She's a receptionist."

"She looks like a bimbo," Grace observed.

My gaze dropped to her not insignificant bosom. "I don't think he wants her for her mind."

Then, as though my attention had drawn his, Sam looked around and saw us. He grinned at me and picked up his scotch-and-water from the bar. I knew it was scotch because that was pretty much all he ever drank—Glenlivet specifically. With his glass in one hand and the blonde's elbow in his other, he began steering her toward our table.

Jenny ogled them. "He's bringing her *here?* He's bringing his date to sit with Mandy?"

"He probably wants my stamp of approval," I murmured.

"You two are strange," Jenny said.

"We're *friends*. Just friends. Why is that so hard for you people to wrap your minds around?"

Grace watched them approach as well. "His bimbo isn't happy," she decided.

I agreed. The blonde's jaw seemed a little too set, her eyes too narrow.

Sam finished propelling her toward our table. He pulled out the last chair for her and snagged a seat from the next table for himself, then he placed it on the opposite side of the table from the bombshell.

"This is Tammy," he said. He deposited his glass on the table and shifted his chair to face mine. "I had a thought on our Woodsen stalemate. What we need to do is get them back together. They're shaky parents individually, but as a team they might be almost solid. Especially if we can convince Larson to appoint some kind of supervisor to look in on them from time to time. I think Lyle has a sister who lives something like two doors down."

I opened my mouth, shut it, then tried again. On the second effort, I found words. "Where do you get these ideas? We're *divorce* lawyers, Sam. We're supposed to break people up. It's what we get paid for."

"I'll kick in my fee if you do."

"I *can't* kick mine in. I have partners to report to." I was being cranky. I was still stinging from what he'd sprung on me in court.

"Just give it some thought," he urged. "We should try to save them for the kids' sake. Besides, I believe strongly in the sanctity of marriage."

I snorted. "Unless it's your own."

I realized too late that his ex-marital status wasn't common knowledge. The look Jenny gave him was amazed. I could only imagine that having traipsed down the aisle once in his life lent Sam a little more potential in her eyes.

"You were married?" she asked quickly. "I never knew that."

Sam cast me a wounded look. "I left McAllen, Texas, after my divorce and came here. It was too painful to stay."

Jenny's gaze went kind and misty. In a moment, I thought, she would begin stroking his hair and cooing things like *poor baby*.

"Mandy decided that I was the one who ended the marriage, and I've never disabused her of the notion," he went on.

It stung a little because I *had* assumed that.

"Why?" Jenny asked, looking between us. "Why wouldn't you tell her the truth?"

"Because there's something emasculating about being tossed over for another man and—worse—being slow to recover from it."

"You told me that," Tammy said suddenly. "You told me you were divorced." The rest of us looked at her. I think we'd forgotten she was there.

"Which just goes to show," Grace murmured, "that Sam doesn't mind appearing emasculated in *your* eyes."

Ouch, I thought. Like I said, Grace can be brutally honest.

I pulled the subject back to what I figured was safe territory. "About the Woodsens," I said quickly. "I don't think Lisa has hooked up with anyone new yet."

"Lyle hasn't, either," Sam replied.

I thought about his suggestion. "He'd be the hardest to convince. He was the one who filed for divorce in the first place."

"She's a paranoid schizophrenic. She woke up one

morning and decided he was an extraterrestrial. It was making his life hell.''

''She didn't mention that.'' There was a *lot* Lisa hadn't bothered to tell me. Then it hit me. ''An *extraterrestrial?*''

''From Pluto. No mundane Martians for our girl.''

''Excuse me,'' Tammy tried to interrupt.

I laughed aloud. ''She told me that when he got drunk he would chase her around the house. Maybe that was what tipped her over into planetary delusions.''

Sam perked up. ''Were they wearing clothes, do you think?''

I had just sipped more wine and it backfired up my nasal passages. I coughed and he clapped me on the back.

''If Lisa stays on her medication and Lyle forgoes a six-pack now and again, it could work,'' he insisted.

''Between the two of them, one might be sane and sober for the kids at any given time,'' I agreed when I could finally talk again. ''The supervisor idea has some merit, but we'd need to have random blood tests for the children's sake, too. You know, test him for blood-alcohol content, and her to make sure she's still on her medication.''

''I'll sound him out on it in the morning,'' Sam said.

''I'll do the same with Lisa. But I'm *not* going to my partners about kicking in my fee.''

''Excuse me,'' Tammy said again.

''We've got trouble,'' Grace murmured and eased her chair back from the table a little. I barely glanced at her.

''Are you going to be in court tomorrow?'' Sam asked me.

''In the afternoon. I'm arguing a motion at one-thirty.''

''So am I. Get there early and I'll buy you a hot dog from our favorite vendor.''

''The one with the spider monkey?'' His name was Julio, and he was the only one who had fried onions on his cart.

"It's a chimpanzee," Sam corrected me.

"No, it's not—" Then I broke off because it happened.

I caught a quick movement out of the corner of my eye, a flick of Tammy's wrist. Then something pale and pink floated over the table in a pretty arc. I reared back in my seat just in time to avoid it. Then her drink was in Sam's face, dripping from his chin. He didn't look good in pink.

He came to his feet, sputtering. "What the hell was that for?"

"You don't love me!" Tammy's voice went to screech volume. "You can't even remember that I'm sitting here at the same table with you!"

Grace rose to her feet. "Okay, that's my cue. I'm going somewhere else."

Jenny just looked stupefied.

"Who said I loved you?" Sam looked at me a little wildly. For help, I knew.

Tammy's face contorted until she managed to squeeze tears from her eyes. She was so young—I really hadn't caught that before. I actually felt a little sorry for her. She'd need a lot more seasoning before she was ready for the Sam Cases of the world.

I stood and reached for her. I was thinking that I should guide her away from the table, maybe to the ladies' room, where she could calm down. Then I spotted Frank Ethan over her shoulder.

The evening was going to hell in a handbasket, I thought. I should have just listened to Sylvie Casamento and gone straight home to my daughter after court. I hadn't seen Frank since the night six weeks ago when I'd discovered that he kissed like a fish. He didn't frequent McGlinchey's—but he knew that I did. Which more or less equated to the certainty that he was here hoping to find me.

Sam recognized him. "Hey," he said. "Isn't that the

corporate dude who used to stand outside our building and check his watch so he'd knock on your door at the exact time he said he'd pick you up?''

''Shut up.'' I spat the words just as Frank started toward me, his arms spread wide and his mouth puckered up fish-style. I caught Sam's sleeve and backpedaled. ''Time to go.''

He was trying to dry his face with a bar napkin. He threw it back onto the table. ''Sounds good to me.''

We turned together and headed for the door. Or rather, Sam headed for the door. I walked into a wall of blue chambray and a snarl of chest hair at its opened collar.

''Ms. Hillman?'' chest-hair asked.

Sometimes you just *know* something and there's no getting around it, even when you'd prefer ignorance. Blue chambray or not, this guy was a sheriff's officer. I'd met enough of them in ten years of practicing law to recognize one when I ran into his chest.

I tried to step around him. I knew he wasn't allowed to detain me, not for what he wanted to do. But he didn't have to. He slid the papers he was holding into the open side flap of my purse.

Service acquired.

Sam tried. He'd only been in Philadelphia for six months, but he'd passed our Commonwealth's bar exam with flying colors and he knew the ropes. He tried to knock the papers out of the guy's hand before they landed. Sam was quick, but the deputy was quicker.

Sam swore once the damage was done and more or less dragged me out of the bar by my arm. I stopped on the sidewalk, pulling back against his grip, and I drew in a steadying breath.

''Okay, okay,'' I said. ''I'm all right now.''

''How can you be after that?'' he demanded.

"If it makes you feel any better, then I'm a puddle of Jell-O."

"Jell-O is solid," he pointed out. "It can't be a puddle."

"It's not so solid that it doesn't jiggle."

He thought about that and finally gave me the point. "What did he serve on you, anyway? Are you getting disbarred?"

I choked at the mere thought. "No."

"How do you know without looking at the damned papers?" He was more upset about this than I was, I realized.

"Because the bar association sends their axes by certified mail in this state," I explained. At his startled look—one that asked how I knew that—I added, "It happened to a guy in my office once."

Besides, I didn't have to look at the papers because I already knew what they were. Now that they'd finally turned up, I realized that I had pretty much been expecting them ever since Millson Kramer III had tossed his hat into the political arena a while ago. I'd guessed then that Chloe and I would become his official campaign skeletons-in-the-closet.

To appreciate this, you'd have to know Mill. He's the proving ground for the fact that too much IQ is not necessarily a good thing. He's clinically a genius and my daughter is a shining testament to that. Chloe grasps it all— math, science, concrete concepts and those of an airier, more abstract variety. She's dazzling. Mill, on the other hand, tends to be so captivated by his own calculating thoughts that he has the charm and disposition of a wet dishrag. He is, however, very exacting, orderly and methodical. So I'd known that Chloe and I were probably on his to-do list of things to clear up so he would become highly electable.

We'd been seeing each other on a comfortable basis for

a little over a year when I got pregnant. I wasn't appalled when I found out about Chloe. I'd always wanted a child, though this wasn't exactly the way I'd envisioned it happening. I knew I would be swimming upstream by going ahead with parenthood on my own, but I was reasonably sure I was good for the challenge. And Mill provided an excellent gene pool, being intelligent, attractive, well-bred and, best of all, indifferent.

After I decided that I wanted the baby, I also realized that hooking up with Mill on a legal basis for the express purpose of her existence would be a mistake of monumental proportions. Regardless of the fact that I arrange divorces and negotiate custody disputes for a living, I strongly believe that marriage is supposed to be forever. And the comfortable pseudorelationship I had going with Mill was not the sort of thing forever is made of. In fact, when I realized that, I was a little ashamed of myself for letting it progress for as long as it had.

In the end, I trusted in the fact that Mill was so utterly self-absorbed, he wouldn't try to take the idea of parenthood too seriously. He wouldn't try to make our relationship more than it was because of the baby. I knew that if I declined his proposal of marriage and asked him to go away, he'd go away. I was right—he did, with a few snide comments for casual observers—until now.

Now he had decided to run for city council, and the whole business of Chloe would make him look less than stellar in the eyes of Philadelphia's more conservative voters. I knew this was a custody suit even without taking the papers from my purse, and I was definitely not going to do that. Not yet. On top of Grace's bizarre opinions about me having sex with Sam, and the Woodsen matter of schizophrenia, I was in no way planning to address the issue of my daughter's parentage before morning.

I opened my mouth to tell Sam this, then McGlinchey's door opened behind us. Sam tugged my keys from my hand. I tried to hold on to them as we started jogging toward the parking lot, but he twisted them free of my fingers, anyway.

I yanked on the passenger door once he had unlocked it. I dropped inside and looked over my shoulder. Whoever had come through the door after us—if it had been either Tammy or Frank—they weren't following us. And the deputy didn't have to. He'd already accomplished his dirty work.

Sam found the little button on the side of the driver's seat, and he moved the seat backward with ruthless intent. I could never get it into the right position again when he did that. He shot the key into the ignition, revved the engine and looped around onto Pine Street. We headed toward the outskirts of Society Hill. Mill lived in the district. Sam and I could only afford to come close.

"You're not very good at this, you know," I told him.

He angled a glance my way. "At driving?"

This is something else I've learned from thirty-five years of living: never *ever* criticize a man's driving, no matter how bad it is. It's a testosterone thing. "Actually, I meant dating. Keep your eyes on the road." I closed my own so I wouldn't have to note how fast we were going.

"I'm a great dater." This came out with predictable evidence of that same testosterone.

"No, Sam, you're not. Practice does not always make perfect."

"It strikes me that this is a little like the pot calling the kettle black."

I opened my eyes again. "I hardly ever date!" I protested.

"That is my point." He swerved around a cab and we veered north onto Third Street.

"What's that supposed to mean?" I straightened in my seat. Damned if the man couldn't get my ire up. Plus, he'd managed to hit on a topic that I'd already been under fire for through half the evening from Grace and Jenny.

"It means that maybe if you did more of it, you might be in a position to judge my tactics," Sam said. "It means that you might figure out that a guy who has an obsession about time is probably going to be a little anal retentive. And he just might be the type to come at you in a bar with his arms open wide, puckering up his mouth like some kind of overblown fish."

I was just outraged enough that I didn't know which comment to respond to first, but I'd be damned if I'd admit that Frank Ethan really did kiss like a fish. "I happen to appreciate a sense of punctuality and responsibility," I said.

"Yeah? What about that day you canceled all your appointments and played hooky so you could show me the Liberty Bell?"

"That was *you*." As soon as it was out, I considered biting my tongue off. Grace's voice whispered nasty little observations in my head again.

"Which means...what?" Sam asked.

I wasn't going to answer that. "I fail to see what this has to do with Frank," I said stiffly. "Besides, there's no such thing as an overblown fish."

"Yes, there is. There are those ones that puff up occasionally for some scientific reason I can't remember right now."

"Like Tammy's chest?"

"Leave her chest out of this."

"That's tough to do, Sam. It's so...out there."

He took his eyes off the road again to glare at me. "What's wrong with you tonight?"

"I'm fine." Grace was wrong with me, I thought, her and her absurd opinions about me and Sam.

"You're not fine," Sam said. "You're being caustic."

"At least I don't tell people I love them on the first date. Or did you do it on the second?" We'd reached the parking lot that I used and he drove my car into a space. The Mitsubishi rocked on its shock absorbers when he hit the breaks too hard. I tried not to wince.

"I did *not* tell her that I loved her," he said.

"Well, you must have done something to put the idea in her head." I got out and slammed the door. "In the throes of passion, maybe?"

"I never even got around to passion with her!"

My heart shifted a little. Damned if I cared. I grabbed my keys from his hand and started up the street toward our apartment building.

"So what about that scampi?" Sam asked, following me. "Since we're both home now and we've semi-resolved the Woodsen thing, we might as well eat together."

"Bribe me and I'll consider it."

"You want me to pucker up like a fish?"

I turned and walked backward to face him. "For the record, Frank kissed like a...like a..."

"Words fail you?" he said when I couldn't quite continue.

"I'm trying to reach for the perfect superlative."

"I hope you come up with it before my hearing starts to go."

"There are just so many to choose from."

He reached around me and opened the outside door of our building. I pivoted back to face forward and we crossed the black-and-white marble vestibule to step into a fern-filled hallway. My apartment was on the first floor, his was one floor above mine.

"Come on, Mandy. Feed me," he said. "I've got some wine I could contribute. I bought it because I was going to try to lure Tammy back here tonight."

"Ah, leftovers. Sam, I am so flattered."

"I'd rather share it with you."

Everything inside me rolled over. Slowly, sweetly. It was purely Grace's doing, of course. I had been absolutely fine when I'd been hating Sam in Judge Larson's courtroom two hours ago.

"Go get the wine, Sam," I said, a little tired of fighting off images of how he would claw. But I watched him move up the stairs with that slow, prowling way he had of moving, and I found myself thinking that on so many levels he seemed absurdly unaware of his own appeal. Either that or he took it for granted. I had never quite figured out which it was.

I went into my own apartment and closed the door behind me. The telephone was ringing. I jogged across the living room into the kitchen and grabbed it. It was Sylvie Casamento.

"It's after six o'clock," she said immediately. "You said you'd be home by six o'clock."

I looked at the clock on the wall in the kitchen. It was two minutes past the hour. "I had a wonderful time," I said. "Thanks for asking."

"Did that man find you?"

"Which one? The blue shirt, or the one with the fishy mouth?" What difference did it make? They'd both nailed me, but I wanted to know which one of them had come here looking for me first.

"He was wearing blue," Mrs. Casamento said.

"Then, yes. Thank you so much for your help. You can send Chloe down now."

Mrs. Casamento lived in my building on the second floor across from Sam. I went back to my apartment door and into the hall, and I collected my daughter.

I sent Chloe off to take a bath. Back in the kitchen I stared at my purse, at the papers stuffed into the side flap.

Over the years, from conversations at preschool, playgrounds, and PTA, I have come to the conclusion that single mothers share a near-psychotic obsession with being a good parent. Maybe this is because statistically we are expected to fail, to produce serial killers and assorted other prison inmates. Our children cannot possibly thrive in a broken home. To prove those statistics wrong, we obsess. And obsession can be exhausting. This is why, when your seven-year-old stares at you with guileless eyes and swears up-and-down on the life of her Barbie that she did her homework at the babysitter's, sometimes you believe her. You do it because you want the hard part of your day to be over and done with. You've earned your wage, you've paid the gas bill. If there's not food on the table, then at the very least it's in the refrigerator waiting to be warmed up, or it's in a takeout bag on the counter. So you take your child's word at face value until you begin to shoo her out the door the next morning and you realize that she fibbed…just a little. The homework is *half*-done. You're late for court and she's late for school and there's no way to backtrack and fix this. Now her teacher is going to know the truth. You are actually a bad parent in sheep's clothing. Your child is doomed for the penitentiary.

This is why I ended up opening the papers right then, after all, instead of waiting for morning. Part of it was that I might be considered a bad parent for not reading them right away. The other part was that I really wanted the hard part of my day to be over, and I knew that wouldn't happen unless and until I knew exactly what Mill was up to.

Chloe was in the tub with the door open so I could hear if the splashing stopped—that way I'd know if she was drowning. I scanned the papers and they were pretty much what I had expected. Mill had decided that he wanted Chloe to live with him.

My heart did a dive. I read the papers again before I went to the phone and dialed Mill's number. This is another thing about single parenthood—if a man fathers your child, it doesn't matter if you haven't laid eyes on him since the moment of conception. You will never forget his phone number.

"Have you lost your mind?" I demanded as soon as Mill answered. "You don't want this."

"Amanda." Other than Sam, he was the only person in my life who ever dared to call me by my given name. I wondered briefly what the implications of that might be. One was the father of my child, and the other was my…well, my platonic friend.

"This wasn't our deal," I grated finally, staring at the papers in my hand.

"No," he agreed. "But a father can't actually sign away his parental rights, can he?"

He was right. A parent is a parent is a parent. Though I had a consent order with his signature on it wherein he solemnly swore never to intrude in Chloe's life if I promised never to ask him for a dime of child support, I'd always known that if he chose to get involved, that piece of paper wouldn't amount to a hill of beans.

The fact that he knew that, too, told me that he had been boning up on his family law—Mill specializes in corporate and tax law. Either that, or the attorney he was using for this had informed him of the fact.

I was starting to feel sick.

"I want my daughter," Mill said. "I want a relationship with her."

"Oh, the hell you do." It was knee-jerk, out before I could stop it.

There was silence. I took that as a good thing. Maybe he was thinking that I wasn't snowed. Or scared. Though, actually, I was a little—a lot—of both.

"Mandy, it just doesn't look good," he said finally.

I realized that he would probably be taping our conversation by now—it's a neat lawyer trick. As long as words are spoken on a telephone line—which is technically a public medium—they're legally up for grabs. So I took a new tack. "It's the election thing, right?" I asked. "Mill, I understand. Okay, then. I'll marry you."

I was gratified by a gargling sound. "I beg your pardon?"

"You asked me once, then you withdrew the offer. And I was so young and foolish at the time. Now I've realized the error of my ways. Marry me, Mill. Please."

Chloe chose that moment to wander into the kitchen wrapped in her favorite, too-pink Barbie bathrobe. I tried to shoo her away but she wouldn't go. I had him, I knew I had him, but I couldn't push my advantage with her listening on.

"I heard you were seeing someone," he said suddenly.

"You did?" I couldn't fathom how that rumor might have gotten started. Then, with his next words, I got it.

"That lawyer who lives in your building," he clarified.

My heart stalled a little. Things always managed to come back around to Sam lately, didn't they? "I'm not seeing him," I said. "We're just friends." This was starting to sound like a mantra, I thought.

"That might have changed the whole complexion of this issue."

I almost laughed aloud. Mill would always be...well, Mill, I thought. No, he didn't want Chloe. He was just trying to find an easy way out of our seven-year-plus mess. If Chloe had another father figure in her life, then maybe he wouldn't have to do the job. He couldn't be publically chastised as much for not remaining a part of our lives.

In an odd way that made me sad.

I was about to say so when Sam came banging at the door. I wasn't sure why I didn't want him to hear me talking to Mill about this. Maybe because I didn't want him to know there was suddenly a major crusade afoot to push us together and the entire city of Philadelphia seemed to be in on it.

"I'll get it, Mom!" Chloe shouted. Then, a heartbeat later, "It's Sam!"

"I've got to go," I said quickly.

Mill overheard. Chloe's voice can be like a siren when she's happy. "Sam?" he asked.

"The pizza guy." I hung up the phone fast.

"I have two bottles," Sam said, stepping into the kitchen. He held them both in one hand. In the other was his Glenlivet. That told me I could have the wine to myself—he wouldn't be sharing it.

"Was it going to take you that much to get Tammy into—" Then I broke off. Chloe was leaning against his right thigh, looking at me expectantly.

"Get Tammy into what?" she asked. Then she looked up at Sam. "Who's Tammy?"

"Never mind, rug rat." But Sam knew where I'd been headed with my comment. "One was for before," he told me, "and the other was for after. I'm good. I don't need much help."

Funny thing about a woman's body. It has a mind of its own. You can react even when your brain is utterly sane with the understanding that reacting is stupid. It happens viscerally. I imagined ''good'' with Sam and when something rolled over inside me this time, it wasn't in my gut. It was a lot lower than that. And after it rolled, it tightened up.

Damn Grace. I rubbed my forehead again.

''Neck rub?'' he asked, noticing.

''Just uncork the wine, Sam. And hurry.''

Chapter Three

I blame Sam's wine as much as I blame anything else for what happened next. By nine o'clock, when Chloe was tucked into bed, my eyes were closed and my head was tilted back against the sofa cushions. My feet were propped on the coffee table. So were Sam's. He was on the other end of the sofa.

"You know what the problem is?" he asked me suddenly.

I made the kind of noise in my throat that said I hadn't a clue what he was talking about, but that he should go on, anyway.

"With dating," he clarified.

I opened one eye. "Ah, *that* problem. Your way or mine? Excessively or rarely?"

"I don't date excessively." He sat up straight, indignantly. "Saturday night comes every week. I just like to use it accordingly."

"Sam, you date on Monday, Wednesday and Friday, too."

"My point is that too much or too little of this dating business is equally frustrating."

He was staring down into his scotch glass now. His expression was serious. After a day filled with Grace's observations and Mill's custody petition, Sam's suddenly pensive mood worried me.

"You go out with a woman for the first time and she expects all these subtle little things to immediately click right into place," he continued. "Talk about pressure."

"As opposed to men," I asked, "who don't give a damn about things clicking one way or the other?"

He looked over at me and his face took on that offended look again. "That's not true. We give a damn."

"Before or after you catch sight of the finish line?"

"Both."

I rolled my eyes to show my opinion of that. "Continue. What little things?"

"Mental stimulation. Good conversation. Mental stability. Sexual attraction. Everything is supposed to happen all at once, and men are looking for that, too. I mean, some of us want it and some of us run like hell when it's there, but it's still an issue."

Suddenly, I was sure that Grace had repeated to him everything I'd told her earlier about my own over-thirty-five theory, my three-Cs rule of thumb—companionship, comfort and conversation. This was a little spooky.

"Have you been talking to Grace?" I demanded.

Sam looked around my living room as though expecting to find her there. "Not since McGlinchey's. Why?"

"What did she say to you?"

He looked at me oddly. "You were there. You heard the whole conversation. You were part of it."

"You didn't talk to her privately?"

"When would I have done that?"

"I don't know."

"You're really acting strange tonight," he said.

I grabbed the wine bottle from the coffee table and topped off my glass. "Having your daughter's father sue you for custody can do that to a woman." I'd filled him in on the problem after dinner when Chloe had gone to her room to watch television.

Sam waved a hand negligently. "I told you I'd handle that."

"And I told you no thanks."

"You're too close to it to represent yourself."

And *he* was closer to it than he knew. I could only imagine Mill's reaction if Sam—the man I was reputedly seeing—appeared with me in court. "Get back to your point," I prodded him. "You were philosophizing."

Sam slanted another look my way. "Okay. The thing is, somebody is always waiting, wanting, hoping for all those little things to click into place and coincide."

"The mental stimulation, the conversation and the animal attraction," I said to clarify.

"I didn't say animal. Who said anything about animal?"

I realized I had claws on my mind again. "Well, that's what we're all looking for, right?"

His brows climbed his forehead. "Are you?"

I definitely wasn't going to get into *that* discussion again. "We were talking about you, Sam."

"All right. Fine. We'll call it animal attraction. But it never happens, you know. Either you get the mental stimulation going, but then the animal business is missing—or it's there, but the woman turns out to be a Looney-Toon, emotionally unstable. Or she thinks you're great and you think she's about as interesting as a can of vegetables."

I got stuck on the emotionally unstable part. "Like Tammy?"

He didn't argue it. He just shrugged. "Then you're left trying to wriggle free without hurting anyone's feelings or wearing some pink drink," he said.

He was like that, I knew. He worried as much about hurting women as I did about bad parenthood. "You looked ridiculous, by the way."

He didn't rise to the bait. He lifted his glass and swallowed the last of his scotch. "I just get tired of it, Mandy. But it's like some kind of...of addiction. We keep scrambling after it because we need that male-female thing going on in our lives. And the need makes us keep going out there, bashing our heads against walls, smashing ourselves all up, getting drinks tossed in our faces, just because we had the audacity to look for a partner who's on the same wavelength."

"Wavelengths are shifty little things," I agreed.

He stood and went to the kitchen to retrieve his bottle of scotch. When he came back, he bent and picked up his shoes from my living room floor. Then he stood at the door, armed with all of it. "On that note, I'm going home," he said. "Thanks for dinner."

Suddenly I felt an overriding need to set everything back to the way we had been in the courtroom that afternoon. I wanted to banish Grace's insane observations and Mill's innuendoes from the air. Maybe I just figured that by reminding us of what we were supposed to be, we would be able keep it so.

"You know, it's really great to have a male-type friend," I said. "It's nice to talk like this, to get a masculine perspective."

"That's me," Sam said shortly. "Male-type." Then he left. Quickly.

I frowned after him. I knew him well enough to understand that somehow or other, I had just hurt him. But how? Then my heart hit the wall of my chest. Did he not *want* to be just a male-type friend anymore?

I shook my head. This was Grace's doing. Such a thought would never even have occurred to me five hours ago.

Or maybe it was the wine, I thought. I'd had too much of it. I narrowed my eyes to focus them on the door he had just passed through. There was only one door there, so I was not drunk. Nope, I was fine.

Either way, now that I was alone, a million little demon thoughts came spewing out of the recesses of my mind to hoot and holler. Most of them wore little T-shirts labeled Sex and Sam. It came to me then that I probably wasn't going to be able to sleep until I knew why he'd been insulted by what I'd said. I got to my feet, still looking at the door. I put my wine down on the coffee table. The Sex and Sam goblins were jumping gleefully up and down by now, clapping their hands. A tiny, sane part of me told me to go to bed *right now*. So, of course, I listened to the demon-goblins.

I peeked into Chloe's room. She was sound asleep. I tiptoed in, kissed her forehead, then I closed her door quietly behind me. I left my apartment and stood in the hall, looking at the stairs to the second floor.

If I came right out and asked him if he wanted to be more than just my male-type pal, I knew I was going to get my pride kicked hard. For one thing I wasn't his type physically—not a blond hair in sight. For another, if he'd had any romantic designs on me whatsoever, I figured he would have acted on them a long time ago. We'd known each other for nearly six months, and Sam is definitely not the reticent sort.

That realization made me sane again. I started to turn back into my own apartment, but then I saw his legs appear on the landing. The top part of him was chopped off by the next level of stairs.

"Sam?" I said, to be sure.

"What are you doing down there?" he demanded.

"I was coming to your apartment."

"No need. I'm right here. So you can just stay where you are."

Talk about one of us acting odd. "Okay."

"Why were you coming to my apartment?" he asked.

"I don't know." I shrugged, though he couldn't see it. "I was just...thinking."

"That's a very dangerous thing to do at this hour."

I looked at my watch. "It's only ten o'clock."

"Yeah, but that makes it something like three in the morning in parts of Europe."

"Okay. So what are *you* doing on the stairs at three in the morning in parts of Europe?"

"I'm not sure yet." Then there was a very long, very quiet pause. "I guess I was thinking, too."

Somehow, in that very moment, I knew I'd been right. He'd definitely been offended by what I'd said, unhappy about being classified as a male-type friend. "About time zones?" I asked, in case I was wrong.

"About us."

I'd been expecting it, but I think my heart actually vaulted over its next beat anyway. "Are you drunk?" I asked. I'd ruled myself out—now I needed to make sure he was sober, too.

He took some time to think about it, and I imagined he was probably squinting at doors, too, just to be sure. "No," he decided finally.

I inched toward the stairs, leaving my door open so I

would hear Chloe if she woke up and called me. He headed down. We reached the bottom tread at the same time and I dropped to sit there, but he kept standing beside me.

"I was thinking that maybe we could give each other a kind of break for a while," he said finally. "From dating. You know, we could do things together."

"What kinds of things?" I asked.

He scowled down at me. "I don't know. Just... uncomplicated things. Things that don't involve pink drinks or timing devices like Frank Ethan's watch. We could swear off chasing the opposite sex for a while if we keep each other company in the interim. We could assuage all those male-female urges without the issue getting too complicated."

It wasn't me who needed the break, I thought. Grace had been right. I'd pretty much been on a dating hiatus since I'd met him. But I decided that it might be prudent not to mention that, because there was a lot in this for me. I could put up a good front for Mill, I realized. If he thought I really was happily involved, maybe he *would* back down on this whole custody issue. I can rationalize anything, even the irrational.

"Let me make sure I've got this straight," I said. "We'll do things together for a while—uncomplicated things—while we swear off dating until such time as one or both of us feels up to plunging back into the pool?"

He looked relieved. "Yeah. That's it exactly. So...what do you think?"

"Define *uncomplicated* first."

"I don't know. Dining, drinks, companionship. Sex."

He shoved that last part in quickly, and my air stopped somewhere midway in my chest. Well, I thought, this would certainly put Grace's opinions to rest once and for all. I could claw my heart out with him for a while and get it out of my system.

"That's the whole point of this!" he said when I didn't answer immediately. I thought he sounded stressed. "Without the sex, we're right back out there bashing our heads against the wall looking for the whole enchilada! Damn it, male-type friends can have sex, too!"

Ah, I thought. Bingo. Am I perceptive or what? "Of course they can," I said quickly.

"This would be a mutually gratifying situation," he said. "Not a relationship."

"We already have a relationship."

"But we don't have a *relationship*."

I thought about it. "True." I got to my feet. "Okay."

"Okay?"

"It sounds reasonable to me." I was breathing again, but just barely.

"So when are we going to start this?" he asked.

"Tomorrow? It makes sense to begin with a brand-new day, doesn't it? And we could each have tonight to change our minds."

"Are you going to change your mind?"

"Probably not."

"Neither will I." He laughed. He sounded self-conscious. Then he started to turn up the stairs again and he paused. "I'm still good for that hot dog tomorrow if you want to get to the courthouse early. Maybe we should each bring a couple of...I don't know...ground rules for this...this..." He trailed off completely this time, sounding lost.

"Nonrelationship?" I suggested.

"Arrangement."

I nodded. It was as good a word as any I could think of. "You want bylaws?"

''They could be our arrangement bill-of-rights-and-wrongs,'' he said.

''Should we write them down and affix our signatures?''

He laughed again, but his voice still didn't sound quite right. ''Sure, if you want.'' Then he went upstairs.

I watched him go. When his legs disappeared around the landing, I came to the amazing discovery that I no longer possessed legs of my own. They'd gone hollow.

After a while, I wobbled back to my apartment. I checked on Chloe, still snoozing, barely moved. This is another parent thing, but I think it's the same whether you're single or with a mate. You check your young repeatedly while they sleep. I don't know what exactly it is that we expect to have happen to them while we're not actually looking at them. It's just a compulsion, and maybe it's a selfish one at that. Because in the back of your mind, you know that the only way you can really settle down and get some rest yourself—or write lists, as the case might be—is if your child is genuinely zonked for the duration of the night.

Since Chloe appeared to be sincerely zonked, I went to my briefcase, found a legal pad and a pen, and carried them back to my own bed with me. Impulsively I took the last of the wine and the shrimp, too. Two hours later I was surprised by how hard it was for me to come up with the ground rules Sam wanted.

Who needed guidelines? I thought. I figured we'd just pretty much stay the way we were, except we'd...do the sex thing. I'd get to touch him with impunity. I'd finally get to drive my fingers into that great, dark hair of his, touch it when it fell down over his forehead the way it did. I'd get him—and Grace's theories—out of my system.

Still, I figured I needed to come up with my own bill of rights if only to keep in the spirit of things, so I spent much of the rest of the night on my list. I still wasn't satisfied with it when I tucked my car into the municipal parking lot at twelve-thirty the following afternoon.

Sam was already standing on the corner beside the hot-dog vendor. The spider monkey—or chimpanzee, or whatever it was—was perched on his shoulder. Sam should have looked ridiculous. Instead, something airy filled my legs at the sight of him.

I got out of my car and rooted in my trunk for my briefcase, wondering if this wobbly-leg business was going to be a new phenomenon while our arrangement was in place. I could only hope that it would go away as things wore on.

His back was to me and he didn't see me approach. I was able to step up behind him before I spoke. "Boo."

He turned. The monkey began chattering. It swiped an eerily human hand in my direction and I jumped back. I did not like the beast. However, like so many females, she was crazy about Sam.

"She has a crush on you," I said.

It was an opinion I'd shared before, but this time Sam wiggled his brows at me. "Jealous?"

"I am beside myself with anguish. Where's my hot dog?"

"Anguish obviously doesn't affect your appetite."

"Not a bit." The vendor held a hot dog in my direction, gooey with melted cheese and fried onions, just the way I like it. The monkey made a grab for it. "Back off," I warned. "Mine."

"See?" Sam said to Julio, the vendor. "She's jealous."

I took a bite. "I was referring to my meal. He's paying this time," I said to Julio. The poor guy's gaze was whipping back and forth between us now. He seemed confused and wary.

"We have an arrangement," Sam told him, then he looked at me again. "By the way, it's started now, right?"

Things danced inside me. I managed to nod. "But if you call me something like *doll,* I'll clock you." It was one of the few rules I'd been able to come up with last night. No saccharine endearments. I'd included this mostly because I'd overheard a good many of Sam's over the last six months, and they all tended to be nauseating.

He shook his head seriously. "Doll? I don't think that particular term has ever passed my lips." He bit down into his own hot dog. The monkey did not try to take his.

"Yes, it did," I said. "With that redhead."

"What redhead?"

"A couple of months ago. The one in the rust-colored spandex. We arrived home at the same time—me and Frank and you and her. And when you opened the door for her, I distinctly remember hearing you call her *doll.*"

"Oh, that redhead. Of course I did. That was her name."

I laughed. "Doll?"

"Eee. Doll-y." He grinned that crooked grin. "So do we have a marriage or what?"

The last bite of my hot dog jammed in my throat. I swallowed hard to push it down. Last night he'd been calling this thing an arrangement, and now he was talking about *marriage?* I felt like I'd fallen asleep in the theater and woken up at the end of the movie. "Come again?"

"The Woodsens," Sam explained. Then he lifted the little monkey from his shoulder. "There now, darling," he cooed to her, giving her back to the vendor. "I'll be back before you know it." He picked up his briefcase from the sidewalk and headed toward the courthouse steps.

The Woodsens, I thought. He was talking about the Woodsens. Of course he was. I paid the vendor without even thinking about it—because Sam hadn't—and I went after him.

"Did you talk to Lisa?" he asked when I caught up.

"Yes. She's says she'll attempt a reconciliation rather than lose her kids." We were back in lawyer mode. There was a great deal of comfort to be found there. Not that I didn't want to proceed with our arrangement. I did. But I was finding that it was a little like walking a tightrope, and every once in a while it just seemed best to step down and plant my feet on solid ground again.

"It's never going to work if that's her attitude," Sam said.

"He dumped her and filed for divorce over a simple medical problem!" I protested.

"Simple medical problem?" Sam laughed as we trotted up the steps. "Is that politically correct for running around the house naked?"

"Only when your partner perceives it as an invasion from Pluto."

We stopped in front of the big oak doors. "Lyle's going to need more of an enthusiastic response than that," Sam insisted. "That's all I'm saying."

"And he'll get it. Eventually. She's just going to make him jump through a few hoops first."

"See all the games and garbage we can avoid with our arrangement? Doll?"

I laughed, but I think it came out a little hoarsely. "What else are we avoiding?" I asked him. "Did you decide on your ground rules yet?"

"Sure. They didn't take much thought."

For a brief moment, I hated him. "Great," I said. "So you go first."

"All right. No sleepovers. Also no sharing of tooth-brushes. Those two sort of go hand in hand."

I frowned. They fell into my "companionship" category, but I had been getting by without that sort of thing for a while now and I figured I could keep on doing it. "Okay." But then my curiosity got the better of me. "Why not?"

"It's just part of keeping it uncomplicated," he said. "It will be neater if we just keep all that cuddly stuff out of it. You know, that's always where I get into trouble."

"With cuddly stuff?"

"Yeah. That's the point of this, right? We're *friends*. We don't have to cuddle. We don't hold hands. We're talking sex and companionship here. Period."

He didn't seem awkward with it today. He really had it down. "My turn," I said, and I latched on to the rule I'd mentioned earlier—in part because for a moment I couldn't remember any of the others. "None of those endearments of yours. Absolutely no...you know...darlings and dolls and snookums and babycakes."

"Honestly, Mandy, you're not the babycakes type."

I wasn't sure if I was insulted or pleased. I decided not to try to figure it out.

"No complaining or handing out guilt trips," he said, ticking off another rule on the fingers of his free hand, the one that wasn't holding his briefcase.

Now I was insulted. "When have I ever done that sort of thing?"

"You haven't. Yet. But that was when we were just...you know, us. Now we're getting into uncharted territory so I'm just putting it out there. If I decide I want to stay in some night and read, there can't be any whining and making me feel bad about it. Also, it works both ways. You get to go to the gym like you're always doing without me busting your chops because I wanted to see you."

My head was spinning. But he was right. It made a certain amount of sense, I supposed. He wanted to take a break from the whining and the guilt trips. That was the whole purpose behind this thing. That, and getting him out of my system.

"Your turn again," Sam said.

I dredged through my memory. "I, um, don't have to run around picking up the apartment just because you're coming over." It sounded as lame now as it had last night.

"You never do that," he pointed out. "Your living room is a Barbie metropolis."

"Uncharted territory," I reminded him.

He frowned. "Okay. No picking up."

"And Chloe comes first. She's my top priority."

"Of course she is. And, anyway, that's part of *my* rule. No whining or guilt trips if you prefer to spend time with her."

I nodded. So far, this was very...civilized, I thought. "What else?"

"It's not necessary for us to touch base every day."

"Sam, we've been touching base every day for the entire six months I've known you." For some reason, this was starting to bother me.

"But things are different now, so if it should ever happen that we *don't* touch base for some reason, there won't be a major conflagration."

"No conflagrations," I repeated.

"And nobody's going to go falling in love," he said. "That's the big one. I don't need to be going *there* again."

I finally laughed at that. It came up from my belly. "I think you're safe, Sam. I've already seen you at your most impressive and it hasn't overwhelmed me. I've also seen you at your worst. Wearing pink, for instance. Or remember when you broke your finger putting in my air conditioner? You howled more than a woman giving birth."

"The hell I did." He scowled. "Anyway, this brings us

back to throwing drinks and timing devices like Frank Ethan's watch.''

''Exactly where we came in,'' I agreed.

''Right.'' He opened the courthouse door for me.

I stepped inside, but then I turned back to gape at him. ''You never open doors for me.''

''That was before, when you were one of the guys. Now you're my girl.''

''I'm—'' I broke off. Somehow, it seemed diametrically opposed to everything we had just discussed.

''Figuratively speaking,'' Sam explained.

''Oh. Of course.''

I knew then that I had to get a grip. This wasn't going to work if the world kept tilting on its axis with everything he said. I was supposed to feel clinical and practical about this, not light-headed and weak-kneed and on the constant verge of passing out.

''They're meeting for lunch right about now,'' Sam said, looking at his watch. ''Or at least they are if she agreed to see him.''

''Who?'' I asked dazedly.

''Lisa and Lyle Woodsen.''

''Where?'' And what the hell difference did *that* make?

''The same restaurant where they had their first date. So where's ours going to be?''

I grabbed my wits about me halfway across the lobby. ''I have show tickets for Atlantic City this weekend.'' No, I thought immediately, that wouldn't work. It would be better to take Grace or Jenny along, because that sort of occasion would almost necessitate an overnight. Would one of us sleep on the floor? Would we take two separate rooms? How would *that* fit into our rules?

''I was thinking more along the lines of tonight,'' Sam said while I was picking at the problem.

Tonight? That was…soon.

I looked at him. He grinned that crooked, bad-boy grin, and I knew—suddenly I just *knew*—that he realized how flustered I was by all this. And he liked it. I decided I was damned if I was going to let him keep yanking my chain.

That was the only reason I did what I did next in full view of a lobby bustling with lawyers, litigants and various law enforcement personnel. Okay, maybe Mill had a little to do with it, too. I knew it would get back to him. I caught Sam's tie with my left hand and gave it a tug until he stepped closer to me.

"Hey," he said, startled.

I kissed him hard on the mouth. That had been my intention anyway—one strong *smack* to reestablish my upper hand. But then something happened. A rolling kind of jolt went through me. Because while I'd meant to smack, his mouth turned out to be as soft as a wish, and I stayed a little too long. At some point while I lingered, he obviously recovered from his surprise…and I forgot all about Mill.

His tongue slipped fast, neatly, past my lips, tangling with mine. It teased a moment. Then it was gone. I reeled back.

"Sneak preview," he said, and winked at me. "Good idea." Then he left me standing there like a dumbstruck idiot and headed for his courtroom.

Chapter Four

I have no recollection of being in court that afternoon, though I know I must have been because I billed Robert Awney for my time. The man was grinning when he left the courthouse. His wife had left him and he'd never gotten over it, so he took her back to court once a year, trying to change his child support or his visitation, just to harass her. Celia Awney Neulander's expression was predictably murderous as she stalked off.

I stood on the cold, aged tile of the lobby floor watching them go, then I looked around for Sam. He was nowhere to be found. I found myself thinking about our arrangement again, and I was suddenly swept by the conviction that it would never work. Nothing between us would ever be as simple as he was making this whole thing out to sound. We both had our egos. We were both strong-willed. Each of us had a decided preference for being in charge. This was going to be a tug-of-war, I thought.

I decided that what I really needed to do about the situation was talk to Grace. I whipped around, swinging my briefcase like a deadly weapon, and headed for the elevator bank instead of the lobby doors.

I found her at her desk outside Judge Castello's chambers on the sixth floor. She was snarling into the phone at someone who apparently mistook her for a woman who cared about the terms of his parole. I waited for six minutes and during that time, Grace told the caller no less than eight times that he ought to get a lawyer who would then tell it to the judge.

She hung up the phone a little too hard and looked surprised to see me. "If it's five o'clock already, then this must be my afterlife."

I hated to disappoint her. "I need to talk to you," I said. "About Sam."

Her brows did a slow slide up her forehead. "Have you decided to claw with him?"

I think I gave a jerky little nod before I shook my head.

"Which is it?" she asked. "Yes or no?"

"Yes. But I'm having doubts now."

"That would make you an idiot."

I glowered at her. "I should have gone to Jenny with this."

"Jenny would already be out buying floral arrangements for your wedding." Grace stood from her desk. "This requires coffee," she decided.

I followed her out of the chambers area to the balcony that overlooked a lot of empty air all the way down to the ground floor. I generally avoided standing near the railing because it made me dizzy. Grace went right over to it and leaned against it, folding her arms over her chest, utterly unperturbed by the fact that if the wood suddenly gave way, her life would be over.

"What happened to the coffee?" I asked, surprised.

"This can't wait for the elevator." The cafeteria was on the third floor. "I want to hear what you two have been up to."

I cleared my throat. "Well, it's an arrangement," I said. "It's...uh, sex. Only." But that wasn't entirely true. "Also companionship," I added.

"Conversation?" she asked.

"Of course." I scowled. "We're hardly going to claw with our lips sealed."

"Comfort?"

Suddenly I saw where she was headed with this. I threw my hands up in surrender.

"Am I to take it that you two talked about this," Grace asked, "set some guidelines and decided to get naked together?"

"We..." I trailed off. "That's about the size of it."

"It's about time."

"You don't think it's odd that we discussed it first?"

"You're both lawyers. This is what lawyers do."

"We made bylaws, too."

She nodded as though this made all the sense in the world. "Less chance of chaos and misunderstanding that way. So what's the problem?"

"My motives aren't the purest." There—I said it aloud. After all, confession is supposed to be good for the soul. "I'm not doing it to dodge the dating pool," I admitted. "I haven't been *in* the dating pool for a while."

"So dodging the dating pool is the motivation behind all this?"

"It's Sam's." We finally set off toward the elevators. "What's yours?"

"It's entirely possible that I just want to rip his clothes off," I admitted.

I said this just as the elevator doors slid open. There were three people inside. An elderly woman gasped mildly. An overweight man in red suspenders grinned at me. The child with him seemed to have no reaction to my comment whatsoever.

Grace sailed into the elevator car without a qualm. I followed, feeling ridiculous.

"How long is this arrangement supposed to last?" she asked me.

"Can we finish discussing this when we get to the cafeteria?" I looked left and right to find that we still had the rapt attention of both the other passengers over the age of ten.

The elevator doors slid open again, and I fled through them, refusing to look back. "Until one or both of us decide we want to move on," I explained finally.

"This will get him out of your system so you can finally start dating again. You know, you've been hung up on him for a very long time now," Grace observed.

I frowned. Teenagers got "hung up," I thought. Cinderella had pined for Prince Charming, and Snow White had been prepared to sleep forever without that kiss. I, on the other hand, was a thirty-five-year-old professional just stuffed to the brim with common sense and independence. I did not get "hung up" on anyone.

"So when does this deal start?" Grace asked when we reached the cafeteria.

"Maybe tonight."

"Ah. There's the floor that makes the feet feel cold."

"I'm not hung up and I don't have cold feet."

"Mandy, you're jumping around like a ballerina here. Whose idea was this anyway—yours or Sam's?"

I thought about it as we collected our coffee. "His."

"That makes it even better."

We sat at a table and reached for the sugar canister at the same time. We both took our coffee black except when we were at the courthouse. The brew there is abysmal. I got to the little packets first and plucked out a whole handful of them. We divided them up, four apiece.

"I have another ulterior motive," I said suddenly. "I'm thinking maybe it will get back to Mill that I'm seeing someone."

Grace very rarely made a move that wasn't smooth, but this almost made her snort her first sip of coffee out her nose. "What does Mill have to do with it?" she asked.

"He's suing me for custody of Chloe."

She went very still. "Bastard."

"It's the election."

"Of course it's the election. That's what makes him a bastard."

I felt the tension continue to uncoil and relax inside me. That's the thing about friends. The good ones, the real ones, don't just talk you down when you're nervous about something and they don't just reserve comment about why you need four sugars in your coffee and what that might do to your health. Real friends are always on your side. If you take it into your head to shoot someone, a real friend will help you hide the body before she asks you why you did it.

"What are you going to do?" Grace asked me now.

"Tear him limb from limb and use him for fertilizer."

"You should ask Sam to represent you," she said. "He's got that amazing winning percentage."

A lot of it had come at my expense, too. "He offered," I said. "I think if Judge Larson is going to hear this, I'll probably take him up on it." The complexion of things had changed since we had talked about it last night and I had declined his offer. We had an arrangement now and I *wanted* Mill to know about it. And Larson would probably give Sam the moon and the stars if he batted those blue eyes at her just the right way.

Grace finally drained her coffee—courageous soul that she is—and stood. "I need to get back upstairs. The criminal element calls. If tonight turns out to be the big night for you two, would you like Jenny to take Chloe off your hands?"

Some people might have thought it odd that she would offer up her roommate's services that way. I was used to it by now. "I'll let you know."

"Don't use Mrs. Casamento," she warned. "She'd be knocking on your door on an hourly basis, and that would be very tough on the libido."

"Sam's or mine?" I asked, standing as well.

"Sam's. Yours is so primed, a scud missile couldn't take it out."

I didn't even try to argue that one. I had been ignoring the little shock waves he created inside me for quite some time now. So I just nodded again. My neck was starting to hurt from all the up-and-down jerks I'd given it in the past twenty minutes or so, but I knew I could probably count a good neck rub in my immediate future.

We went back to the elevator bay, and Grace rode up while I headed down. When I hit the lobby again, I rooted my cell phone out of my briefcase. I called the office and told my secretary that something personal had come up so I wouldn't be back today. It wasn't really a lie. This was definitely personal with a capital *P*.

Wine had gotten me into this, I decided, and wine would get me through it. I stopped at a liquor store on my way home and hit the front door of my building at the precise moment a cab pulled up to the curb, toting Chloe and three other classmates whose mothers I'd made kiddie-travel arrangements with for purposes of school. It was my week to pay. Mrs. Casamento was waiting at the curb to collect Chloe for me and I took back the money I'd given her for the taxi.

"I'm home early today," I explained. Then Chloe bulleted out of the taxi and threw herself into my arms. I caught her neatly and didn't even come close to bobbling the bottle of Cabernet I'd bought.

"How come, Mom? This is cool!" Chloe shouted. I felt a spasm of guilt that she was so glad to see me. I wasn't around after school nearly enough.

"Hard to make a living if you don't work normal hours," Sylvie Casamento judged.

"I don't get paid by the hour," I assured her. "It's okay."

"Thing is, *I* count on this money every afternoon," she complained.

She didn't, I know. Her long departed husband had left her pretty comfortable. And if I went ahead with the Sam thing, I thought, then she would more than make up for this insult to her pocket book in extra baby-sitting hours. "I'll be sure to compensate you eventually," I promised her vaguely.

Chloe and I went inside.

"Feel like hanging out with Jenny and Grace tonight?" I asked her.

"Where are you going?" She'd learned the art of diverting questions from me.

"You first," I said.

"You're pulling rank, Mom."

"Exactly. Hold my briefcase for me while I find my keys."

"They're right there in your hand."

Okay, I was getting rattled again. The soothing, Grace effect was starting to wear off.

"So...where are you going?" Chloe persisted once we were in the apartment.

"I'm just going to hang out with Sam for a while." I deposited my briefcase on the sofa and toed off my high heels.

"So how come I can't stay home with you guys?"

How do kids do it? How do they zone right in on the one question you don't want to answer? "We're...going out," I lied.

My cell phone started ringing inside my briefcase. It sounded like a reprieve.

"Go do your homework," I said to my daughter.

"I don't have any."

"How can you not have any? Since when do second-graders not have homework?"

"When we have a substitute."

I found my cell phone and headed for the bathroom with it for a little privacy. I closed the door behind me and put the phone to my ear. "Hello?"

"Where are you?" Sam's voice asked. How had I known it was him?

"I thought you weren't supposed to ask me that. I thought that was one of your rules." His smooth, off-the-cuff bylaws for this arrangement bothered me again for a second. "Where are you?" I countered.

"In the courthouse lobby. Larson's clerk said you were in and out by two."

"Awney," I said. He knew about the guy—those motions always got slapped down by the judge inside of thirty minutes.

Sam gave me a brief pause. "Come out and play," he

said finally. "Meet me at McGlinchey's. Wear nothing, and we'll get this new deal of ours on the road."

I'd heard much more romantic suggestions in my time, but heat zinged through me anyway. It literally *flashed*. I leaned closer to the bathroom mirror and peered at my reflection to find that my cheeks were actually pink.

"Sure," I said a little breathlessly. "Just let me just get out of this suit."

His next silence was long by Sam standards. He's usually very quick off-the-cuff. "Wow," he said finally.

"Don't go all gaspy on me yet. I still have hose on."

"Mandy, you're doing something to me here."

My stomach rolled over and my legs went hollow again. *That* part, I thought, was really going to have to stop. "Hold the thought," I said. "I still have to arrange for a baby-sitter."

"I'll hold the thought *and* a table," he promised. "Just hurry."

I disconnected, then I think I wove around in little circles on the bathroom floor, staring blankly at the walls. I finally ended up near the edge of the tub and I sat there. My nerves had been pulsing with every heartbeat all day, and now they were haywire. I had to get a grip.

I finally got to my feet and went to the telephone in the kitchen. If Sylvie Casamento was pleased at the idea of being back on baby-sitting duty today after all, then she'd willingly die before she'd admit it.

"When will you be home?" she asked immediately.

"It doesn't matter," I told her. "Either Grace or Jenny will come by to pick up Chloe well before then."

"So where are you going, anyway?" Chloe asked from behind me when I hung up.

I sidestepped the question again. "You really don't have any homework?"

"Nope."

Past experience should have taught me to check, anyway, but my mind was already on who and what was waiting for me at McGlinchey's. "All right," I said. "Upstairs with you, then."

"You're going out right *now?*"

No, I'm going to get naked first, I thought giddily. "Soon enough. Come on. Let's go."

I ushered her as far as the steps. Mrs. C. took charge of her on the first landing, and I went back into my apartment and poured a full glass of the wine I'd bought.

It took me an hour to get Grace on the phone to tell her that things were a go after all, then to shower and dress. Thirty-nine of those minutes were spent in front of my lingerie drawer. One of them was spent in front of my closet.

The white silk blouse, the jeans and boots that I chose for the occasion were the easy part. But what I was going to wear *under* all those things? This was another matter entirely. I finally went for the Wonderbra and matching thong panties, which I wore only on special occasions. In my life, *special* when linked with the word *occasion* usually only means *dressed up*. It means that I am probably going to wear the slinky little black dress that I'd managed to steal from Saks Fifth Avenue for a mere eighty dollars on sale, and which was now the epitome of my wardrobe. I had never paired the Wonderbra with jeans and a blouse before. Nor had it ever gone on with such malice aforethought—that is to say, knowing that I intended to take it off again sometime before I brushed my teeth for the night.

This is all by way of explanation for the fact that I spent another five minutes turning this way and that in front of my cheval mirror in order to determine if the thing really did give me extra cleavage. I decided that Playboy was not going to come knocking on my door anytime in the foreseeable future, but the end result was something I could live with.

I finished dressing, slashed on lipstick and fluffed my hair. I left my apartment and caught a cab because I'd already had two glasses of the wine—those demon grapes again—and I didn't want the worry of driving. The taxi carried me toward McGlinchey's at what felt like warp speed—and I was suddenly, inexplicably calm.

It could have been—maybe even *should* have been—the most awkward experience of my life. As I've said before, I'm basically a traditional sort of woman. This was really pushing the envelope for me—getting together with a man for the express purpose of having sex with him. But—and this would be my downfall later—I discovered that it felt exactly right because Sam was the one waiting at the other end of this cab ride. I felt good in my skin.

The taxi spit me out in front of McGlinchey's. I swept inside, and Cinderella never had a finer moment. Then reality crashed in on me. Sam was waiting for me as promised, but he hadn't gotten us a table yet. This was because he was standing at the bar surrounded by no less than four adoring fans of the female persuasion.

Then he looked up and saw me. I know this sounds sappy, but his eyes lit. He grinned, one of his fast ones, and a world of knowing was in his eyes for a fraction of a second that had my heart doing calisthenics. He cut out of the throng and came toward me. I've wondered a lot since that night if I have ever been as happy as I was in that one moment, with endless possibilities ahead of me, most of them involving Sam.

"Those are clothes," he said, reaching me, then he ducked in for a quick kiss. *That* was new. "How was your day?" he asked, and that wasn't. He'd asked me the same question every afternoon for six months now, and I liked it because I knew he was genuinely interested.

"Awney's happy," I reported.

I could feel the women he'd left glaring at me. I admit it—I felt a little smug at my good fortune. There are worse things in life than being joined by a really good-looking man in public.

Then I saw people get up from a nearby table. "Quick. Dive."

Sam looked over his shoulder. He grabbed my hand and dragged me toward the seats just as they were vacated. "Good eye," he said as we claimed them.

I noticed that he kept his chair on the opposite side of the table this time. What did that mean? I tried not to wonder about it.

"How did that lunch go today?" I asked. "Have you heard anything from the Woodsens?"

"You were right. She's making him jump through hoops. He's complaining, but he's doing it."

"This will work, then."

I had another glass of wine and he nursed a scotch before he asked me where I'd stashed Chloe for the evening. It had never mattered before because we had never been concerned with her interrupting us. So this was another new wrinkle and it made warmth pool in deep parts of me.

"Grace has her," I told him. "Well, technically, Jenny. But you know how it goes." Grace has a staked interest in not appearing to be too much of a pushover. I knew from past experience that while she might have put Jenny up for the job of baby-sitting tonight, Jenny would be hard-pressed to pry Chloe free from Grace's grasp.

"Will they be keeping her overnight by any chance?" Sam asked.

I knocked back the last of my wine. "Overnight is against our rules, pal."

"Was that one yours or mine?"

"Yours, I believe."

"Can I change it?"

I thought about it. I didn't give a damn about holding to the rules, but I thought Grace might know a thing or two about the pratfalls of being considered an easy touch. "No," I decided.

"What if we start and don't want to stop?" he asked.

My stomach literally flipped over inside me. "Hey, they were your rules. Live with them."

"Okay, snookums."

I laughed, then I leaned across the table. If I prolonged this too much, I would end up fluttering right out of my seat, I decided. "Sam," I said. "Could you be persuaded to take me home now?"

He shot to his feet. "Where's the waitress?"

"Two paces behind you." I thanked my stars that it was Jenny, still on duty.

"Hey, guys," she said by way of greeting.

Sam shoved a twenty-dollar bill at her abruptly. "We'll catch up on the change later," he told her. "In fact, just keep it. I'm feeling magnanimous."

"You are?" she asked, startled. "Why? I don't get it."

He didn't answer her. He already had my hand and was pulling me out of the bar. I looked back over my shoulder at her. "By the way," I called, "you're baby-sitting to-night."

I knew the exact moment that she understood what was going on. She looked surprised, fiercely pleased, then wistful.

Chapter Five

Sam was disgruntled by the fact that I hadn't driven to the bar, and missing the opportunity to stomp on the clutch of my car dimmed his mood just a little. Boys and their toys, I thought, following him to the curb. A cab finally stopped for him and he got in first. So much for his new gentlemanly knack of holding doors for me.

"You're paying for this," he said when I slid onto the seat beside him.

"How is that fair?"

"You left a perfectly good vehicle sitting in a parking lot a block from our apartment building."

"I also have a perfectly good career," I pointed out.

He looked sideways at me. "What does that have to do with anything?"

"I'm attached to my license to practice and I figured I would be drinking tonight. A DUI would seriously derail my life."

He looked startled, then contemplative. "You were planning on getting drunk tonight?"

"I didn't say that."

"You're nervous about this."

My pride kicked in hard and fast. This was right there in the same ballpark with Grace's opinion that I was "hung up" on him. "Of course I'm not. Are you?"

"Not at all."

"Well, good. Me, neither."

"Then why were you planning on getting drunk?"

"I didn't say I was going to get *drunk!* I never get drunk!" Then I noticed in the rearview mirror that the driver was grinning at us. He was a jovial-looking guy to begin with, roughly the shape of Santa Claus if my view of him from the waist up was any indication.

"How long have you guys been married?" he called back to us.

"We're not married," Sam told him. "We're just having illicit sex."

I choked on my own breath. "Keep this up and you'll talk your way right out of our arrangement," I whispered.

"Not likely." He grinned at me. "You want this as much as I do."

I had alternating reactions to that. The first was that I was entirely too transparent for my own good. The second was that he was admitting *he* wanted it a whole lot, too—which was a very nice thing indeed.

The cab stopped at our building, and we went to my apartment by unspoken accord because I have furniture. Sam, on the other hand, has always gone about decorating pretty much the same way he went about dating, which is to say that he shops a lot but he rarely commits. His apartment contains the barest of essentials and he seems happy that way.

We made it inside and behind my closed door without being intercepted by either Chloe or Mrs. C., which was something I'd worried about a little. If it had happened, in the immortal words of Ricky Ricardo, I'd have had some 'splaining to do. Why had I shipped my daughter off if I was planning to be home tonight? I locked my door behind us.

Nerves were beginning to jump in my stomach again, but they were mostly of the perplexed variety now. How exactly were we supposed to get from the ground we'd always enjoyed over to that exciting new potential ground we'd planned on?

I looked to Sam for some guidance. This had been his idea, after all. But he only turned on the television as he did every time he stepped into my living room.

I went to the kitchen and came back with the wine. He was still standing in the middle of the living room, poking at the remote control.

"How do you get the kiddie handcuffs off this thing?" he asked.

I had recently invested in digital cable. It was awesome—for an adult, but not for a seven-year-old. I'd yet to tune in to any of the spicier channels, though I kept thinking I would—purely for the edification, of course. Still, the range of premium networks was something I didn't want Chloe glueing herself to, so I'd put the requisite childproof locks and bars on the controls. I put the wine on the table and snagged the remote from his hands, clicking it into grown-up mode. The channel flashed to a scene of a half-naked woman running down a street, screaming at the top of her well-endowed lungs. I lowered the volume a little.

When I looked Sam's way again, he'd poured the wine but he was still standing. I'd never known him not to just drop down on my sofa and put his feet up on the table.

Then it hit me like a revelation—for all his game talk, *he* didn't quite know how to get from here to there, either.

That touched me in a tender spot inside that probably would have been better left untouched. It made my breath feel a little shallow. I went to the sofa first—my usual end—and patted the cushion beside me. Self-explanatory. Sam grabbed his wineglass off the table and he finally sat.

''I've seen this one,'' he said, gesturing at the television with his glass.

Code Normal, I thought. ''Then change it.''

He picked up the remote again and began scrolling through channels as only a man can do. Grace and Jenny and I have discussed this phenomenon at length, and you probably have, too. We figure that it's true—men *do* come equipped with an instant radar-detection system that allows them to identify a program in two-fifths of a second. Somehow they know the full scope and details of any program they glimpse before female eyes can even actually see it.

Sam went through a minimum of 150 channels in sixty seconds, telepathically absorbing whole-show descriptions. I decided it was time to take matters into my own hands.

''I think we should be touching or something,'' I said.

He cut a look at me out of the corner of his eye. ''Touching how?''

''Not cuddling,'' I said quickly. ''Cuddling is against the rules.''

''All other kinds of touching preclude television watching,'' he pointed out.

I lifted my brows at him. ''You came here to watch my television?''

''Well, you've got a great cable system.''

I was amazed. Then it hit me again that he was a little unsure of himself here.

I grabbed the remote from his hands. He gave it up easily

enough, which lent some credence to the fact that he was not currently on his best stride. Then I lifted his arm and found my way beneath it, against his side. I draped his arm around my shoulders again once I was settled.

"This is cuddling," he said.

"No. It's relaxing."

He honestly seemed to think about it before he nodded. "Okay. That'll work."

I looked up at him to grin, and that was when he kissed me.

His stride was definitely back. And instantly mine was gone. He didn't kiss me the way he had in the courthouse lobby. This time he put his full attention to it. I knew whole moments—maybe for the first time in my life—where I felt I was the only thing that mattered in the universe. That alone is something I will never regret.

When it finally started happening, it happened fast. Intensely. Desperately. As if we had both been underwater for a long time and had finally been given a chance to breathe. He tasted like an elusive dream I was just beginning to remember. He kissed exactly the way I liked, hard and without apology, deep and without hesitation, wet and encompassing but not sloppy.

I was in heaven and would gladly have died there if he'd given me any chance at all to consider it. But I was too caught up in feeling things, so many things, all at once. What thoughts I did have were in and out of my head like lightning, some flickering, others spearing through and illuminating places that had always been dark before. There was one flash of Goldilocks, communing with the bear she liked best, and I thought, Oh, yes, this is just right.

His hands found my skin under the silk blouse that hid the Wonderbra. And I didn't feel cold, the way Mill had accused me of being. One of the spears of lightning I experienced had to do with the fact that I'd never made love before without…well, without considering what my next move ought to be. For instance—now my hands are here, so next they ought to go there. It had always been sort of an orchestrated dance, to be accomplished just so. No one had ever taken me outside of myself before, but Sam literally stole my ability to think.

His hands were perfect—but then, I'd known that from all those platonic neck rubs. Their charm and finesse didn't end with my vertebrae. They were strong, then gentle, tentative, now sure. And wherever they went, wherever they slid, I felt reaction in a layer deep beneath the surface of me. It wasn't even subdural—it was like shock waves reverberating deep, deeper still, heating all the little cells they bounced off.

To this day, I can't tell you where the Wonderbra went or when it actually came off—if he liked it or if I really could have bounced into McGlinchey's naked or in serviceable white cotton and gotten the same response. I remember thinking about his just-right hands, and I remember a moment of frisson when his weight settled on top of me. Somewhere in the process of losing clothes, I'd ended up on my back on the sofa. I had another Mill flash-thought—more like a chain reaction of them, actually—and they were an epiphany: I am normal. This feels incredible. I am not a cold fish. I knew then how much Mill's criticisms of me had hurt. I knew that in some measure I'd actually believed him.

There was heat down low at the core of me, and it kept getting hotter and tighter. It wasn't a star spiraling out of control but gathering in on itself instead, intensifying, pumping with a need to explode. Or maybe implode. I didn't feel as if I was going to come apart. I felt as if I was about to go home.

I had one moment of panic. It came when he filled me, because that was perfect, too. Then I found myself wondering how I was ever going to learn to live without this again.

This was an *arrangement,* and by definition it was temporary. But now that I had found this, now that I had experienced it, anything else would be second best, and I knew—even then I knew—that I would never settle for that. I wanted this, exactly this, with Sam, and nothing else would do. I wanted it even with all his rules. I wanted it on whatever terms I could have it. I just...wanted

It took me a long time to get my breath back afterward, even longer for the tingly sensation in my limbs to subside. I am not much of a talker after sex under the best of circumstances, and I couldn't actually remember ever going breathless and tingly before. So I said nothing for a long time.

Then little by little I became aware of the fact that *Sam* wasn't saying anything, either. My heart started thudding all over again, just about the time it was getting back to a normal rhythm. I wondered if *he* was usually a talker after sex. It stood to reason that he was—he rarely shut up in any other scenario. I decided this was definitely out of character for him.

Something was wrong.

I started to panic. Then he hummed. Maybe it was a moan. Maybe it was a sigh. But it was noise regardless, and it came from his vocal chords, not my own.

I let myself breathe again, then he asked, "Where do you keep your antacids?"

I struggled to sit up, pushing him off me. I nearly landed him on the floor, but he recovered in time to save himself. "Sex with me made you *sick?*" I demanded.

He found his usual end of the sofa and stared at me. "Where did you get that from?"

"You were quiet!"

"I always get quiet when my stomach's burning."

"That's what I mean! There's a definite link here between orgasm and antacid!"

"I was really geared up for this, Mandy."

I felt like an idiot even while I felt a smile pull my mouth wide. "Oh," I said. "Well, that's good."

He kept staring at me as though he was waiting for something more.

"What?" I said.

"So can I have the antacids?" he asked again.

I jumped up from the sofa, remembered that I was naked and swiped his shirt off the coffee table. I punched my arms into the sleeves as I headed for the bathroom. Then my own stomach started to unsettle. I was pretty sure I had just nudged up against breaking a rule: thou shalt not nag, bitch, complain, or call one's arrangement-lover on the carpet over asking for antacids at a delicate moment.

"That wasn't in his rules," I muttered aloud as I rooted in my medicine cabinet. It was perilously close to *no whining or guilt trips,* but that had been in conjunction with one of us having other plans. It had nothing whatsoever to do with one's stomach being adversely affected by sex with the other party.

I wondered if maybe he'd just been worried about his own performance. He hadn't actually said *how* he'd been geared up, after all.

I forgot about the antacids and shoved my fingers into my hair. I was making myself crazy with this. Then a knock came at the bathroom door.

"What?" I called out, finally grabbing the antacids.

"Are you hiding in there because it wasn't as good for you as it was for me?"

My grin came back. That was *definitely* the sound of someone else making himself crazy with this.

I went back to the door and pulled it open to push the antacid bottle at him. He headed back to the living room ahead of me, gloriously naked. My tongue wanted to cleave to the roof of my mouth as I watched him. That's another thing about men, a thing I actually envy them. They can be three-hundred-pound Sumo wrestlers, but they never seem to have a single qualm about how they look naked. It never occurs to them that a jiggle here or an extra bulge there might not be a *good* thing. They don't suffer the female need for draping. For most of *us,* an artful sweep of cloth here or there to hide various physical flaws is the way to go. I'm reasonably sure that even Grace, as gloriously beautiful as she is, has never strolled across a room stark naked and felt good about it.

I finally hurried after Sam to find—to my great dismay—that he was no longer undressed. He'd put his boxers back on.

He sat and picked up his wine. "So what were you doing in there for so long?"

I blinked at him. "Where?"

"The bathroom. Did it involve…you know…thinking about what we just did?"

"Oh, that."

He looked alarmed. "How exactly do you mean 'Oh, that'?"

I decided to be honest with him—well, halfway honest. His ego clearly needed it, but I needed to hold some cards. "It was fantastic, Sam," I said, curling up beside him again. "There's something to be said for arrangements."

He grinned. "Yeah, there is, isn't there?" Then he relaxed. "Where's the remote?"

"I don't know. Who had it last?"

"I think you did. Which would put it…"

I leaned forward to look on the floor. It was under the coffee table, lying between my Wonderbra and my jeans. I started to reach for it.

As I said before, Sam has a way of moving like smoke. He can drift from place to place with utter male grace. I leaned over and reached and he sort of drifted into me. Or over me, as the case might be. I found myself on my back on the sofa again and he was nibbling at my mouth.

I liked it. In fact, I loved it. If I had been even remotely sane that night, I would have known right then, in that moment, that I was in way too deep over my head. I would have known that I was *beyond* "hung up" on him. But I just teased his lower lip with my tongue instead while he talked.

"Do we really want to watch television?" he asked.

"Um…maybe not."

"I feel like a kid in a candy store."

My heart vaulted as he kissed me fully. "Me, too," I said against his mouth.

"I actually really was thinking about television before you…you know, leaned forward like that."

"How did I lean forward?"

"The way you always do. But you never did it half-naked in my shirt before." He began doing interesting things to my lower lip.

"Not true. I've borrowed your clothes a lot." His sweatshirts were just big enough on me to be the epitome of comfiness.

"But you always had something on under them," he said. "At least I thought you did."

He was working his way down my throat now. I had

never in my life felt anything so divine. "I was naked under them. I'm always naked inside my clothes."

"Stop being a lawyer and splitting hairs."

"And be what instead?"

"Mine." Then he heard his own voice. "For now," he said quickly. "Just for now."

"For the life of our arrangement."

"Exactly. And a really great arrangement it is, too."

The first time we'd made love, we'd both been really driven. This time was so agonizingly slow, it tore the breath from my body *before* it was over. We talked like that for ten minutes, mouth to mouth, nibbling and licking between words. That time, more than the first time, I was exquisitely aware of every inch of his skin against mine. I can't tell you where his boxers got to any more than I could account for the activities of my Wonderbra the first time around. And this time he was talkative afterward. Maybe we were just finally falling into a rhythm together, or maybe his stomach felt better.

"What are the odds that you have any of those shrimp left from last night?" he asked almost immediately.

"Just for the record, that's up there with after-sex comments like 'Where's the antacid?'"

"Both are permissible under arrangement bylaws," he said.

"In that case, the answer is no."

He pushed up a little, resting his weight on his elbows to stare me in the eyes. "What do you mean, no? There was a whole bowl of them when I left here last night. Where'd they go?"

"I polished them off while I was making my list of rules."

He seemed startled. "How long could that have taken?"

Hours. "I also watched a late movie, chewing all the while."

He thought about it. "So there's nothing around here to eat?"

"You want me to feed you, too?"

"You always did before."

Too late, I realized I should probably have put that in my rules: no little-woman scenarios, scurrying off to the kitchen after sex to feed and care for my man.

"Peanut butter and jelly," I offered, knowing he hated any combination thereof.

"Let's order out for Chinese," he decided predictably. Then he eased off me. I felt lonely without him.

I sat up. "I'll flip you for the tab," I said.

"We don't have to do that. I'll grab this one."

I sighed. "I know you, Sam. You tore up Lyle Woodsen's bill, didn't you?" Being a solo practitioner, he didn't have the luxury of partners to fall back on. He wouldn't have drawn a paycheck this week.

He shrugged in a way that said it all. "Yeah, but I picked up a DUI charge and an estate yesterday."

"You won't get paid on the estate until it settles. I'll buy."

Sam's jaw came forward. This is another guy thing—their pride is even more precarious than ours sometimes. I think this is especially the case after they've just had sex with someone. They experience a distinctly overriding need to beat their fists against their chests and to drag home some bacon—even if they never plan on seeing the woman again, even if it's just paying for the pizza on that one occasion. Or the moo goo gai pan, as the case might be.

"Never mind," I said finally. I definitely wasn't in the mood to argue about it, and I didn't want him spending the money over something so unnecessary. "I'll just cook something."

He perked up. "Naked?"

I narrowed my eyes at him. "You've been talking to Lyle Woodsen again, haven't you?"

"I think he was the one who always ran around un-clothed, not Lisa."

I wagged my brows at him. "Feel free."

He laughed and grabbed my hand, tugging me off the sofa. "We'll make it a joint effort."

He wasn't dressed. I decided that in order to keep in the spirit of things, I really wouldn't do it, either. I'd just suck in my tummy. It's my personal opinion that that part of my anatomy went to hell in a handbasket when I had Chloe. For that matter, I never needed a Wonderbra prior to her birth, either. My breasts had once stayed up all by themselves.

Sam didn't seem to share my opinion in either quarter. I'd barely gotten the makings for a salad out of the fridge when he caught me from behind and started nuzzling my neck.

I sighed and leaned back against him, and we never ate.

Chapter Six

Sometime after nine o'clock, Sam went upstairs to collect Chloe for me. When they returned, she was wearing the full repertoire of Grace's cosmetics bag. She hit our apartment like a pinball, bouncing off walls and furniture, and I figured that she'd had a healthy share of sugar during her visit, too, maybe even some caffeine-rich chocolate.

"Where did you guys go?" she squealed, doing a flying leap into my arms.

To heaven. "McGlinchey's." I slid her back down to earth. "Time to hit the tub, kiddo."

"But I already took a bath upstairs."

"Okay, just wash that stuff off your face, then."

"Mom! I'm bee-yoo-tiful!"

"Yes, you are," Sam agreed.

Chloe beamed at him, then she curtsied. It was something she'd picked up recently in ballet lessons.

"Don't encourage her," I warned, "or I'll make you wash her pillowcase when she smears lipstick all over it."

"I always do my laundry down here, anyway," he said, shrugging. "What's the difference?"

He had a point. I wondered suddenly how such a routine would fit into our new rules. Wasn't it a little like sharing toothbrushes?

He grabbed Chloe and spun her up and around to sit on his shoulders. "Come on," he said to her, then he added in a stage whisper, "We'll run the water real loud and maybe we can fake her out. Maybe she won't even notice that you still have all that gunk on your face when we come back from the bathroom."

"It's not gunk!" Chloe protested.

"Beautiful gunk," Sam corrected himself, then he headed off down the hall with her.

I watched them go and I had a sudden pang that hurt. I could not lose her to Mill. For the better part of twenty-four hours, I had done a pretty good job of not dwelling on that possibility, or the lawsuit. Mill had crept up in my thoughts here and there, but he always did. He was my best and my worst mistake. He'd given me Chloe, after all, but now he wanted her back. *Damn him.* I swallowed an emotion that tasted bitter and decided that I needed more wine to wash it down.

Sam returned from the bathroom, winking at me exaggeratedly. A moment later Chloe followed him and I saw why. Her hair was soaked all around her scalp line, but she still wore every trace of Grace's makeup.

"Thank you for cleaning her up," I said to Sam. Who cared about pillowcases, anyway?

Chloe giggled. "He did a good job, Mom."

"I can see that. Are you *sure* you don't have any homework?" I asked again.

She shook her head hard, and her long, dark hair swirled—the part of it that wasn't plastered to her skull.

"Okay, then," I said. "You can have half an hour of Nickolodeon before lights-out."

"Cool!"

She did a U-turn on one heel and raced back to her bedroom and the television there. I watched her and had to swallow hard again.

"It's not going to happen," Sam said, reading my mind. "You're not going to lose her."

I knocked back another mouthful of wine. "That reminds me—we need to talk about this."

"You're going to let me represent you after all."

I shouldn't have been startled. We had been on the same wavelength so often over the months that it was a miracle we didn't have bruises from bumping into each other there. But I'd been pretty adamant about this, so it surprised me. "How did you know?"

"I figured it would take you just about a day to remember that Larson really likes me."

"We could pull another judge in the rotation," I pointed out.

He shrugged. "It wouldn't matter. I played golf with Judge Shannahan last weekend."

That didn't actually make me happy. "You played golf with one of our judges? No wonder you win so many cases."

"It's called schmoozing." He poured himself more wine, as well, then he scowled a little. "You know, I should just leave a bottle of Glenlivet down here."

"Is that in keeping with our rules?" I asked.

"I don't remember anybody saying anything about scotch, Mandy."

"I mention it because it seems a little like blurring lines, you know, infiltrating."

"Infiltrating what?"

"Each other's lives."

"With scotch?"

He made it sound stupid—but, hey, toothbrushes were never mentioned in any of my rules.

He pushed his wineglass at me. "Here. You drink this. I'm going upstairs for my Glenlivet, and when I get back and Chloe's tucked away, we can talk about the thing."

Thing was as good a description of Mill as any I could think of, so I nodded and went to snuggle Chloe into bed. Later, when Sam came back and she was asleep, I coerced him into watching an old rerun of *Bewitched* with me. I have always envied that thing Elizabeth Montgomery did with her nose. How glorious would life be if I could just wiggle my own and make Mill disappear along with all the Barbies populating my living room?

"Okay, here's what we're going to do," Sam said, flicking channels even before the *Bewitched* closing jingle started playing.

"Hey," I protested. "I like that part."

"You're procrastinating."

I was. "All right, what are we going to do?"

"First, I'll swing by Larson's chambers for a little tête-à-tête tomorrow morning."

"You've been tête-ing with Larson? I knew it."

He gave me a long-suffering look. "You're changing the subject again."

I sobered suddenly, feeling something cold wash through me. Maybe he saw something in my eyes, because he said, "Hey, hey," real quietly and pulled me close. I snuggled into his arms and his rules could be damned.

"She's all I have, Sam," I said. "Chloe is what I *am*. She's all I ever wanted."

"I know."

"I'm afraid I wouldn't know how to wake up in the morning without her."

"I won't let it happen."

"You're not God."

"You're kidding, right?"

I nudged a fist into his ribs, which effectively put an end to the snuggling. He straightened and I sat up, too.

"About this tête-ing you and Larson are going to do," I said, getting back to the scary thing that I had been trying to avoid.

"I'll find out if your matter is on her docket," he said. "If it's not, I'll move on and take it from there. If it is, I'll let her know how angry it makes me that Kramer is doing this to you and to that little girl."

"Does Larson know we're friends?"

He gave me an incredulous look. "Mandy, everyone knows we're friends."

Well, if they didn't, I thought, they would soon—after news of our kiss in the courthouse lobby this afternoon got around. "Right. Then what?"

"That, along with all my spectacular legal moves, should be enough."

"You're not *that* spectacular, pal."

"I'm injured. You said it was as good for you as it was for me."

"I meant in the courtroom."

"So I *am* spectacular in bed?"

I threw a sofa pillow at him. "Larson is holding my life in her hands and you're thinking about sex?"

"We don't know if it's Larson yet or not, and I often think about sex."

"How often?" I asked, curious. I just barely stopped myself before I inched onto forbidden-by-the-rules ground and added: *with whom?*

Sam started to look wary. "What do you mean, how often? Now and again. Once in a while."

"Once in a sixty-minute while, or once in a twenty-four-hour while?"

"Closer to a once-in-a-minute while."

"Are you serious?"

"No. But it was worth the look on your face."

I was running out of pillows to throw at him.

"So how often do *you* think about it?" he asked.

Before or after our arrangement? "Three times a day." That was generally as often as he gave me neck rubs or appeared at my door unexpectedly.

"You beast," he said.

I laughed.

"You know, those black sweatpants you have do it for me," he added suddenly.

I have not often in my life been flabbergasted, but I was then. And things inside my blood started catapulting. Because if I understood what he was saying, then he'd thought about sex with me well before our arrangement. In woman-speak, that meant something.

"The really old ones with the bleach stain on the right thigh?" I asked to be sure. Had to be, I thought, because they were the only black ones I owned.

"They're too big on you," he said as though that explained it all.

They were. "I lived in them while I was pregnant," I explained, "so the waist stretched out."

"Yeah."

Yeah? What was I missing here? "They're my grubbies," I added. "That's why I've kept them all this time."

He nodded. "You wear them on Sunday mornings while you do the crossword puzzle."

"And they turn you on?"

"Especially with that yellow kangaroo top you've got."

That was when I began to understand. The yellow top with the kangaroo on the front was actually a T-shirt I'd destroyed in the wash. It had shrunk, and now it didn't quite hit my navel lengthwise. As for the sweats, the elastic was shot enough in the waist that they more or less rode my hips. All in all, it was a very comfy ensemble and it left maybe four inches of skin exposed, but if I'd been planning to inspire him to great sexual heights, I never would have thought of it.

"Thanks," I said. "That's nice."

His eyes narrowed. "Are you going to go all mushy and female on me?"

That was exactly what I was doing. "Of course not. It's against the rules, isn't it?"

He watched me a moment longer, then he apparently decided that my response was safely unmushy. "Okay, then. About Mill."

A bucket of cold water could not have had a greater dousing effect on me. "Around these parts, we call him 'the bastard.'"

Sam frowned. "I never heard you say that."

"I do it mostly in the company of Jenny and Grace, and out of Chloe's earshot—for obvious reasons. But I've said it more often lately."

"When was the last time he saw Chloe?" he asked.

"When she was five months, two weeks and six days old."

"You *remember* that?" He seemed astounded. "That's amazing."

"Not really. What was the phone number of the first girl you ever kissed?"

"It was 555-6093. Beth Brickman. Gorgeous, tall, strawberry blonde."

"I rest my case," I said. Men and women really aren't so different after all—their priorities are just in different stratospheres.

"Okay—five months, two weeks, six days," Sam said. "No way in hell are any of our judges going to award him custody of a seven-year-old girl he hasn't seen since then."

I knew that—intellectually, anyway. "Mill probably out-earns me four-to-one. He's a partner in one of the most established, ritzy and nose-in-the-air firms in the city."

"Doesn't compete with the mental and emotional stability of the child," Sam countered. And he was right again. Our commonwealth judges cared about *that* much more than income. Still, I persisted. "His family has Philly clout."

"Where's your family from?" Sam asked suddenly.

I realized that there was actually something I had never told him about myself. Then again, my family is something I very rarely discuss.

"They're not in the picture," I said finally.

"Why?"

I shrugged.

"Why haven't we ever talked about this before?" he asked, reading my mind again.

"It's no big deal. You don't know my checking account balance, either. You don't know *everything* about me."

"It was $4108.00 three days ago," he replied, "but you hadn't actually made the last deposit yet, and I figure you've unloaded a bunch of that since then because yesterday was the first of the month and you would have paid bills."

I stared at him, stunned for the second time that night. "You have no way of knowing that."

"Sure, I do. You spilled your purse on my living room floor last Tuesday night when you dropped off my dry cleaning."

"And you filched my checkbook register?" It had gone missing—now I knew why.

"It flew under my sofa."

"You actually cleaned and found it there?"

"No. I saw it go under and I decided to let you leave before I fished it out. I wanted to find out how much more money you make than me."

"That's low." But the crazy thing was, I loved his honesty.

"I intended to tell you. It just didn't come up until now."

I knew that was the truth, too. "Shouldn't we have some secrets here?" I asked.

"Why? It's just an arrangement."

In that moment, said in just that way, it hurt. But I rallied. "So *do* I?" I asked after a moment.

"Do you what?"

"Make more money than you do?"

"Oh. No."

"And you were going to let me buy the Chinese food tonight?"

"No, I wasn't. But I really did give Lyle his fee back. I'm in a slump."

I decided to play this turn of events to my advantage. "So I don't have to pay you for representing me in this Mill mess, right?"

"Mandy, get real."

That response could go either way. It was very noncommittal. "I could get one of my partners to do it free," I pointed out.

"Except you're the only attorney with your firm who practices family law, and that's why you're up for a partnership next year."

Was there *anything* he didn't know? "Where'd you hear that?" I asked. "I didn't tell you that. I only found out myself two days ago."

"Judge Shannahan told me," he said. "Over golf. He's tight with Leonard Custin."

Custin was my firm's senior partner. "I need to start golfing," I said.

"Maybe not. You'd look dorky in those shorts. They come down to the knees. You're more built for speed, Mandy."

My knees went back into unsteady mode, and I was sitting. What did that mean? "Thanks again, I think." Then I hastened to clarify, "That wasn't mush. It was just pure female gratification."

"I got it," he said.

"So what are you going to charge me for this?"

He grinned. "Not money."

"Sexual favors?"

"All in keeping with our arrangement," he explained.

"What if our arrangement doesn't last until the hearing?"

He scowled at me like I was being ridiculous. "The hearing is only four weeks away."

But for some reason I couldn't let it go. "Theoretically speaking, Ms. Right could cross your path at four o'clock tomorrow," I persisted.

Something happened to his face then. I wasn't expecting it, and I couldn't quite define it. Was he sad? Pensive? Angry? Had I crossed a rule line somehow without knowing it? "Mandy," he said finally, "the last thing in the world I want is Ms. Right. I really thought I'd found her in Shelly, and I never want to go through that again.''

Ah, I thought. His ex-wife. I remembered that I owed him an apology. ''Sam, I'm sorry I assumed you were the one who ended your marriage. It's just that from the time I first met you, you've always been so…I don't know. Free-wheeling.''

''I never was until she got through with me.''

It was one of the saddest things I'd ever heard anyone say. That kind of betrayal—the kind that made you change your whole modus operandi—was tough.

He was being honest enough that I thought I owed him a piece of myself, too. ''My dad left when I was six,'' I said suddenly. ''So I guess I don't trust men much.''

''You trust me.''

I realized with something that rocked me a little that I really did. ''Yeah.''

''Where's your mother?'' he asked.

''To this day I'm not entirely sure if she went up or down,'' I admitted.

''She died?''

''My second year in law school.''

''So you have no one?''

''I have a very rich, very snotty sister in Seattle. We don't talk.''

''I have a brother,'' he said.

I hadn't known that, either. ''Is he rich and snotty?''

''He's a dead-broke cowboy who loves his beer.''

We were crossing a line here. I knew it as I stared into his eyes. Something inside me yelled, *Lighten up!* And something else said that he really was the only person in the world I'd trust my every secret with.

We were one day into our arrangement, and I could already feel it coming apart at the seams. None of our rules had addressed secrets, I thought. Maybe they should have. This was a little scary.

"So what do you want for representing me against Mill?" I asked again to change the subject. "You know, in light of our arrangement?"

He sat back against the sofa cushions and drained the scotch he'd brought down from his apartment. "Can you ever have Chloe stay somewhere overnight? Is that possible?"

I jolted. Sure, it was possible. But... "That's against our rules. *Your* rule specifically."

"I just want to be able to keep going sometime, a little later than eight o'clock, anyway. We can't keep playing around if she's in the bedroom."

This was the second time today that he had alluded to an overnight. This, too, "meant something" I thought, but I wasn't sure what. "Keep her safe from Mill's clutches," I said, "and I'll arrange it."

He grinned. "Throw in those stretched-out black sweatpants and you've got a deal. I can't tell you how many times I've thought of peeling those off you."

I decided to wait until morning to check Chloe's book bag to nail down the homework situation. I started to lock up and turn the lights off, then I realized that Sam's Glenlivet bottle was still on the coffee table.

I picked it up to take it to the kitchen, then I paused in mid-stride. There was a rule-hitch in here somewhere, I thought. In fact, just as I had told him, this scotch business was rife with rule-breaking possibilities. If I put it in a cupboard with my precious stash of special-occasion Chambord, that would be too cozy, wouldn't it? Storing our stuff side by side in my apartment was long-term, comfortable, antiarrangement. But if I left it out on the kitchen counter, that would be like saying I was just waiting for him to pick it up and go again, which I definitely was not. I finally turned around and went back to the living room, perching it high on a shelf of the entertainment center. I stepped back and studied it there.

Good enough.

I finally caught a few hours of sleep. The alarm jarred me awake again at six and for a moment I just looked up at the ceiling, letting my eyes take their time about focusing. I love the first five minutes of every day. I'm not sappy enough to tell you that I lie there and rhapsodize about all the possibilities ahead of me. I just mentally pick up the threads of my life from the day before and do a little plotting and planning for the hours ahead. It's a quiet, lazy time—often the only private time I'd have all day.

That morning I did something that was too rarely a part of the ritual. I remembered the night before and I grinned ear to ear. It occurred to me that what had happened with Sam was a little like finding an absolutely perfect pair of new jeans. You go shopping for them knowing that you're not going to find them, not on this trip, maybe not even on the next. Then…serendipity. There they are, and they fit like a second skin. Of course, the down side to this is that you never want to throw them out. The seat wears thin, the seams go to light blue, and the hems fray, and you still can't part with them because they were perfect once.

That realization and all its implications wiped the smile from my lips at the same moment Chloe's face swam into my view. She was standing at the side of my bed, peering down at me.

"Um…Mom," she said.

Those two words are some of the most alarming in the English language. Couple them with the fact that this child never voluntarily wakes much before eight o'clock, and we've got trouble. Something was on her mind.

"What?" I asked warily.

"I need a fruit that starts with my name."

My eyes were very focused now. "You need *what?*"

"Hold on."

She scampered from my bedroom again. She was going to get something from her book bag, I realized—the book bag that I hadn't checked last night. Would I never learn?

I got up and rummaged in a drawer for sweatpants to pull on under the T-shirt I'd worn to bed, and I came up with the black pair. I felt a good strong thump in the center of my chest and grinned again—but it only lasted a second. Chloe was back, waving a piece of pink paper. The sad truth is that if Shania Twain really "felt like a woman" in that song, then she probably didn't have children while she was singing it.

I took the paper and read it. "Is today the third?" I asked. That was the due date for the fruit.

My daughter nodded solemnly.

"And this was assigned yesterday?" I *knew* this pink piece of paper had not been in her book bag two days ago.

"Sort of...maybe...last Friday." She was doing a good job of studying her toes. "I forgot to bring it home until yesterday."

I was getting a headache and it wasn't even six-thirty yet. "And nowhere in the three times I asked you about homework last night—nowhere in all that did a memory of this fruit business surface?" I demanded.

Her face came up and her chin jutted. She got that from me. "It's not *homework,* Mom. It's an *in-class* project."

When I was in second grade, we had reading, writing and arithmetic, and anything that was sent home with us was called homework. Also, very little of it involved my mother making a side trip to the supermarket before she went to work. Then again, my mother rarely worked. She basically just drank and ruminated about my father, sometimes in angst, sometimes in fury.

Today Chloe had to take a fruit to school that began with the first letter of her first name. "You need a cantaloupe," I realized.

She nodded earnestly.

"And this teaches you what?"

She shrugged. "It's science."

"Unless you're going to dissect this thing, there's nothing scientific about it."

"Mom, I *need* it."

And there went my morning. We scrubbed last night's makeup off her face while simultaneously brushing our teeth. She squealed a little when I yanked her hair into a ponytail a little too hard. I was rushed again.

We finally hit the door. I was hopping up and down on one foot, trying to get my other shoe on, when I lost my balance and stepped on Barbie's sports car. I swore mildly when I felt a run tear up the back of my heel. I hurried back into the bedroom to change hose, yanking my skirt up to my hips to drag off the ruined pair of stockings. Then I had a thought that gave me fierce pleasure. I'd dearly love to see Mill deal with this sort of thing if he won our court battle. "Ha!" I said aloud. The custody he wanted so badly would last maybe two days by my reckoning. Then again, he'd probably just have his maid take care of this cantaloupe business. And remembering his maid, I realized that she'd probably already have one in residence, tucked into the fridge for just such an emergency.

I put my shoes back on and hurried to the front door. It was nearly a quarter to eight. We'd just make it, I thought. I took my cell phone out while I drove—something I try conscientiously never to do—and called the other mothers that I normally did the taxi-pool thing with.

Every last one of them already had a food product with a first letter that matched their child's name. I felt small. I told them all to car pool without me today without explaining why.

There was a produce market between the courthouse and Chloe's school. I parked, shoved change into the meter and jogged inside. Five minutes later I found myself shouting at the clerk. "What do you mean, you don't have any cantaloupes?"

"They're not in season," he said.

"What's in season that begins with a *C?*"

He looked at me like I had lost my mind. I was on the verge of it. "Carrots?" he suggested. "They're always in season."

"It has to be a *fruit*. It's the food chain. And she's a fruit."

He backed off from me warily. "Maybe you could change her to a vegetable."

I shoved my fingers into my hair, thinking. Then it hit me. "Cherries!"

"Got them," he said, obviously relieved.

I jumped back into the car with twelve minutes to spare before Chloe had to be in school. "Ta-da!" I said, pulling the cherries from the bag.

Chloe's face lit up. "Mom! They're not just a *C!* They're a *Ch!*"

Sometimes we win, I thought.

I pulled away from the curb and headed for her school. By the time I landed in the courthouse lobby, my clients were waiting for me. I mentally divide my case load into categories of "ugly"—like the Woodsens, where even the easy answers are iffy—and "sweet," which is not actually preferable. The Conovers were on the "sweet" list. Good people, just married, and he wanted to adopt her child by a previous relationship. They made cow eyes at each other a lot and they used all those endearments I'd warned Sam away from in my own rules.

The paperwork was in order so it was an open-and-shut hearing. There was no protest from the child's natural father, and I was out of Larson's courtroom less than an hour after I got there. For the first time since Chloe had appeared beside my bed that morning, I found a chance to really breathe. I stopped just outside the courtroom door and leaned back against the wall as I watched the Conovers leave. They were smiling at each other beatifically, but they hadn't made any cooing noises. At least, they hadn't done so in my hearing.

"Amanda."

The voice that spoke my name was like a slap out of the blue. I jerked off the wall and looked around a little wildly. Mill was standing in front of the water cooler, looking my way.

It struck me then that I had never really felt any extreme emotion for him one way or the other—until now. Resentment and anger caught me by the throat. I can't even tell you that it was entirely pure and justified, a mother-tigress-defending-her-young sort of thing. That was part of it, of course, maybe even most of it. But just beneath the surface of that there ran an undercurrent of what Mill had said about me as a woman—of all the things I had realized in Sam's arms last night.

"Go away," I said shortly. "You're not anyone I want to see."

He sighed heavily and approached me instead. He really is a good-looking man. He's not of Sam's caliber, doesn't have Sam's roguish charm, but he can hold his own. He's tall, imposing, with sharp hazel eyes and a strong jaw. His dark hair was beginning to go a little gray at his temples, and it looked good on him the way it rarely does on a woman.

"I'm sorry," he said.

"No, you're not."

"I was really hoping there wouldn't be any hard feelings between us over this."

I stared at him. I couldn't believe what I was hearing. "How could there *not* be?"

"You've been raising her by yourself all this time. I thought perhaps you'd enjoy having a breath of freedom again."

Had he always been so cold? I shook my head because I wasn't sure. "I don't want my freedom. I want my child."

He didn't answer. His eyes coasted up and down me— critically, I thought. I found myself thinking that I was glad I had changed my stockings that morning instead of just zapping the run with clear nail polish and hoping it didn't ride all the way up my calf. I had on my favorite suit, too— the black pin-striped one.

"Why do you look different?" he asked suddenly.

Sam, I thought immediately. Maybe I was glowing or something. But that was ridiculous. A woman didn't suddenly just bloom because of one night of great sex with a really good friend. "In fact, you look fantastic," Mill continued. "I like your hair like that."

I'd let it grow lately to collar length and I wore it tucked behind my ears. "Stop trying to soft-soap me," I said.

"I was just stating an opinion."

"You've got an agenda, Mill. You've always got an agenda going on."

He looked genuinely hurt. "We parted on good terms, Mandy. At least, I thought we did. Why this bitterness?"

"I was fine until you pulled this nonsense. You've got to know that I'm not going to let Chloe go, Mill. Not without a fight that will leave your ears ringing. Not just so you can have a clean election.''

I shouldn't have been surprised when he held out a con-ciliatory hand. Mill doesn't argue. It's beneath him. He's upper-crust Philadelphia/Mainline bred to the bone, and he doesn't cause a scene. Ever.

I backed off so he wouldn't actually touch me. ''What?'' I asked suspiciously.

''Mandy, please. Let's sit down somewhere and talk about this.''

''She doesn't even know you, Mill! Have you even con-sidered what this would do to *her?*''

He ignored that. ''Can't we come up with a compromise? I was going to suggest that on the phone the other night before you cut me short.''

I thought back to that conversation. ''The pizza guy came,'' I remembered.

''If that's what you call them these days.''

I narrowed my eyes at him. ''Was that a joke?'' Humor has never been his strong suit.

Mill gave half a smile in appreciation of his own wit. ''You said you weren't involved with anyone. So, yes, I was joking.''

Sometimes opportunity just gapes at you. ''I lied,'' I blurted.

I had the pleasure of seeing him look genuinely taken aback. ''You did? Are you are seeing someone?''

''Yes.'' And I prayed that Sam would understand why I was elevating our arrangement into a full-blown rela-tionship.

Mill seemed troubled by that, when I had expected the exact opposite reaction from him—like maybe he'd be re-lieved that there was a man in Chloe's life after all and he would drop the suit. ''Is it serious?'' he asked.

"Oh, very." I made another mental apology to Sam.

"I'd still like to have coffee with you and discuss all this."

What did one have to do with the other, I wondered? He was playing a game here, I thought again, but I couldn't quite put my finger on what it was. Then I saw Sam come off the elevator.

He noticed me, grinned, then he recognized Mill and he went poker faced. I wasn't sure they'd ever met, but as I've said before, most lawyers in Philadelphia have either passed each other in these hallowed halls, bumped into each other at McGlinchey's or slept together.

I headed for Sam at the same time he started toward me. "Darling," I said, lifting my face for a kiss when we collided.

He seemed startled, but then he planted his mouth on mine and talked against it. "What's going on?" he asked in an undertone.

"I need your help here. Just follow my lead. *This* lead." I cuddled against him.

"Gotcha." He kept an arm around my shoulders and turned to Mill, then he let me go to hold out his hand. "I don't believe we've ever formally met," he said. "I'm Sam Case, Mandy's attorney."

Mill grasped Sam's hand in one of those more-smooth-than-macho grips. "Millson Kramer," he said.

"The Third," I added inanely.

Mill shot me an odd look before he glanced back at Sam. "Am I to understand that you deliver pizza on the side?" he asked.

Of course, Sam had no idea what he was talking about, but as I've mentioned, he thinks on his feet very well.

"Only for preferred customers," he said in his best Texas drawl.

I wanted to kiss him again. The only thing that stopped me was that this time I wouldn't have been doing it for show.

Chapter Seven

The next day was Saturday.

I'd been burning the midnight oil with Sam for three nights running at that point, and I'd decided that nothing short of nuclear holocaust was going to move me from my bed before a decent hour. When I woke at eight, I just snuggled deeper under the covers and closed my eyes again. This state of affairs lasted for approximately fifteen minutes before I felt the mattress shift as someone sat on the edge of my bed.

I opened one eye warily. It was Jenny.

"This isn't Kansas," I told her in one of those sleep-rough voices. "There are no roosters here. You took a wrong turn."

"I brought coffee," she offered.

That changed things—a little. I opened both eyes. "Why?"

"I want to hear everything about what's been happening with you and Sam."

"At quarter after eight on a Saturday morning?"

"I have to be at the art museum by nine," she explained.

I opened my mouth and closed it again. I wanted to go back to sleep more than I wanted to know why she was going to the art museum at such a ridiculous hour.

Chloe padded into the room next to state the obvious. "Mom, Jenny's here."

I gave up then. I pulled myself up against the headboard and took the coffee mug from Jenny's hand.

"Everything," she repeated, sweeping that long, gloriously straight, sun-blond hair back from her forehead. The color is real—I happen to know that it doesn't come out of a bottle. I'd often thought that she looked as if she should have been born and bred on the California coast, not on a farm outside Topeka.

"We have an arrangement," I said, sipping the coffee. Then, when Chloe left and went back to her Saturday-morning cartoons, I added, "We're taking a break from the opposite sex for a while. With each other."

"I already know that part. That's what *he* said. I want the inside scoop."

"Sam talked to you about this?" For some reason that startled me. "What exactly did he say?"

"That he wished he'd thought of it a long time ago."

Maybe all those tossed drinks had had to add up first, I thought. Then again, he'd said he'd been lusting after my black sweatpants for a while. "That's not bad," I decided.

Jenny grinned, showing even, white teeth that were almost too perfect—and *they* were real, too. "You two are great together. I've always said that."

"Well, it's just an arrangement."

She waved a hand dismissively. "Call it whatever you want—the man is smitten."

I choked a little on my coffee.

"You'll hang out together for a while," she decided, "then fall head-over-heels in love and the next thing you know Chloe has a little brother or sister. Or both."

"Not everyone wants a passel of kids, Jen," I said quickly. "Besides, I'm past childbearing age."

"Oh, you are not."

I had to steer her straight. I didn't want her getting her hopes up. She hadn't seen the expression on Sam's face the other night when he'd mentioned his ex-wife.

"It probably won't happen that way," I said gently, though I didn't know if I was being gentle for her sake or my own. "I don't think Sam will ever go down that sort of primrose path again. If it happens, I think he'll just be floored suddenly and out of the blue by someone. She'll blindside him. He'll find himself at the altar before he wakes up from his daze."

"Well, that's romantic, too. But it kind of leaves you out in the cold." Jenny frowned.

"It's okay," I lied. "What we're doing now is pretty terrific."

Her eyes lit again. "So was it great?"

"Spectacular," I said.

"Stupendous?" she asked.

"Gifted."

She blinked. "What?"

I realized that I had spoken aloud and flushed a little. "Sam is very…gifted," I explained. Or maybe it was just the way we fitted together.

Jenny let out a little sigh. "This is just too cool." Then she looked at my bedside clock and stood. "Oops, got to run."

I finally asked. "Why would anyone in their right mind go to an art museum at nine o'clock on a Saturday morning?"

"Single fathers who have visitation on Saturdays are looking for something to do with their kids." She tapped a finger against her temple to show that she'd thought this out.

"They go to fast-food restaurants and the zoo," I said.

"Not if they're intellectuals."

"Divorced parents usually put their own intellectualism on hold until after college graduation," I explained. "Their kids' graduations, I mean. I'm a divorce lawyer. I know these things. Any and all highbrow intentions fly right out the window in the face of hungry, whiny kids and a kitchen stove, especially where men are concerned."

Jenny came back to the bed. "You're saying that I should go to Mickey Dee's instead?" She seemed disappointed.

"If I were you, I'd go there first. Then I'd try a park a little later in the morning."

She thought about it. "That's nice. A walk in the park. I could go for a guy who makes time for a thing like that."

"Uh, Jenny." I cleared my throat. "You'll probably find what you're looking for tossing a football or Frisbee with his kids, not walking around looking at flowers."

She sighed and turned away, then she stopped again and looked back at me. "You gave me this idea, you know. You and Sam and this thing you're doing with the rules. I realized that I needed some guidelines, a planned approach. I was just...I don't know, flopping around like a fish on the lakeshore, waiting for someone to pick me up and toss me into the frying pan."

I winced. Jenny was hell on analogies. I also thought of that old adage about how Mr. or Ms. Right usually doesn't turn up until you quit looking for them. "Don't work on this too hard," I suggested.

She crossed her arms over her chest and leaned back against the doorjamb. "Here's the thing, Mandy. Call me a simple country girl, and that's fine. It's true. I'm just not you, and I'm not Grace. I don't want to be a Superior Court judge or a high-powered attorney."

"I'm not high powered." I felt vaguely indignant. "I spend almost as much time chasing down cantaloupes as I do working."

"I want children. I *love* kids."

Something gentle tugged at my heart. "You're young yet, Jenny. You've got plenty of time."

She pushed off the doorjamb. "I just figured I'd better get started on it now. I don't want to wake up some morning and realize I've overslept and that I'm waiting for the bus in my underwear."

That analogy I didn't get at all. "Good luck," I said, meaning it.

She left and I looked at my bedside clock, wondering if I could doze off again for another half hour. I slid back down under the covers and closed my eyes just as Chloe's voice rang out from the living room. "Mom! Sam's here!"

I sat up again fast. He came into my bedroom and my jaw dropped. "What do you have on?" I asked. He was wearing yellow slacks.

"I'm golfing with Judge Shannahan," he said. "It turns out he has your case."

My heart cringed a little. I had really started hoping for Larson because of her affinity for Sam's blue eyes. "When did you find this out?" I asked.

"Yesterday afternoon, but I didn't tell you last night because I didn't want to ruin our time together."

We'd gone out to dinner and then to a movie. And he

was right—the news would have wrecked my mood. We both knew his luck ran best with Larson.

"Golfing with a judge is not the normal way one goes about winning a case, Sam," I said, worried about his technique now.

"It's just one little part of my repertoire." He leaned in suddenly to kiss me.

I reared back. "No kissing before a toothbrush."

For an insane moment I thought he looked hurt. But hurt had no place in our arrangement. We had ruled out every possible potential for hurt.

"I used mine already," he said finally, easing away again.

"Good, because you're not allowed to share mine."

He sat on the edge of my bed. My mattress was seeing more traffic this morning than the Walt Whitman Bridge. "So what are your plans for today?" he asked.

"Chloe needs new sneakers, and I either have to hire a cleaning service or wash my kitchen floor myself. What are yours?"

"Schmoozing with the judge, then I thought maybe we should sit down and put our heads together and write a response to Mill's petition."

That was important. The Court calendar only gave us until Friday to submit it in order to give Mill's attorney time to rebut.

"I also distinctly remember you mentioning something about having show tickets for Atlantic City this weekend," Sam continued.

I gaped at him for a second time since I'd seen the yellow slacks. So much had happened this week—my world had been turned upside down—and I had forgotten all about the show tickets.

"That's tonight!" I scrambled out of bed.

"You look great in your underwear," Sam said, grinning.

I looked down at myself. I was wearing panties and the yellow kangaroo top. Which would have been great, would have presented some interesting possibilities, but my daughter was in the other room watching cartoons. It wouldn't do for her to find her mother half-clothed in the company of her best male friend.

"Oh, hell," I said, and shot for the dresser, yanking a drawer open. Sam made no comment and I glanced over my shoulder at him as I found a pair of shorts. It struck me that he understood exactly that I wasn't suffering a sudden bout of modesty and that it was nothing personal—I was thinking about Chloe. In fact, he got up and closed the door for me.

"Thanks," I said. "Do you want to go to the show? That's assuming I can scare up a baby-sitter at the last minute."

"Sure." Then he added, "Sylvie Casamento lives for your dollars."

"But Chloe doesn't like her enough to stay there overnight."

We both went still and looked at each other at the same time.

"Are we staying overnight?" Sam asked finally.

"It could be your no-little-girl-at-bedtime reward for representing me in court," I pointed out.

"True. Would you be packing the black sweatpants?"

I gave a jerky little nod.

"It'll probably be late by the time the show is over and it's an hour's drive back to Philly," he said. "Yeah, it makes sense for us to stay overnight. Jenny will watch Chloe, won't she?"

I knew she would. "So how does something like this fit into our rules?" I asked.

"Well, for one thing, we'll each take our own toothbrushes."

I think I laughed a little. "But we ruled out overnights."

"This qualifies as extraordinary circumstances."

"Not *that* extraordinary," I said. "We're not talking about Bermuda here, just Atlantic City."

"Are you trying to change my mind?"

Not likely. I bit down on my tongue hard enough that it hurt. "I just want to get everything ironed out arrangement-wise first."

Sam grinned again suddenly. "You're great, Mandy. You're about the only woman in the world this could possibly work with." He wagged a finger back and forth between us.

My heart kicked my ribs. I wasn't sure if that was good or bad.

"Okay, let's come at it from this angle," he suggested. "How would we have handled this back before we had rules?"

That was easy. "We would have shared a room to cut down on expenses."

He nodded. "You would have taken the one bed and I would have taken the other."

"So that's what we'll do, then. Assuming we can get a room at this late point."

"I'll take care of that, and you take care of the baby-sitter. What resort is this show at, anyway?"

"The Tropicana. It's Three Dog Night." I love vintage rock and roll.

"Okay. I'll try the Trop first. Worst-case scenario, we might have to walk next door to another hotel after the show."

"Sounds like a plan."

He went to my bedroom door, then he paused. "You know, you never mentioned that no-kissing-before-a-toothbrush thing in your bylaws," he said suddenly. "I don't know if it's fair to start adding new rules now."

I'd been right—something about that *had* bothered him. "I didn't mention it because I thought it was precluded by the no-overnights rule," I explained. "It's also kind of covered by the no-mushy-stuff rule."

"Okay. Then I'll keep it in mind."

No, don't! I wanted to shout it. I could change my mind. But he was already gone.

I heard the front door open and close as Chloe called out a goodbye to him. I went immediately into high gear. I had a lot to accomplish before we drove to Atlantic City.

"Sit, stay," I said to Chloe as I jogged through the living room.

"Where are you going?" she asked without taking her eyes from the TV. I backtracked to make sure it really was cartoons she was watching, that I had returned the kiddie controls to the cable system last night.

"Upstairs to Grace's apartment," I answered, satisfied with what was on the television screen. Jenny would already be at Mickey Dee's with her binoculars, but Grace would be home.

"She'll kill you, Mom. It's not even nine-thirty yet."

That was undoubtedly true, but I decided to risk it.

I had to bang on their apartment door three times before Grace answered. It is a testament to our friendship that I don't hate Grace. Any woman who can look good in a granny nightgown, with sleepies in her eyes, ought to be shot on sight.

Then I registered what I was seeing. "What are you wearing?" I demanded. It was turning out to be a strange morning clothingwise, first Sam in yellow and now Grace in flannel.

She turned away from the door. "I get cold at night. Who died?"

Chloe had been right—nothing short of an untimely death was justification for waking Grace before ten o'clock on a weekend morning. "I need a favor," I explained.

She headed for the kitchen. I followed her and found her turning on the coffee machine. "I need overnight accommodations for Chloe," I said. "You know, she really barely tolerates Mrs. C. She'll howl if I ask her to stay there through tomorrow."

"With good cause," Grace said, watching the coffee drip. "Short notice," she observed.

"Emergency," I corrected. "Why else would I knock on your door at this hour?"

"Tonight is still several hours away."

"I need to know if I'm going or not so I can shop. I need something to wear tonight."

That got her attention. "Where are you going anyway?"

"Atlantic City. The Three Dog Night concert."

"*You're* a dog for not inviting me. You've had those tickets for weeks now."

"I couldn't take you without slighting Jenny, and I could only get two tickets. Besides, you can't do for me what Sam does."

She might have smiled if the hour had been a little later. "Send Chloe upstairs for the night, then. I'll tell Jenny she's on duty." She paused and frowned. "Where is Jenny, anyway? Why didn't *she* answer the door?"

"She went to the park to look for sperm."

"Ah."

Grace poured the coffee. We sat at the kitchen table and sipped. We didn't need sugar for her coffee.

"If you need a dress," she said finally, "I've got a closetful of them. You could probably borrow something."

Friends, I thought. Aren't they great? "I'm two inches taller than you are, Grace. Anyway, I was thinking more along the lines of new lingerie."

"Well, I won't share my underwear with you."

I laughed. "I need a new Wonderbra. Sam has already seen the old one. And I'll bet you don't have one of those. You don't need one. Yet. Until you have a baby."

"I'm not having any babies," Grace said. Her voice went unusually toneless.

I stared at her. "Are you serious?"

Then it struck me how very little I knew about her past. I hadn't known that Sam had a cowboy brother, and I didn't know where Grace had come from before she'd hit Philadelphia except that she did have a trace of an accent. And all I knew for sure about Jenny's past was that she had grown up with cows and somewhere along the line she had learned how to make a mean berry cobbler.

I scowled down into my coffee, thinking about that. Then I realized that this was probably why we were all so happy with each other. It's the secrets thing again. We'd started fresh when we'd found each other. We had no preconceived notions. If someone knew you when you were six, they'd also know if you once got caught in class picking your nose. You're scarred for life by that memory. You could turn out to be the president of the United States, but that person would still have that image tucked into the back of their mind. When you meet each other in your twenties and thirties as we all did, you're more inclined to take each other at face value.

Grace reached for some sugar packets she'd brought home from the courthouse and I knew she did it without thinking. Her mind was somewhere else.

"The world is overpopulated," she said finally.

"Well, Philly is," I agreed. "Not so much Topeka, so I guess it depends on who you talk to."

She dropped the sugar packets without opening them. "Mandy, I am one of seven kids. I have nine aunts and uncles, and those are just the biological ones. My forebears did enough procreating for all of us."

I held my hands up. "Hey, I'm not espousing the joys of motherhood. It's not for everyone. I spent yesterday morning hunting down cantaloupes."

"Do I want to know what that means?" Grace asked.

"Probably not."

"Then finish your coffee and go buy a fantastic new bra. What color is the one he's seen already?"

"White."

"Borr-ring."

I nodded.

"For an overnight in Atlantic City, you'll want black," she advised. "Or red. Red is always good, especially if it's silk."

"Well, it's not really an overnight," I explained. "I mean, it is, but it isn't. We'll use separate beds, though not separate rooms."

For the second time in a week, Grace's coffee almost came up her nose. "You're going to have sex then jump in different beds to sleep?"

"It's in the bylaws."

"This is complicated."

I thought about his expression over my no-kissing-before-a-toothbrush rule and I agreed wholeheartedly. "You don't know the half of it," I said.

"I thought this whole thing was brilliant in the beginning. If more people thought out rules ahead of time, there would be a lot fewer relationship problems in the world.

But this throws me off a little.'' Then she shrugged. ''If the rest of it works, who's to say that jumping into different beds to actually sleep is wrong?''

''Exactly.'' But something shifted inside me. I drained my coffee and stood. ''I have to go shopping.''

''Are you taking Chloe or do you need Jenny to watch her this morning, too?''

''I already told you—Jenny's at the park. Besides, I have to take Chloe with me. I need to buy her sneakers.'' I figured I could still get half of my chores done today, though the kitchen floor was probably a loss. ''I'll send her upstairs around three o'clock.''

I hurried back downstairs, thinking about a woman who slept in red granny nightgowns and didn't want children. My own child was still glued to the TV when I got back to my own apartment.

''Teeth-brushing time,'' I announced. Toothbrushes were really starting to dominate my life.

''This show is almost over, Mom. I want to see the end first.''

I learned a long time ago to pick my battles. ''Okay, but I want to see you dressed and standing in front of the bathroom mirror by the time I get out of the shower,'' I warned.

Ten minutes later I turned off the water and pulled back the shower curtain to find her brushing away. I grabbed a towel off a hook on the wall.

''Where are we going?'' Chloe asked.

''To buy sneakers.'' And red silk underwear, I decided.

It was two o'clock before we got home with a bag of new clothing for Chloe and one full of lingerie for me. Somewhere in all the shopping, it occurred to me to wonder why I was spending $77 and some change on a bra and panties for what was just an arrangement, but if nothing else it felt good to indulge.

By ten minutes past three, Chloe was upstairs with Grace and I was standing naked in front of my closet, my bag of new undies in hand, wondering what I was supposed to do now. We were sharing a room and normally, since we would have that room in the first place, I would just check in and dress for the show once we got to Atlantic City. But would that seem too relaxed and comfortable with each other, under these arrangement circumstances? Should I just put on the red silk and the little black dress now?

Then I heard a knock at my door. I grabbed my robe, pulled it on and went to answer it. Sam was already standing in my living room because I had neglected to lock my door. He doesn't usually wait for me to actually answer before he comes in.

"The show is at eight o'clock, right?" he asked. "We need to get on the road."

"That's five hours from now." I felt a little grumpy because of this latest decision about how to dress. These rules were starting to wear me out.

"It's four and a half hours, give or take," he said. "But we need to leave time to check in and change our clothes and relax a little first, right?"

I sighed. He had just solved my dilemma. "Okay," I said. "Let me just go pull on a pair of jeans."

He followed me when I headed back for the bedroom. I tossed my robe on the bed, and then he was all over me.

He came at me from behind, his arms wrapping around my waist, his mouth going to my neck. I remember lifting my right hand and plunging it into his hair the way I'd always wanted to. I had the hope of holding his mouth there forever because it really felt delicious. Then our momentum drove us forward so we landed on my bed, wrapped around each other.

"Then again," Sam said, "how much time do we really need to check in and change our clothes?"

"Half an hour?" I suggested.

"Max," he agreed.

"Sam," I said as his hands cupped my breasts.

"Mmm?"

"This is so good."

"I know."

Our arrangement was still young, but I was learning little things about him that I'd never known before, like the fact that he felt a need to progress with lovemaking in a certain order. He'd admitted to me one night that as long as he kept with his game plan, he knew he was probably satisfying his partner. That vulnerability had struck me as deeply as his admission about his ex-wife.

I decided then that arrangement-lovers have an obligation to rock the boat every once in a while. After all, under our bylaws, complaining was not allowed, hurt feelings were anathema, and we'd always be friends regardless—so what was the harm? When he got to the part where his mouth was lowering to my breasts, I sat up, put my hands against his shoulders and pushed him back.

He looked alarmed. "What is this?" he asked.

I didn't answer exactly, though I let my mouth do the talking.

I nibbled on the rest of him the way I'd been nibbling on his mouth. That first night when we'd held a whole conversation with our lips pressed together had inspired me and we kept talking.

"What's your favorite spot to be touched?" I asked.

His voice came back low, vibrating. "That one. No, that one."

"Make up your mind."

"Keep going and I'll try to decide."

I did. Then I rose up on top of him and sank down again, taking him inside. His hands had my hips but then everything changed. He reached up and took a handful of my hair and somehow I found myself flipped over, with him on top of me and his mouth on mine. He seemed hungry and fierce, demanding something, though I wasn't sure what it was. It didn't matter, anyway. I would give him anything.

We were both quiet again afterward. I was starting to learn that sometimes we were and sometimes we weren't. And if antacids found any place in the conversation, it wasn't necessarily a statement on my femininity.

After a while, Sam asked lazily, "How badly do we want to see that show?" He was playing with my hair and had that look in his eyes that said he was gearing up for another go-round.

"The tickets cost me $150," I answered.

"Oh. In that case, I'm going to get dressed again now."

In the end we managed to leave my apartment by 4:30. I went upstairs to hug Chloe one last time, then we were off. We were halfway across New Jersey on the expressway before Sam brought up the subject I'd been trying not to ask about—his morning golf game.

"Shannahan is going to recuse himself from your case," he said.

I jerked my head around to look at him. He was driving. "He's taking himself off? Why?"

"He says you've appeared in front of him too many times and he likes you."

"He *does?*" Shannahan always tended to snarl at me when I had the temerity to set foot in his courtroom.

"He says that your heart is always in the right place and he doesn't want to decide anything that involves your daughter."

"So where does that leave us?"

"Not with Larson. She's recused on it, too."

I couldn't believe it.

"*She* likes *me,*" Sam said, "and she knows I like Chloe. She pretty much has the same issues as Shannahan."

"Oh, this is bad," I muttered, worried.

"Not really. I've decided to transfer the whole thing out of county."

We could probably do that easily, I knew, since both Mill and I practiced in Philadelphia. But I'd really been banking on having an in with one of our own family court judges.

Sam veered around a slow-moving car. "If we go out of county," he said, "then Mill's reputation—and his family's—won't come into play so much."

That was true. And if we took all that stuff out of it, I was in pretty good shape.

"I'll file a change-of-venue motion first thing Monday morning," he said.

Which would buy us another four weeks before trial so all the paperwork could catch up, I thought. I liked that for Chloe-and-Mom reasons, and I liked it for Sam-and-Mandy reasons, as well. Theoretically, at least, Sam would be less inclined to get blindsided by Ms. Right if he was preoccupied with saving my maternal life. There was also the fact that if we succeeded in bumping the whole issue back a month, it would take Mill perilously close to election time. A win then—even making the overture of taking me to court—might still buy him some last-minute election applause, but if Sam and I could swing one *more* postponement after that, the election would be a nonissue. I couldn't help thinking that Mill would give up if that happened.

Sam started singing one of Three Dog Night's greatest hits. I'd never noticed before that he couldn't carry a tune.

"Stop," I said, planting my hands over my ears.

"Ouch," he replied. "That was criticism."

"It's allowed in the bylaws."

"I don't remember that part."

"Didn't one of us say something about honesty?"

We laughed and talked and everything was right with my world until we arrived in Atlantic City. We were crossing the Tropicana's lobby on the way to the check-in desk when Sam skidded to an abrupt stop to stare down a long, wide, tiled corridor.

"What?" I asked, looking that way myself. I saw a gift shop at the end of all the space.

"Chloe would love that," he said.

That was a five-foot-tall doll with long, lanky limbs and a bowl of fruit for a hat. It was in the gift shop window. Something happened inside me that was absolutely and entirely against the bylaws. It was soft and squishy.

"She told you about the cantaloupe," I said, eyeing the fruit-hat.

"Cherries," Sam replied. "She told me that you aced it with a *Ch.* Plus I think that doll is one of those things that you can strap to your feet and dance with. She does ballet, right?"

"Right," I agreed.

"I'm going to buy it for her." He headed down the corridor. "I love that kid."

My knees went weak. I found myself wishing that he loved me, too. And that was the moment when I started understanding the truth—I was already in love with him and I really wanted us to be a family.

Chapter Eight

Looking back now, I know that that night was the beginning of the end of our arrangement. Something so wonderful shouldn't be able to turn into a death knell, but there you have it. For just this reason Grace is very suspicious of anything that too closely resembles bliss. Not only can such occasions kick off heartache, they often do.

Jenny, of course, would jump off a cliff if the man of her dreams promised her that it wouldn't hurt, but most of us have the good sense to recognize the peril inherent in euphoria. We know that heaven rarely lasts forever, so whatever follows is bound to tweak the heart a bit. So I'll admit it—that weekend in Atlantic City, I did a Jenny swan dive. I went right off the cliff. The thing is, Sam never promised me that it wouldn't hurt.

Not only did we have time to change clothes after we checked in, but we had time to loll. Lolling is one of my favorite things to do because I have the opportunity to do it so rarely. We found our room, dropped our overnight bags and looked around. It was perfect. There were the requisite two double beds—I breathed a little sigh of relief at that because it meant that there would be no awkwardness later. I would just get up—or he would—and nonchalantly wander over to that other bed and call out a good-night.

There was also a courtesy bar, a sitting area and two televisions. "Now you can't make me watch *Bewitched*," Sam said, motioning at the second TV.

"You can't make me watch *Star Trek,* either," I countered.

He gripped his head in his hands as though he was in pain. "How can anyone *not* like *Star Trek?*"

"There are too many little nuances and references and terms involved with it that I don't understand."

"You're a lawyer," he accused.

"What does that have to do with Klingons? They're Klingons, right? Or was that some other show?"

"You're brilliant," he said.

"Thank you very much, but I fail to see what that has to do with extraterrestrial beings."

"You should be able to understand the nuances and references," he explained.

"Maybe it's one of those things where you have to enjoy what you're trying to learn."

"Like a mental block?"

"Right." I went to the liquor cabinet and peered inside. "No Glenlivet," I reported.

"That's okay. Do you know what they'd charge for those little bottles, anyway?" Sam went to the bed and flopped down on his back, locking his hands behind his head.

I remembered our conversation about how he'd snooped

into my checkbook. "Don't worry about it," I said. "You're loaded."

"Not this month."

I went back to the nightstand to find a remote control for the nearest TV. "Who's paying for this little shindig, anyway?" I asked. He'd used his credit card to reserve the room, but that didn't necessarily mean anything.

"You are," he said complacently.

"I bought the show tickets," I pointed out.

"Then I guess I am."

"Fair enough." Arrangements are just so easy and equitable, aren't they? I dropped down onto the bed beside him to turn on the television.

As luck would have it, *Bewitched* was on the first channel I clicked to. I sighed happily.

"Give me that," Sam said, trying to take the remote from my hands. "Go watch this on your own television."

"This *is* my television." I tugged the remote back. "That one over by the sitting area is yours."

"I'll flip you for this one."

I thought about it. The choice was between *Bewitched*...or lolling with Sam. "Let's compromise," I said.

"Flipping *is* a compromise."

"I meant we could watch something besides *Bewitched* or *Star Trek*, or anything else involving aliens for that matter." Meanwhile, the *Bewitched* jingle was starting to play. I was gaining ground.

"See, this is what I don't get," Sam said. "What do you have against alternate universes? It's not just *Star Trek* that you don't like. It's space in general."

"This world gives me enough trouble."

Then something happened to his eyes. I've seen it happen in court when a new angle or a great argument suddenly occurs to him. They get brighter somehow. And he does this thing with his mouth where it's like he wants to grin but he can't do it without tipping his hand.

"What?" I asked suspiciously.

"A witch is an alien."

"Samantha is a *good* witch."

"All the same, you're not going to encounter her walking down Broad Street. Because she's an alien. Ergo, you like aliens."

"I like witches who can clean with a twitch of their noses and turn irritating people into frogs." I thought that if I actually had the talent myself, he'd be looking around for a lily pad right about now. We were still doing a tug-of-war over the remote control.

"We shouldn't be watching TV, anyway," he said suddenly.

That surprised me into letting go. He immediately started flicking channels.

"We should be...I don't know, doing something instead of just lying here," he went on. "Neither of us gets away all that often. We should take advantage of it."

"What would you like to do?" I asked.

"I don't know. Maybe we should visit the casino."

We'd taken a walk through it before we'd come upstairs. It was like a funhouse maze down there, lots of rooms, all mirrored, all containing far too many blinking contraptions. "I got a little lost in there," I confessed.

He lifted one shoulder in a shrug. "We could do the boardwalk then."

"Fog was coming in when we got here. It'll be damp and dreary on the beach."

"Then I guess we'll just lie here for a while and watch—"

I grabbed the remote back and flipped channels, landing on a movie. "HBO," I finished for him.

"That's a compromise?"

"Exactly." Just to be on the safe side, though, I surreptitiously dropped the remote on the floor on my side of the bed so he couldn't easily get to it.

I'm not sure where the next hour went. We talked, we laughed, and at some point Sam started fishing for the remote again. I slid off the bed to sit on it and keep it safe, and that clued him in as to what I'd done with it. We wrestled for it and I lost.

At seven o'clock I finally left the bed to fish the little black dress out of my travel bag. It's made of some flexible knit that is truly amazing. No matter what you do to it, it doesn't wrinkle. I pulled my sweater over my head and Sam grinned.

"This will work," he said. "It brings to mind something we can do." He wiggled his eyebrows at me.

"Not if we want to make the show on time," I said vaguely, tossing the sweater onto the bed.

It wasn't that the idea of ripping off the rest of my clothes and falling back onto that bed with Sam didn't have even more appeal than a couple hours of vintage rock and roll. My hesitation was purely because a realization was starting to nudge at the edges of my mind and I wanted to put everything else on hold for a moment so I could think about it.

As great as the sex was between us, we'd just spent the better part of an hour goofing off, and the subject hadn't…well, come up, I realized. I wasn't sure what that meant. My first guess would have been that I simply didn't inspire Sam to uncontrollable passion—except I knew now that he'd spent months with those black sweatpants on his mind. And once we got down to things, there was never any question about his desire or passion or lack thereof. So if we hadn't spent the last hour groping each other, I decided, then it was because this thing we had going on between us was so multifaceted. It thrived on conversation and companionship as well as sex.

My three Cs rule again. It was just what I had told Grace I wanted, when we'd been talking in McGlinchey's, but I felt a little like someone had chop-blocked me in the back of the knees, anyway. This was why every other relationship I'd ever had had failed. To be fair, there had been precious few of them. Like I said earlier, I tend to take things seriously and stick around for the long haul. All the same, every one of those relationships had been lacking in one respect or another.

With Mill, it had been a largely intellectual liaison. I'd enjoyed his mind—period, end of story. I'd kept waiting for that to ignite things in the bedroom, but it never really did. Before that, there had been someone I'd hooked up with while I was in law school. He, too, had lasted awhile. Jorge had been sexy in that heart-stopping way Latin men can master—but drawing decent conversation out of him had been somewhat like pulling teeth. He'd dropped out the second year.

This was the first time in my life I'd enjoyed the full package, I realized. No wonder I was falling in love with Sam.

The thought ripped the breath from my throat and, apparently, it did things to my complexion, as well, because Sam stared at me. "Are you all right?" he asked.

"Dandy." My voice was a croak.

"Then how come you look like you're going to pass out?"

I recovered. "Your idea about sex just swept me away."

"Except we don't have time now," he pointed out.

"Right," I agreed. "And longing always makes me dizzy."

He grinned. "You long for me?"

"In rare, vulnerable moments."

"That'll do."

But it wouldn't, I thought. This wouldn't do at all.

I peeled out of my jeans and found the little black dress again. I pulled it on over my head. "I need the bathroom first so I can resurrect my makeup," I said quickly.

He didn't argue. He was happy—he had the remote again.

I went to the bathroom and locked myself in a little unsteadily. You've got to understand that at this point in my life, my opinions on love aren't all that far removed from Sam's feelings about finding Ms. Right. The sad truth is, love is not a peachy-keen, gooey, fine sensation. It's needy and it's greedy. It gets hungry and it demands to be fed and cared for. It's like a puppy that shows up on your doorstep one morning. Even though the last thing you ever considered was acquiring a pet, it looks so damned cute sitting out there that you let it in. The next thing you know, it's sleeping in your bed and hogging your covers. It whines for a bite of your pizza. It makes messes on your floor. And since it has a lifespan significantly shorter than your own, you know that sooner or later it is going to leave you alone with a broken heart.

Once you let it inside, though, once it crosses your threshold, you're done. The key is not to open the door in the first place—if you're smart enough and quick enough to catch yourself before you commit that irrevocable act.

My door was wide open, and suddenly I didn't want to leave that bathroom. I was scared. I was terrified by what was happening between us and where it might—or might not—lead. That time in the Tropicana bathroom was the closest I came to chickening out with Sam.

I'll never know if I really would have done it because

he chose that moment to pound on the door. "I've got one of those woman mysteries going on here," he yelled in.

"What?" I demanded.

"I want to know how you can do the makeup thing when you left your little purple bag full of gook and smell-good stuff on the dresser."

I had, I realized. I'd fled in here without my cosmetics case. I went to the door, opened it, and held out my hand. Sam dropped the bag into it.

"Why does sex make you hide in the bathroom?" he asked.

"What?" I didn't get it.

"The first night—remember?—you went looking for the antacids and you locked yourself in the bathroom. And you just did it again now."

"We didn't have sex just now," I argued. But he was pretty close to being on target. It wasn't sex that often made me scurry to the nearest closed space, but it did happen whenever I didn't feel very sure of myself.

"We talked about sex," Sam pointed out.

"There is absolutely no connection. You're overanalyzing."

"Hey, I know a trend when it jumps up and bites me on the nose."

I leaned into him as if I was going to do just that, then I kissed him instead. It was quick, friendly. There was nothing at all in that kiss that might reveal to him that I had fallen in love with him, or to remind myself of that knee-buckling fact.

"Go away," I said, pushing out the door again so I could close it, "or we're going to be late for the show."

And what a show it was, too. I confess that I am one of those who turns the volume up full throttle on the stereo when I clean, so being surrounded by live Three Dog Night vibes was to die for. Sam finally got his Glenlivet, and at one point I actually stood up and danced beside our table. I didn't make a spectacle of myself—a good many other people were doing it, too. And at least I'm not a grandmother, as one of them was.

When I dropped back into my seat, Sam was staring at me. "What?" I asked in a break between songs. "I don't have to be on my best behavior. I'm not trying to impress you. This is just an arrangement."

He flashed a grin. "Hey, it rings my chimes. Next song, I think you should get up on the tabletop."

"I'd need several of what you're drinking first."

"No problem." He signaled a waitress and I laughed. I declined the scotch but I did have another glass of wine.

After the show, Sam gave twenty-five dollars to one of the video poker machines in the casino, and I put ten dollars on a roulette table and got thirty-seven back. Sam had his arm around me and his hand on my hip, and he was leaning forward to watch the ball spin and bounce. When it landed in my favor, I wanted time to just stop. I wanted to live in that moment forever.

"I didn't know you were lucky," Sam said, sliding his hand down to catch mine as I took my money and turned away.

"Damn, another secret down the tubes." But I grinned.

"We don't need them, anyway," he said. "This is just—"

"An arrangement," I finished for him, because it didn't hurt so much when I was the one who said it.

He nodded.

"We never ate," he said after another moment.

My stomach rumbled in response. "Do we want to spend exorbitant prices on a casino restaurant?"

"Sure. You got the tickets, I got the room, so now it's your turn again. I don't care what you spend."

I was struck by a brainstorm. "Okay," I said. He still had my hand, and I started tugging him out of the casino.

"Okay? Just like that?" he asked.

"If I'm paying for dinner, then I want you naked while we're enjoying it."

"People will notice."

I laughed.

"However, if you're going to take your clothes off, too, I might be game," he continued.

"It's a possibility." We crossed the lobby and I led him toward the elevators.

"Ah," he said as he understood. "I knew there was a twist."

We went upstairs to call room service. To his credit, he started dropping clothes as soon as we crossed the threshold. He was trying to get mine off me while I sat cross-legged on the bed and read the room service menu.

"Steak Thai Taicu," I said, trying not to shiver when his mouth found my collarbone.

He paused in his ministrations. "What the hell is steak Thai Taicu?" he asked.

"Beats me, but they have a restaurant here called Wellington and Chan's." I showed him the page in the room's services book. "A steakhouse with Asian-fusion cuisine," I read aloud.

"Fusion sounds like something we'd do to an enemy nation. Give me that."

I sighed and gave up the book. I missed his mouth on my throat.

"How does one lacquer a chicken?" he asked after a moment.

"Same answer I gave to your last question. Beats me."

"And how do shrimp get fragrant?"

"Out in the sun too long?" I guessed.

"We've got to try this."

"Yeah. We do."

So we ordered up the steak and the chicken and the shrimp and we had a feast sitting Indian-style on the bed. Sam found some interesting uses for the Thai noodles. He more or less adorned me with them. Then he ate them all up.

We laughed and loved and sometime in the wee hours of the morning, we finally fell still and quiet. I knew I had to get up and change beds. And I had every intention of doing it. But my limbs were leaden and I kept putting it off. This is how it came about that when we opened our respective eyes again at ten after nine the following morning, they were very close, to say the least. In fact, we were wrapped all around each other.

"Oops," I said, because my first thought was of our shattered no-sleeping-together rule.

His first thought was of my rule. "I know, I know," he said, rolling onto his back. "No kissing before toothbrushes. Would that be your toothbrush, my toothbrush, or both?"

I had to think about it. "Mine, definitely. But let's be fair and say both."

"Fair is good," he murmured, still sleepy. But then he turned into me again to pull me close. I forgot all about toothbrushes.

All in all, we ended up back in Philadelphia far too soon. And this is when I had my premonition. The funny thing about it is that it was totally unwarranted—but I guess that's why they call them premonitions. We'd just come off a fantastic evening and everything was normal between us. There was no mention whatsoever of our broken sleeping-together rule or my oral-hygiene one, and I took that to be a very good thing. So, at first, I figured that missing Chloe accounted for the sudden urge to cry that was crowding my throat. We don't spend all that many nights apart.

"You're quiet," Sam said as he parked in the lot near our building.

If I told him that I felt on the verge of tears, he would probably think I had lost my mind. It was that weird. "I'm fine," I said.

"You look funny."

I stuck my tongue out at him.

"Funnier," he agreed.

"I want to see Chloe. What will I do if I lose her, Sam? One night without her is all I can stand."

"It's not going to happen. I'm on the job."

Then I told myself that I was feeling misty-eyed because all the nastier realities of life were crashing back in on me after a really good night away. And I believed it—then. But now, looking back, I know exactly what it was. Somehow I had the feeling in my gut that it was the last overnight getaway we were ever going to take together.

We dropped our bags in our respective apartments and went up to the third floor to find Chloe. Sam had the doll he'd bought her strapped to his feet. She squealed when she saw it and ran to take it from him.

"I wouldn't be caught dead in that hat," Grace commented, looking at it.

The three of them had been curled up on the sofa, watching television. Or maybe they were playing Monopoly. It was hard to tell. The game was out on the coffee table but only Jenny seemed to be paying any attention to it. She'd just landed on Park Place and was counting out her remaining money with fierce concentration.

"Did you have fun?" Chloe asked at full volume.

"We had a great time," I told her.

She waltzed off with her new doll. "Thank you, Sam," she called over her shoulder. "She's bee-yoo-tiful."

"You're welcome," he said, then he looked at me. "I guess I should go feed the cat or something."

I frowned. "You don't have a cat."

"I know, but there should be a reason that I need to go back to my own apartment now." I couldn't think of one— except, of course, our rules. He usually came downstairs on Sundays to share dinner with us, but we'd just spent the past twenty-four hours together and even though that wasn't specifically mentioned in the bylaws, it seemed awfully cozy to tack on even more time.

I also thought that he looked as if he wanted an out. This is what happens when you fall in love with someone—at least early on, in the beginning. You plunge into that land of vulnerability. Knowing full well that the person you love has just gained the atrocious power to rip your heart out and stomp on it, you tend to consider the worst in any given situation. You're ready for the ripping and stomping to begin.

So I said, "I wasn't going to cook a big dinner tonight, anyway."

Sam just shrugged. "I'm going to watch the ball game, then. Maybe I'll give you a holler later."

Ha, I thought. He *had* been looking for a way out of spending the afternoon and evening together, too. "Whatever," I said indifferently, because complaining when the other person had other plans was definitely against his bylaws.

He must have read something on my face. "You don't like sports," he pointed out.

"I don't *understand* most sports," I clarified. "So I don't know whether I like them or not." Then I realized that it sounded as if I was arguing, as if I was angling for him to watch the game at my place. "I think I'm going to take a Sunday nap," I decided.

I watched his face closely to see if he looked relieved or not. I couldn't tell. "Then call me when you wake up," he said. "That way if you're still sleeping when my game's over, I won't wake you."

Then he was gone. I turned back to the living room to find Jenny, Grace and Chloe all staring at me.

"What was all that about, Mom?" Chloe asked. "Is he gonna eat with us or not?"

"That was your mother losing another brain cell to premature death," Grace said.

"How do you figure that?" I demanded.

"The poor man was just about scrambling to find a way into your apartment this afternoon," Jenny said sadly. "Like a size-ten woman trying to squeeze into a pair of size-six jeans."

"Will you stop with the analogies?" I said a little too loudly. My urge to cry was really strong now.

Grace rarely agreed with anything Jenny said, but this time she nodded. "She's right."

I threw my hands up. "*Now* you tell me this!"

"A woman with your intelligence should be able to figure it out for herself," Grace said. It was the second time in twenty-four hours that someone had expressed appreciation of my mind, but it didn't make me feel any better.

"I couldn't see it! I'm *involved*! You can't see things like that unless you're a bystander!"

"Isn't getting involved against the rules?" Grace asked.

"Yes!" I shouted.

"Well, don't take *my* head off," she replied.

"What am I going to do?" I almost wailed it.

I saw both their eyes widen as they both understood the truth: I'd fallen in love with Sam.

Jenny looked happy, then confused. Grace came off the sofa. "Stay with the juvenile," she told Jenny. Then she grabbed my elbow. "*You* are coming with me for a little talk."

I let her drag me off to the apartment's single bedroom. It was hers because she'd found the apartment first. Jenny used the sofa. On the very rare occasions when Chloe slept over, she used a sleeping bag and the floor.

Grace closed the door behind us. "This is bad," she said.

"I know," I shook my head miserably.

"How could you let this happen? It was supposed to be about sex. *Just* sex."

"But the sex is very, very good." Then I told her what I'd realized last night. "And, damn it, he's the whole package!"

"That doesn't mean you have to *marry* him," Grace said.

"Who said I wanted to do that?" But I had been thinking along those very lines yesterday when he'd gone off to the Tropicana gift shop to buy Chloe that doll.

I sank down to sit on her bed. "This doesn't have to change anything," I decided.

"It changes *everything*," Grace insisted.

"No, it really doesn't. If you remember, my motives when I went into this weren't all that pure to begin with."

"I thought this would get him out of your system. Instead, you've gone and done the exact opposite."

"So what do I do now?" I asked her.

She sat on the bed beside me. "Let me think." After a moment she decided, "It should be okay as long as you never, ever, ever let *him* know about this."

I was appalled. "I'd rip my tongue out of my head first."

"Good. That's the attitude."

"His rules all had to do with keeping me at a distance," I said, thinking aloud. "So I'll keep my distance. Because the minute I start breaking rules and crowd him—"

Grace interrupted me by snapping her fingers. "He's gone."

"Right." My heart sank hard and fast, and I felt like crying again.

"Get a grip, Mandy," Grace said, reading my expression.

"I'm gripping, I'm gripping."

"Grip harder."

I took a deep breath. "I'll toe the line and never let him know."

"That would be my best advice."

"I already screwed up," I confessed. "I didn't go to my own bed last night."

Grace relaxed. "That's not so bad. That was a pretty stupid rule, anyway."

"But it's all part of his thing about keeping me at a distance," I said. "He's not looking for a mate, Grace. Shelly, his ex-wife, really hurt him."

She thought about that. "Was he upset when he woke up beside you this morning?"

No, I thought, he hadn't been. But then, it had been Atlantic City, extraordinary circumstances. Even in woman-speak, it's hard to read anything into that. I shook my head.

"Okay, then, here's what I think you should do now. Go downstairs to your own apartment and take that nap. Then forget to call him."

I frowned. "I hate playing games, Grace. I was never that type."

"Learn," she suggested. "You need to put some distance back into this. What you've got here is a man who meets all the criteria you were talking about in Mc-Glinchey's a while back, and you don't want to ruin it by glomming on to more than you said you needed.''

''Compatibility, comfort and conversation,'' I remembered, as I had last night. I hate it when my own words come back to haunt me.

''You don't want another child,'' she pointed out. ''Or do you?''

I shook my head and told her what I had told Jenny. ''I'm too old.''

''You're not, but that's neither here nor there. Answer my question. Do you want another kid?''

''Of course not. I just want to hang on to the one I have and keep Mill's paws off her.''

''Okay, that's a start. And you don't want a mortgage.''

''No. I love my apartment.''

''If there's somewhere you want to go, but you don't want to go alone, you've always got me and Jenny. So that takes care of the society compliance part.''

It did, I thought, in a manner of speaking.

''So actually,'' Grace deduced, ''you don't want anything from Sam other than what you've already got.''

She's a genius. That was absolutely—almost—true. I sighed. ''I feel better now.''

She stood up from the bed. ''Good. So go take your nap.''

I decided I would bring Chloe into bed with me to watch TV. She would get glued to the screen and I would doze off. It was a routine we followed with some frequency on Sunday afternoons. Then I woke up and I cooked a big dinner. For her, me and Sam.

But Sam wouldn't be coming downstairs tonight. I

squared my shoulders and marched back to the living room. Chloe already had all her overnight stuff packed.

"How do you feel about the Disney Channel on my TV?" I asked her.

"You're going to fall asleep again, aren't you?" she countered.

"Probably."

She grinned. "Okay."

I took her hand and pulled her toward the door.

"Are you going to call Sam later?" Jenny asked.

Grace and I answered in unison. "No."

Chapter Nine

I didn't call Sam and he didn't call me, and I landed in my office on Monday morning in an exceptionally foul mood that didn't improve when Mill turned up just before lunch.

I was having the kind of telephone conversation with a client that always made me want to bang my head against a wall afterward. Kathy Sloane was worried about how certain small but sentimental objects might be divided in the battle for equitable distribution between her and her soon-to-be-ex-husband. I chose my words carefully, implying that sometimes small things get lost. Sometimes spouses haven't seen them for years, anyway, so they don't even notice when they go missing. A woman could easily misplace her grandmother's not-very-valuable garnet ring, for instance, or the photo album of the baby's first year of life. Those things could magically turn up again at a relative's home once the dust settled. Judges are mostly concerned with pension plans and homesteads, after all. Of course, if the ex actually *asked* about the photo album, all bets would be off.

I thought she got it, but then the woman called me back at eleven-thirty to tell me that her rocking chair was stuck in the front door and her pending ex was due to stop by in a few hours to pick up the kids for their time with him. What was she supposed to do now?

I closed my eyes. "Small, Kathy," I said. "I told you *small* things might get lost." The soon-to-be-ex-husband was definitely going to notice a rocking chair stuck in the front door, I thought. I knew I could expect a call from his attorney, sooner rather than later.

When I hung up and opened my eyes again, Mill was standing in my office door.

"What are you doing here?" I asked too sharply. I was still reeling from all of the emotional repercussions of my weekend, and he was the last person I felt like dealing with.

He didn't answer my question. He took a step inside, closed my door behind him and looked around. "You've settled in nicely since the last time I was here," he observed.

I stared at him. I wondered again what he was up to. I thought about standing but I decided that I felt more secure sitting behind my desk. If there had been a bathroom within easy striking distance, this would have been one of those times I would have hidden there, and sex was the farthest thing from my mind. I was a little worried and I was feeling insecure.

"That makes sense," I answered slowly, "because you haven't been here since about a week after I joined the firm."

He stopped in front of one of the prints on the far wall. "I like the Matisse," he said.

"It's fake."

He turned back to me and gave me his practiced smile. "I know."

He would—he had the real McCoy on his living room wall. "Why are you here?" I asked again.

He still didn't answer me. "Is that Chloe?" he said instead.

He was zooming in on my desk now, and I realized why. I had Chloe's second-grade class photo framed and sitting there. I also had two smaller snapshots. One was of me, Chloe and Sam that Jenny had taken eons ago—okay, months ago—during our last real snow storm, and one was of Grace, Jenny and me hamming it up at a party.

I had an almost impossible-to-control urge to grab the Chloe pictures before Mill could look at them—as though by snatching them back, I could keep him away from her, as well. I had to fist my hands in my lap to stop myself from doing it. I let him pick up the school picture.

"You still haven't answered my question," I said.

He put the picture down again and picked up the other one, the snowball-fight picture. "Ah. The pizza man."

"Stop mauling my things and talk to me."

He put the second picture down. "Let's do lunch," he said suddenly.

My heart gave a hard painful tug that might have been another brand of premonition. "Why?"

Mill sighed. "Amanda, let's not be difficult about this."

"Millson," I said, drawing his name out, as well, "it wasn't me who turned up in your office unannounced and reluctant to explain why."

"I just told you why," he said.

"You suddenly had an overriding need to share a meal with me again?"

"Yes."

That took the wind right out of my sails. Then a lightbulb went on in my head and I finally got it—his agenda.

I remembered how he'd complimented me on my appearance last week in the courthouse, and now I understood why. His attorney—I knew the guy and he was one of the best—had probably warned him that getting a seven-year-old girl away from her mother when the mother was the only parent she'd ever known would be a long shot. So Mill was hedging his bets. He was laying the groundwork for a back-up approach. After all, it really didn't matter so much if he won custody—the important thing was that the voters saw him *trying* to get it. And it would be just as fruitful for him to reconcile with the mother of his child.

I no longer felt unsure of myself. I stood up from my desk and walked around it to face him. ''Mill,'' I said, ''you'd be despicable except for the fact that you're so unaware of the fact.''

His smile faded. ''That was an insult.''

''I know what you're up to, and I'm telling you to give it up. I'm involved with someone, anyway. This isn't going to work.''

I noticed that he didn't deny that he was—what was the word Sam used?—trying to schmooze me. ''That could change, Mandy,'' he said. ''You've walked away from relationships before.''

It stung a little, though I knew that he was as wrong about that as he had been about so many other aspects of my personality. I had never walked out on anyone until it had become utterly apparent that the union was a lost cause.

I started to say as much, then something else struck me. If I lost Sam—*when* I lost Sam—he would definitely be the one doing the walking. And it would be a long, long time before I stuck my toe back into the waters of another relationship. I had known that the first time we'd made love, when I'd realized that I'd never settle for less than that kind of connection with a lover again. That scared the hell out of me and it almost had me looking for a bathroom again. Because I *would* lose Sam eventually. By definition arrangements are not permanent. But I didn't have time to think about it because suddenly, the preposterous happened.

Mill clasped his hands on my upper arms and drew me to him. I know it was supposed to have been a passionate move, one that indicated he was swept away by need over seeing me again. The truth of the matter is, Mill doesn't have a passionate bone in his body. When Sam follows a game plan in the physical department, it's endearing. When Mill does it, it's mechanical.

I just barely managed to get my hands up to his chest, but I didn't do it quickly enough. He kissed me.

Then a quick rap came at my office door and it opened. As I've said, Sam always does this. It's not that he's rude; it's more like he's been so much a part of my life that there's not much I could be doing behind a closed door that would bar him. He always knocks once to announce his imminent appearance, then he just comes in. I knew that in this case he would have asked Gina, my secretary, if I was with a client. Gina would have said no, which I wasn't. But neither was I alone.

I was very glad to see him. His timing couldn't have been better. So at first I didn't identify the look of angry surprise on his face. Nor did I have a whole lot of time to study it, because he turned right around and left again without a word.

I started smacking at Mill's hands until he stepped back, alarmed. After all, the door was open now and anyone could see me making a scene. As soon as I was free of him, I jogged out of my office to go after Sam.

I caught up with him at the elevator. He was stabbing the down button repeatedly, like he wanted to hurt it.

"Where are you going?" I asked, a little out of breath. The elevator is at the opposite end of the floor from my office, a bit of a run in heels.

He wouldn't look at me. "Sorry. I guess I mistook you for someone I was having an arrangement with."

Lightning couldn't have struck me silent more effectively. *He was jealous.*

In woman-speak, this doesn't just mean something. It's huge. It's up there with a grade-five hurricane or tornado. It's running for the presidency of the country instead of city council, as Mill was doing. It's gargantuan.

I opened my mouth to point this out. I almost said, "You're so jealous your eyes are turning green." Then I snapped my teeth shut again sharply because experiencing jealousy was probably not something that would amuse Sam. Experiencing jealousy over any woman—even or especially me—would be, in man-speak, an unwelcome occurrence that meant it was time to boogy on out the door and end the relationship...arrangement.

So instead, I said, "That's me, an arrangement at your service. What's up?"

He hesitated for a very long time. I could tell that he wanted to move on as though nothing had just happened. More than that, I knew he *needed* to. But he just couldn't do it. "What did I just see?" he asked after a moment.

The elevator doors opened. Neither of us got on and they closed again. I leaned against the wall and crossed my arms over my chest. "That was Mill working on plan B," I explained.

"Which is?"

"If you can't win the kid, reconcile with the woman."

"Are you going to do it?"

I gaped at him. "Tell me you're kidding."

"Guess not," Sam said at my expression.

"Not," I agreed.

"But you let him kiss you."

"He took me by surprise. I was seriously considering using my knee on him when you opened the door."

He narrowed his eyes a little, studying my face. "Should I believe that?"

I suddenly saw a golden opportunity to prove that I was *not* in love with him. What had Grace said? Never ever ever let him know about it, right? So I veered to the opposite hemisphere from the truth. "What difference does it make?" I asked, lifting a shoulder indifferently. "This is temporary with us, right? If I wanted to go back to Mill, or if I found someone and I wanted to move on, our arrangement would just be…over." It hurt to even say it. "That's the idea behind this, right?"

It took a long time, but his face finally cleared. Maybe it cleared because he *made* it clear. "Right," he said shortly.

"Not that I want to move on," I said quickly. "My point is that if I had enjoyed what just happened back there with Mill, I'd simply tell you and go back to him."

He kept searching my face. "You would, wouldn't you? That's why you're safe."

"Safe as a storm cellar in a grade-five twister." I realized I was starting to sound a little like Jenny with the analogies and I winced.

"People have been known to get plucked right the hell out of those things by the wind," Sam pointed out.

Suddenly my heart went still. I got serious. "I'll take the chance if you do."

Now, looking back, I realize that he never responded. He just leapfrogged right over my words. And Mill made it easy for him because he finally joined us at the elevator after apparently deciding that I would not be returning to my office anytime soon.

He hit the down button with much less ferocity than Sam had, his gaze moving back and forth between us. "Think about it, Amanda," he said. "We should have lunch—or dinner—and talk to see if we can reach an out-of-court settlement on this."

"We can talk," Sam said abruptly and a little beligerently.

I looked at him, startled by his tone. Suddenly he reminded me of a dog with his hackles up—the way all their fur rises along their spines when they see an enemy dog on the opposite side of the street. The next thing you know, the leash is snapped out of their owner's hand and they're snarling their way across traffic, lunging for that other poor beast's throat.

"Sam," I said. "I don't want to talk with him."

"Yes, you do."

I thought he was taking this I'm-cool-I'm-not-jealous business to an extreme, but I let it go. "Okay," I said, "I do."

Mill looked confused by our exchange, then relieved. "Excellent."

"You realize, of course, that all conversations take place in the presence of her counsel," Sam said. "So if you're so keen on dinner, why don't we make it, say, seven o'clock tonight at Mandy's place?"

At *my* place? My heart stopped. Chloe would be at my place! "Are you out of your mind?" I said to Sam. My voice raised several serious notches.

He glanced at me. The look he gave me said *later*.

"Tonight?" Mill took out his little computerized date

book. "Let me change a few things around and I can do it."

"Bring your attorney as well, of course," Sam said.

Mill smirked. "That won't be necessary."

He finally got on the elevator and I rounded on Sam. I was so angry I literally hit him. I smacked a palm against his shoulder, then I smacked my other one against his other shoulder, and I kept doing it until he was backed up against the wall. "What did you just do?" I shouted.

"Calm down. People are watching."

I looked over my shoulder. Our little scene had drawn the rapt attention of the receptionist and two other attorneys. But I was livid. I was also near tears, and I couldn't let up. "I can't believe you just threw Chloe to the wolves like that!"

"Let's go back to your office to talk about this," he suggested. "I'll even kiss you the way he did if it makes you feel any better."

"No, you will not. I'm ready to eviscerate you." But I let him take my hand and drag me back up the hall.

By the time he closed my office door behind us, I was crying. Not bawling, not sobbing, nothing ugly, but I was having to blink very, very hard to keep the tears from spilling over and ruining my makeup before my day was half-done. "What did you just do?" I whispered again, then I sank down on the sofa across the room from my desk. I put my face in my hands.

I felt the sofa cushions shift a little as Sam sat down next to me. "Honey, there's no way in hell you're going to keep him from seeing Chloe now that he's filed this petition," he said.

I opened my fingers a little to peer at him through them. He'd just used an endearment. He'd just broken one of *my* rules. I didn't mind. "Go on," I said.

"If this mess goes to court, you know a judge is going to order visitation at the very, very least. So let's get the initial meeting done on our terms. Home field advantage." He touched a lock of my hair. He'd been doing a lot of that lately, I realized. Was he reminding himself that it wasn't long and blond?

"I wouldn't betray you if someone held a gun to my head," he said.

I sniffed. I knew that.

"With a guy like Mill, this could all come down to a power play. And I want all the power advantages on our side."

It made sense, I thought. But... "You didn't give me a lot of time to brace Chloe for this."

Sam finally sat back and laced his fingers behind his head. "I thought of that. But I didn't want to give *him* a lot of time to prepare, either, to start thinking that he does need to bring his lawyer, et cetera."

The thing is, Sam really is a great attorney, even if he uses a lot of schmoozing and ploys to win. I agreed with him.

"I filed the change-of-venue motion this morning," he said suddenly. "And Larson already called me to say that she's going to judge it on the papers."

That meant she wasn't going to call for oral argument—that the issue was so cut-and-dried she was going to judge it on whatever affidavits Sam filed and whatever Mill's attorney submitted. She'd probably do it early next week so everyone would have time to set forth their various reasons why changing counties was or wasn't a good idea.

"In the meantime, don't use your knee on Mill yet," Sam went on. "Let him think the door might be open a crack for a reconciliation."

I took in a sharp, deep breath. I didn't like the sound of

that at all. I especially didn't like it in light of Sam's reaction to seeing Mill kiss me. I didn't want to do anything
to jeopardize our arrangement. Then again, I would do anything to save Chloe.

"You want me to humor him," I said bleakly. "You
want me to play him along, let him think he has a chance."

"Buy me a week in his good graces to have Larson sign
that order sending this out of county. Then who knows—
if you keep him happy and we can work out some kind of
visitation terms, maybe he'll even back down and withdraw
the motion for custody. When you're nice to me, I'd do
just about anything for you."

My heart vaulted. "I'm always nice to you."

He nodded. "Mostly. As long as you brush your teeth
first."

"I won't kiss him again," I said obstinately.

A shadow passed through Sam's eyes, but he only nodded.

I really hated this. "I don't play games," I said, just as
I had told Grace yesterday.

"Mandy, you're a whiz at playing games. Look what
you do in a courtroom. Just take your personal feelings out
of this and try to think of it as one more case."

When it involved Sam, Chloe and Mill? Not likely. All
the same, I leaned over and kissed his cheek. "Thanks."

"Do toothbrushes have any play in this situation right
now?" he asked suddenly.

I frowned. "Of course not. Why?"

He tackled me and flattened me on my back on the sofa.
And he kissed me within an inch of my life. My office was
seeing a lot of action that afternoon.

"Who's the best kisser?" he asked.

Testosterone time, I thought. I pretended to have to think
about it, which effectively convinced him to kiss me again.

I could have lain there with him forever, but it wasn't plausible and he finally pulled away. I sat up again.

"I've got to go," he said. "I have to be in court in half an hour."

"Why did you come by here, anyway?" I finally thought to ask.

"I wanted to see if you had to be there, too. I was going to buy you one of Julio's hot dogs with all the fried onions. Then I was going to drag you off for some major-league sex and kiss you like crazy, maybe get you over this oral hygiene thing you've got going on."

That new rule I'd sneaked in was really sticking in his craw, I thought. But I grinned. "I like the sex part, but I have appointments here all afternoon." Then that realization had me shooting suddenly to my feet.

"What?" Sam asked, startled.

"I have to get Gina to cancel everything after my two-o'clock meeting. I need to be home when Chloe gets back from school so I can talk to her about this."

I kissed him one more time, then he left and I went to lay the bad news on my secretary. She hated rescheduling appointments.

I met Chloe's taxi sometime after three o'clock, and I growled a little when Mrs. Casamento protested the fact that I was usurping her services again. I definitely wasn't in the mood for the woman. Chloe and I went inside to our apartment.

"Would you like milk and cookies?" I asked judiciously when we were in the kitchen. Laying the groundwork, I thought.

My daughter just eyed me suspiciously. "Why?"

"It's something moms do after school when they're home. They offer their kids milk and cookies."

"Like that old TV show you watch on reruns?"

"Bewitched?" It was true that Samantha was a superb mom—who wouldn't be if she could let some magic fly with her nose and acquire canteloupes and a pristine home?

"No," Chloe said. "The other one. The one with the kid named after an animal."

"Leave It to Beaver?" I thought about it. "Yes, it's exactly like June Cleaver." I took a deep breath and plunged in. "Except she was married to Beaver's father."

Chloe sat down at the table. "I don't get it."

My head was in the refrigerator so I didn't answer right away. Since I had spent most of the weekend with Sam in Atlantic City, I was seriously derelict in the mother-duties department at the moment. I discovered that we were out of milk.

"Tea?" I suggested instead.

"I'm a *kid*," Chloe said.

"But you're growing in leaps and bounds every day." I turned the stove on under the teakettle and got some cups from the cupboard. I would just douse hers with plenty of sugar and make it weak, and it probably wouldn't be any more potent caffeinewise than the chocolate syrup she always stirred into her milk.

Then it occurred to me that if the court caught this act, they would probably snatch her right out of my grasp. "Don't tell anyone about this," I said quickly. "Try not to mention that I'm letting you have tea because I forgot to buy milk."

"Who would I tell?" Chloe asked.

"I don't know. Maybe...your father." There. It was out.

"I don't have one," Chloe said.

"You do. You know that. He's just not here. With us. Living with us." For someone who made a living stringing together persuasive and impressive words, mine were suddenly getting all bollixed up on my tongue.

"He doesn't want me," Chloe said.

My heart broke. Cleanly. Savagely. I left the stove abruptly and went to sit beside her, taking both her hands in mine. "Chloe, I left him. He didn't leave us."

"But he never wanted to see me in all this time, in my whole life." She looked miserable.

How could I have not known for seven years that this bothered her? I felt wretched, bitterly small, horribly ashamed of myself. I had been so busy dancing a double jig, trying to keep up as the perfect single parent, that I'd somehow missed this.

"Honey," I said, "he wants to see you maybe a little too much."

Her eyes widened, narrowed, widened again. "What does that mean?"

I've always told my clients that the best route to take with their kids when going through a situation like this is to tell them the truth. So why was it so difficult for me to follow my own advice? "It means that your father wants you to go live with him instead of me," I said finally.

She looked horrified. My heart broke for her a second time. *Damn, Mill.*

"Mom, no," she said, and I squeezed her hands.

"Don't worry. It probably won't happen. It's a law thing. And Sam is my lawyer."

That made her happy. "That's *great*. He won't let anything bad happen to me."

It was true. Ours might be just an arrangement, and it might be over when Ms. Right finally got around to blindsiding him, but Sam would fall on his sword before he let anything happen to Chloe. "You're right," I said, my voice a little raw.

"So then, there's nothing to worry about," Chloe said.

"Just…one small thing. The man in question is coming to dinner."

"My *father?*"

"Yeah." I felt sick all over again.

Her face was all puckered up. She was thinking. Hard. "Okay. What time?"

"Seven o'clock," I said.

"I better go get ready."

"It's not even four o'clock yet, Chloe."

She stood. We'd never gotten around to the tea, which was probably a good thing. "I have homework," she said.

"And you're *admitting* to it?"

"Lots of homework. Lots and lots of homework. And I should probably do it now because, you know, he'll be here later and all."

"How come so much?" I asked.

"We had a substitute."

"The last time you had a substitute, you had no homework but those cherries we had to go buy and that was assigned days before."

"That was an in-class project. And this is a serious substitute. Billy Craig calls her a Nazi."

Billy Craig was one of the taxi-pool kids, a little older than the others. Still, I was startled. "Do you know what a Nazi is?"

She shook her head. "But Billy says they're super evil."

"That's true. So I doubt if your substitute is one of them." At least, I emphatically hoped not.

"Just in case, I better go do my megatons of homework."

"Megatons," I repeated a little dazedly.

"Megamegatons."

I wondered if I could get out of dinner by claiming that Chloe simply had too much homework. But Sam was right.

Let's nail this tonight while all the power is on our side, I thought. "Better get to it, then," I said.

She scampered off.

I shouldn't have trusted her. The business about the homework should have had all my maternal antennae twitching. But we were still hours away from dinner and I was already emotionally wrung out, so I poured myself a glass of calming wine instead of thinking too much about Chloe's megatons of homework. Then I sat at the table again and put my head down on it hard.

My life was getting complicated. It was really starting to stress me out.

Chapter Ten

Sam arrived for dinner first because I made him come early. I did *not* want to deal with Mill on my own.

I had decided to make my scampi and linguini for dinner, and I'd bought a dozen extra shrimp for our own personal appetizer. We ate them standing up in the kitchen, dipping them into cocktail sauce, hoarding them from Chloe. She dearly loves them and if she'd known what we were up to, she wouldn't have left even one of them for us to split between us.

''Where is the rug rat, anyway?'' Sam asked, chewing.

''Getting ready.''

''For twenty minutes now? She hasn't been out of her room since I got here.''

That *was* unusual, given that she adored Sam and rarely missed a potential moment in his presence. ''She also had a lot of homework,'' I said.

Sam scowled. "She never admits to having a lot of homework. She's up to something."

I was somewhat indignant that he had thought of it when I hadn't—she was my kid, after all. Then I decided that checking on her would be more productive than quibbling about who was right and who was wrong, especially since my nerves were screwed up about as tight as they could go. A minor word skirmish would have all the potential of erupting into a full-blown argument in my current mood. So I put my wineglass down on the kitchen counter and went to Chloe's room.

She was at her desk, writing diligently, when I peered inside. Ha! I thought. I'd been right. "You *did* have a lot of homework," I said.

"Told you."

Mollified, I headed back to the kitchen. I was halfway there when Mill's knock came at the door.

Theoretically it could have been Grace or Jenny, but I knew it wasn't. With his latest agenda, Mill would be trying to catch some time alone with me before Sam arrived. He was nearly half an hour early. I felt pretty smug for out-witting him.

"Hi," I said calmly when I opened the door. It was him, all right.

He held a clutch of roses in his hand. He held them out to me. "For the hostess," he said.

I backed up fast. Then I remembered what Sam had said about playing him along. I reached out and took the flowers. "They're beautiful." There wasn't a wilt or a brown spot among them. But that's Mill, unimpeachable to the core.

"Come on in." I stepped back from the door, and when he was inside, I headed for the kitchen. "Sam's in here," I told him.

I glanced over my shoulder at him when I spoke, so I caught Mill's fleeting frown. If I was supposed to be placating him, I was doing a bad job of it, I realized. I tried a little harder. "Sam, look what Mill brought me," I said sweetly, practically gushing as I entered the kitchen and held the flowers out for him to see.

Playing along with Mill's game might have been Sam's idea in the first place, but he still didn't look happy about the roses. "Great," he said shortly.

"I need to find something to put them in." I U-turned out of the kitchen again.

"Do you still have that Cloisonne vase I gave you for our anniversary?" Mill asked.

"What anniversary?" Sam's voice followed me as I went to the hall closet where I stored things like vases. "You guys were never married."

"A minor technicality," I heard Mill say.

I found the vase. In for a penny, I thought, in for a pound. I stuck the roses into it and returned to the kitchen.

"You kept it," Mill said, obviously pleased.

"Why the hell did you do that?" Sam wanted to know.

"It's pretty," I explained, "and knowing Mill, it cost a great deal of money. I couldn't see sticking it out on the curb on top of the garbage." Oops again, I thought when Mill looked distressed. Wrong answer. "Not that I ever really was tempted to do that," I added hastily.

"Dinner time," Sam said suddenly.

I looked his way sharply. "No, it's not. I haven't even started the shrimp yet. I still have to toss the salad."

"You can do that while Mill and I negotiate this situation."

"I'd like to see my daughter first," Mill said.

My daughter. Coming out of his mouth, it sounded almost vulgar to me. It took everything I had to nod and turn back to the kitchen door to call Chloe.

Her voice came back subdued and polite. "I'm coming, Mom."

I looked over my shoulder, and Sam and I exchanged a look. I was starting to think that he had been right about her after all, and I had been wrong. Chloe was beautiful, smart, exuberant. She was *not* sweet and polite.

She was up to something.

Five seconds later I knew what it was. She limped out of her bedroom sporting a brace that I had been forced to wear for six weeks the year before, when I'd gotten in the way of a mugging on Seventh Street. I'd been shoved to the concrete and I fractured my knee cap. Even with the adjustable Velcro, it was too big for her and it kept sliding down to her calf. As near as I could tell, she'd dragged Saturday's jeans and T-shirt out of the laundry hamper. A musty-clothes smell preceded her. Her hair was wild, standing almost straight up from her head, so she'd gotten into my hair spray, too, and had used it liberally. And was that my beige eyeshadow smeared all over her face, making it look dirty?

I was speechless as she hitched and limped her way past me into the kitchen. She had to have been planning this for hours, diligently gathering up everything she needed so she could do a quick job on herself when the time came. She'd looked perfectly normal when I'd checked on her a few minutes ago.

Mill stared at her. Sam recovered from the spectacle first—as I've said, he thinks well on his feet.

"Chloe," he said disapprovingly. "Have you been outside trying to play softball again? You know how dangerous it is for you with your leg."

I stared at him. He was *condoning* this!

Chloe cast her gaze to the floor. The performance should have won her an Oscar. "Sorry," she muttered, choking up. "I just want to be like normal kids."

Mill finally found his voice. "My God," he said, "what is this?" Then he turned a shocked gaze my way. "You never told me she was…" Words failed him. His voice trailed off.

"Crippled," Chloe supplied for him.

"If you get custody," Sam said, "you'll have to make certain special arrangements—"

I clapped my hands to my ears. "Stop this!" I shouted. It was insane! They had both — the two people I loved most in the world—lost their minds! "Go wash your face and brush your hair," I snapped at Chloe.

She gave a long-suffering sigh. "Well, it will take me a while with this leg. I'll have to walk all-l-l-l the way back down the hall again."

"We'll hold dinner," Sam promised her.

"You'll need to." She limped off again.

"You!" I pointed at Sam and my voice went up another octave.

"What's going on here?" Mill asked.

I spun on my heel to face him. "Think about it! The last thing you are is stupid! Chloe is trying to convince you that…that she's…handicapped so that you don't want her, so you won't take her away from me!"

He looked shocked, genuinely upset, then he did something Mill very rarely did. He laughed. Long and loudly and with utter enjoyment. He laughed hard enough that he had to sit down at the kitchen table and I think—though I can't swear to it—he actually wheezed.

"She's a pip," he said finally.

"Don't tell her that to her face," I warned. All the air had gone out of me. Actually, it was more than air. It was fight, too. "This is a mess," I said helplessly, pulling out a chair and sitting at the table, as well. I looked at him. "Mill, couldn't you *please* just go away again?"

"Actually, I'm rather enjoying myself," he said.

Sam made a vague, growling sort of sound, and I glanced at him. He was glaring at Mill. It struck me again that he was jealous. He had aided and abetted Chloe as if the two of them had some secret, special relationship that Mill could never hope to duplicate—and, in fact, they did. I realized suddenly that he was jealous over her, too. No matter that this meal had been his idea—Mill was infringing on his territory in a lot of ways today.

My heart started to swell, then Chloe came back. She'd washed her face and had tamed her hair, but she still wore the knee brace.

"Jig's up," I told her. "Take that thing off."

"Mom! I can't walk without it!"

"She's right, Chloe," Sam said a little too quietly. "Mr. Kramer knows what you're up to."

I watched her turn slowly to look at Mill. I girded myself, genuinely unsure of what might come out of her mouth next. A moment later I had the consolation of knowing that when push came to shove, my daughter was indeed honest.

"I don't want to go live with you," she said simply.

I was proud of her.

I would have figured Mill to be a disaster with kids. I wasn't even sure he liked them much because they tended to be all the things he wasn't. He was elegant, and they were off-the-cuff. He was snotty, and they were guileless. He was rigid, and Chloe, at least, led with her heart. But he surprised me. He leaned forward to put his elbows on his knees and he rested his chin in his hands to look straight at her, eye level.

"Why not?" he asked. "You don't even know me."

"That's the problem." Her chin came up.

Mill seemed to give that great consideration. "Yes, I can see where it might be."

"I'm not leaving my mom. You can't make me."

"Well, could I visit with you once in a while so you can get to know me?"

She crossed her arms over her chest. "I'll think about it. I really wouldn't mind having a father. But I don't want to leave my mom."

Mill finally looked up at Sam again. "Let's talk now," he said.

They went to the living room. My heart was screaming, *no, no, no!* But I also knew deep within that heart that Sam would give up nothing he didn't have to.

Larson had been right. Sam was emotionally involved here, too. And I trusted him implicitly—even with the most precious person in my world.

I stayed behind in the kitchen and put water on to boil for the pasta. The scampi is a great company dish—also a great long-day-in-court dish—because it's a cinch to make, especially if I go the extra money to have the guy at the market peel them for me. I just slap them onto a baking sheet with some melted butter and oregano and garlic, give them a little squirt with some lemon, and stick them under the broiler for six minutes. Voilà—elegance with minimal pots-and-pans and fuss.

Less than ten minutes later, I called everyone to the table. I don't earn enough to afford an apartment with a dining room, not in the city, not if I want to have any money left over for Wonderbras and sneakers. So I expected some comment from Mill about having to eat in the kitchen, but he surprised me again. He took his seat, and the first thing he said a few minutes later was, "This is delicious."

"She always makes it when she's too nervous or tired

to cook,'' Chloe reported. She was turning into a regular informational chatterbox with him. I tried not to frown.

I couldn't eat. I couldn't swallow. I tried twice, two mouthfuls, and the effort left me nauseous. I let Sam steer the conversation, but he wasn't himself, either. He was decidedly laconic.

At eight-thirty, I sent Chloe to bed. She put up a mild protest, but I could tell she was tired. For all her clever bravado, the whole situation had drained her, meeting a father she'd never known before. I knew this would be the topic of our bedtime conversations for days to come.

When she was safely tucked in with her TV turned on for one last precious half hour of Nickelodeon, I returned to the living room and dredged to the bottom of my cool aplomb. I offered Mill a nightcap.

To my great distress he accepted.

''I don't have much,'' I cautioned, hoping he would change his mind. ''Just the last of the wine from dinner. Oh, and some Chambord.'' I decided that tonight was definitely a Chambord moment. I needed something with a little more kick than the Chardonnay.

''You've got a bottle of scotch right there.'' Mill pointed to the entertainment center and the bottle of Glenlivet I'd put there.

''That's mine.'' Sam bit the words out.

''Ah,'' Mill said, then he waited for Sam to offer him some.

Sam didn't. He'd been forced to share me, to share Chloe, but he was damned if he was going to cough up his Glenlivet.

''I'll have a bit of the Chambord then,'' Mill said finally.

I poured for all of us. Sam was at least gracious enough not to dip into the scotch he wasn't intending to share. Then we all sat in the living room, looking around at each other. I cleared my throat first.

"The negotiations?" I asked. "What did you two decide, if anything?"

"Some visitation for now," Sam said. "Here, with you present, so Chloe can get to know him."

I felt something wither and die inside me.

"Well, we didn't confine it to merely these premises," Mill said quickly.

Sam shrugged one shoulder. "That's a minor technicality."

"Where, then?" I asked suspiciously. "What are you planning?"

"The two of you could come to my place," Mill pointed out.

"I don't want to—" *do that.* I broke off before the words could actually come out. Placate him, I reminded myself.

"Put you out," I finished instead. "She's young. She's very active sometimes. She could break something at your place." He had a lot of precious antiques.

"It's a chance I'm willing to take," Mill said.

Then I thought that if he got custody, he'd have to. "Are you willing to withdraw the motion in exchange for this?" I asked.

"No, of course not. But your man here succeeded in knocking back the hearing thirty days."

I looked at Sam, startled. Had Larson already signed off on the venue motion? He gave me an almost imperceptible nod.

"What's the new date?" I asked him.

"June third."

Days before the election, I thought. If we could manage just one more delay after this, then the election would come and go and Chloe wouldn't be important to Mill anymore.

If we could just stay out of court, nothing would change much for her.

I glanced back at Mill. There was something I had to say. "You can't seriously intend to hurt Chloe this way in the interest of your career." Not even he was that callous. "Do you really intend to uproot her from the only home she's ever known, to push it after she told you flat-out that she doesn't want to leave me?"

"It won't happen that way," Mill said, and once again I realized that he had been boning up on his family law. "There's not a judge in the country that wouldn't allow you several days a week with her if I win. We'd share her, as we should have been doing all along."

In that instant, I hated him. "You didn't want her," I reminded him in a whisper. I didn't want Chloe to overhear this. "You signed her away to me so you wouldn't have to deal with anything messy like paying child support!"

"I signed her away because you asked me to," Mill corrected, "and because I dislike arguing. Now I want to be her father."

Sam made an odd sound, and when I looked his way, he rolled his eyes a little. If Chloe had an Oscar coming for her performance tonight, then he was at least up for a supporting role. I ignored him and focused on Mill again.

I opened my mouth, then I realized that there was absolutely nothing else I could say to him. I had pretty much lost all the way around tonight. He'd walk away from this dinner with something—he would have visitation. I'd gained nothing—not even the hint of a promise that he would back off if I allowed him this much. The fact of that made me more than a little irritated with Sam. When Mill finally left, I rounded on him.

"How was that equitable?" I demanded.

He kicked his shoes off and put his feet up on my coffee

table. He started looking for the remote. "It's all part of kissing his hindquarters."

"I didn't even want to do that eight years ago!" I snapped.

His gaze swiveled to me but he didn't smile. He was definitely out of sorts. "I'm very glad to hear that."

He found an old *Star Trek* rerun and he put the remote down deliberately. I was not going to rise to that particular bait, but if he wanted a fight, I'd give him one.

"I got *nothing* out of this tonight," I said again.

"He consented to the venue change. That's why it went through so fast."

"Of course he did. It doesn't hurt him in the least! Our return date is still a week before the election! The voters are watching all this go on!" Some snippets of it had been reported in the newspapers, and I knew Mill's press agent had leaked them.

"He gave up his political-connection edge in Philadelphia County," Sam pointed out. "And his family's reputation here."

"*We're* the ones with all the connections in family court," I argued.

"You're not being reasonable, Mandy." His jaw was tightening noticeably.

"I'm being eminently reasonable." I just couldn't back down, even though I'd told myself earlier that we needed only one more adjournment after this and we might be home free.

Sam sighed. "Let's just keep him happy and agreeable and get through this."

That was when I put my foot in my mouth. "*You* were the one who was rude."

His eyes left the television and narrowed on me. I did have one heart-stalling thought then, one inclination to back off. I realized that I had never—not once in all the months I'd known him—seen Sam truly angry. I thought that I didn't *want* to see it. But I just kept pushing, anyway. Maybe it was a week of pent-up resentment over all his rules. Maybe it was pure frustration that I couldn't let my heart and everything in it soar free. Maybe it was as simple as the stress Mill was putting me through. It could even have been PMS. But for whatever reason, I ended up doing exactly what I had promised Grace I *wouldn't* do.

I pushed him.

"How was I rude?" Sam demanded.

"You wouldn't share your scotch."

"I don't share my scotch with people I don't like."

"You were jealous," I blurted.

His brows shot high. "Come again?"

I pushed my chin out in the gesture Chloe had learned from me. "You heard me."

"Probably not accurately," Sam said, "because I thought you said I was jealous."

"You've been acting like a rabid dog all day."

"I haven't been around you all day," he said with forced equanimity, "so how would you know?"

"What I saw of you was rabid," I insisted.

"Mandy, are you trying to make me mad?"

"Yes." I thrust my chin out a little more.

"It's working."

"Good."

"Why?"

"I don't know," I admitted. This is what happens when you argue with a lover who is also your best friend. It's hard to lie.

Sam stood and looked around for his shoes. "I'm going now," he said. Then he glowered at me. He even stabbed a finger in my general direction. ''Jealousy isn't part of our deal, you know.''

''Then I guess you broke your own rules, didn't you?''

''I don't give a damn if you want to call him back here and jump all over him tonight. That's your business.''

It cut me to the core. I think I might even have gasped a little because it hurt so much. ''Maybe I will.''

''Go for it.'' He went to the door and stepped out into the hall, then he looked back at me. ''You know, the beauty of this whole arrangement business was that there weren't supposed to be any scenes like this.''

He slammed the door hard when he left. The cracking sound killed me. I wanted to bawl.

I sat on the sofa instead and put my head in my hands. I loathed Mill profoundly for bringing all this on. He seemed as good a scapegoat as any. If he had never filed suit, if he had never wormed his way into my life tonight, if he had just dropped dead or at least off the face of the earth seven and a half years ago, if only, if only, if only...

But the fact of the matter was that I wanted more from Sam than I was getting, or ever likely to get, and it was starting to get to me. If not for that, I might well have been able to handle everything else that was going on.

I was admitting that to myself when the door burst open again. He didn't even give his usual knock of announcement this time.

''I am *not* jealous!'' he practically shouted.

And all the tension, all the angst, drained right out of me. Methinks the man protests too much, I decided. ''Okay,'' I said agreeably. I'd come back to my senses.

''Why would I be?'' he demanded.

I shrugged. ''No reason.''

''There was obviously a reason it occurred to you in the first place.''

''That business with the scotch set me off in the wrong direction, I guess.'' I stood from the sofa.

''You know, you're really acting off-the-wall tonight,'' he said. ''What gives?''

''Being nice to Mill is something of a strain. Can I go to bed now?'' It wasn't late, but I was emotionally exhausted.

He stepped inside, then he shut the door behind him. He crossed to me in a few long strides. He wasn't gentle when he took my face in his hands. He kissed me punishingly, hard. Yep, I thought. Jealous. More testosterone. Marking his territory again. And my heart, on the verge of cracking just moments before, soared.

That's how deep I was in. Something that simple had me flying. I had never flown for any man. I had never cared enough. But if you go blurring the lines between sex and your best friend, you have no one to blame but yourself when the wind catches your wings. You've let that puppy in from your porch, so you'd better damned well get used to the messes and be glad you didn't have too much invested in the way your life used to be.

So I kissed him back with everything I had. I put everything I couldn't say into my touch. I'd opened the door and he had found his way to the core of my universe.

I caught his wrists and started backing up without taking my mouth from his, urging him along with me. When we got to the hall, I tore my mouth from his and went for the hollow of his throat. I let his wrists go, too, and started unbuttoning his shirt.

''What are we doing?'' he said hoarsely, his mouth against my hair.

''I think that's obvious.''

''Chloe's home.''

''Sleeps like the dead.'' In all honesty, though, we had

so far reserved this part of our relationship—make that arrangement—to hours when she wasn't in the apartment. He'd respected my position on that, and he accepted my judgment now.

"I'm sorry," I said suddenly.

"Is this make-up sex?"

"I'm not sure. I don't think I've ever had it before. Have you?"

"I'm not going there."

I was very glad to hear that. I didn't want to envision him with someone else. Then it hit me that if this really was just an arrangement, we should be able to discuss such things without hesitation. His caution made me realize that he knew this was turning into more than an arrangement, too. We were inching onto ground where we really didn't want to have to deal with reminders of each other's past lovers.

It also struck me that he'd been doing just that all night, with the man sitting right there in my living room and asking for a hit of his Scotch. And he was wading into legal battle for the child of that union. No wonder he had seemed rabid.

We passed through my bedroom door with me still walking backward. He kicked the door shut behind him even as he began tugging upward on the hem of my top. Then he paused and remembered to lock the door.

He turned back to me and gathered me up hard and fast in his arms and we stumbled a little back toward the bed. We landed with him on top of me, and his touch became frenzied. That was okay, because mine already was.

"This is definitely make-up sex," he said, pulling my jeans off.

I went for his zipper. "Okay."

His mouth fell to my breasts. He forgot his rhythm, his

routine. He didn't take things in his usual order. His mouth was here, there, everywhere, as though he was claiming me, branding me. I kept arching up against him, and I think I pushed him onto his back and straddled him before he was ready for it. I think if he had had time to cover every inch of my skin with his mouth, that would have made him happy.

It would have made me happy, too, but need was getting the better of me. When I took him inside, there was none of the usual sense of nearing completion. Everything inside me was screaming *more, more, more!*

And Sam gave it. Again. And again.

My heart still stuttered for a long time after I lay spent on top of him. We were skin to skin and I could feel his own heart skittering, too. Jealousy and skittering, I thought. Maybe this would turn out all right after all.

But the fact of the matter was that we were breaking our rules left and right. And that scared me. Because I knew, even then I knew, that with or without Ms. Right's arrival, breaking the rules was one thing that would make Sam move on.

Chapter Eleven

I got home from the office early on Tuesday, which is to say before seven o'clock. I tend to run from one extreme to another when it comes to my work hours. There are those rare, precious days when I call it quits in time to meet Chloe directly after school, as I had on Monday. Most of the time, though, I barely have an hour and a half with her before bedtime, and I hate that. So on days when I have to be in court in the afternoon, when I'm not seeing clients at five o'clock, I try to slide straight home after the last gavel raps.

That's what happened on Tuesday, and I was looking forward to dinner with Chloe. I left the courthouse at four-thirty and gave Grace a lift, stopping at a deli on our way to grab a rotisseried chicken and three scoops of mashed potatoes in case Sam wanted to join us. I was pretty sure I had a can of corn in the cupboard. It wasn't exactly home cooking, but I was able to convince myself that it was nutritious and it required almost zero time in the kitchen on my part.

When we got to our apartment building, Grace headed up to the third floor and I knocked on Mrs. C.'s door on the second to let her know I was back. Then I knocked again. And again. And got no answer.

The woman is not hard of hearing. She's not that old. And even if she were, Chloe should have been in there, I thought. Chloe would hear a pin drop.

Alarm started making my breath feel loose and shaky. When I drew in air, it wouldn't quite fill my chest.

Something was wrong, and I didn't know what to do about it. I know that sounds ridiculous because I'm a smart woman and I spend hours each day instructing people as to what to do in situations similar to this. But when my own daughter wasn't where she was supposed to be at 5:30 on a Tuesday evening, my mind went blank.

I blamed this on Mill. What he was doing to me and to Chloe had me tied up in knots. The idea of humoring him in his crazy bid to get me back could make my muscles stiffen to the point of pain at odd moments. Add to that the whole Sam thing—walking a tightrope with him, trying desperately not let him know what I was feeling—and I was starting to come a little undone.

I finally turned about and rapped on Sam's door across the hall. No answer there, either. Where was he? He was almost always home by now.

I trotted up one more floor. Since I couldn't find Sam— my first choice—I figured Grace could always be counted on to be logical and unflappable in nearly any bizarre situation.

She answered my knock. "Chloe's gone," I blurted.

Grace frowned. "Gone where?"

"She's not at Mrs. C.'s."

"Did she come home from school? Does Mill have her? What did Mrs. C. say?"

"I don't know. She's not there, either."

Grace gave me an odd look. "If she didn't come home from school, Mrs. C. would have called you."

That was absolutely true.

"So they've obviously gone off somewhere together," Grace said.

It was highly unlike Mrs. C. to expend that much energy on baby-sitting, but stranger things had happened. I felt like an idiot. "I'll go back to my apartment and wait for them to call," I decided.

"Mandy," Grace called to me as I turned away.

I looked back. "What?"

"You're starting to scare me a little."

"I'm scaring me, too," I said miserably.

I went back downstairs, clutching my chicken, my briefcase and my mashed potatoes. As it turned out, I didn't need to wait for them to call. When I let myself through my own door, I found Sylvie Casamento seated on my sofa. When she'd started baby-sitting for me, I'd left a key with her in case Chloe ever needed anything from inside the apartment.

"What are you doing down here?" I demanded. "Where's Chloe?"

"Dressing." She didn't take her eyes from the talk show she was watching on my television.

My first thought was that there'd been some kind of an accident, that Chloe had spilled something on herself or gotten her school clothes incredibly dirty somehow. Then again, Chloe rarely minded being dirty.

"Why?" I asked more carefully. "Why is she dressing?"

"For dinner."

This was starting to feel like an episode of *Twilight Zone*. "Damn it," I snapped, "would you please look at me while we have this conversation?"

Her gaze finally came to me. "There's no need to swear."

I would have disagreed with that, but I just wanted answers. "I want to know what's going on here," I said.

Mrs. C. grunted a little as though she'd been grievously insulted. "I was doing you a favor," she said. "I brought her downstairs early and let her get ready. I was saving you time."

"Time for *what?*" Then I dropped everything I was holding onto the coffee table and drove my hands into my hair, scraping it back from my face. "Never mind." I'd talk to Chloe.

"You owe me thirty dollars," Mrs. C. said as I started toward the hallway. "You could probably give me a bonus, too, for bringing her downstairs early."

She didn't trust me to pay her at the end of the week. I had to do it every day. And ten dollars an hour was outrageous—the after-school program at Chloe's school only charged twenty dollars up to six o'clock. I paid her because I liked being able to come straight home at the end of the day, knowing that Chloe was already here, safe and sound. Sad as it is, the fact remains that schools are not the safest place in the world anymore.

I dug in my briefcase for my wallet and gave Mrs. C. the money—minus the bonus. My expression must have warned her off from mentioning it a second time.

I went to find Chloe. I did one of those Sam things. I knocked once on her bedroom door and opened it before she had a chance to respond. What met my eyes was just as bizarre as the knee brace and the lacquered hair the night Mill had come to dinner. She was wearing a dress.

Chloe does not do dresses. For all the Barbies littering our apartment and Barbie's various accouterments, my daughter is essentially a tomboy. Mostly what she does with the Barbies is pretend they are policewomen and race car drivers. She'd live in jeans if I let her. Well, I do let her, but I make sure that at least half of them are pink, white or red. And I generally make her wear girly tops and sweaters.

Now she stood staring at me in a much-too-small teal organdy dress I'd bought her to wear to a friend's wedding last fall. It strained over her skinny chest.

"Hi, Mom," she said.

I found my voice. "What in the world is going on around here?"

"We're going to my father's for dinner," she informed me.

I felt something go *ping!* in my head, the first warning that I was about to come really unglued. All the same, I thought I replied with a great deal of calm. "No, we're not."

"Yeah. At seven o'clock. Miss Mildred is making spaghetti."

This time I felt a double *ping!* "How do you know the name of Mill's housekeeper?" I asked.

She looked at me like I was dense. "He told me."

"When?" I knew he hadn't said a word about it last night.

"When he called me at school today to invite us over for dinner."

I was suddenly so livid I was shaking. Not only had he gone behind my back, but nowhere in those negotiations with Sam—nowhere—had Mill been given the right to call my daughter's school. In fact, until and unless we ultimately landed in court so he could shred the legitimacy of the agreement we'd signed seven years ago, he was expressly forbidden from doing any such thing. Give the bastard an inch, I thought, and he stretched it out to a mile.

I needed Sam for this. Where the hell was he, anyway? I glanced at my watch. It was pushing toward six o'clock now. He was almost always home by this time.

"Take the dress off," I said to Chloe.

"But—"

"Now!" Yes, I thought, oh, yes, I was losing it. I never yelled at her like that.

"Are you mad at me?" Chloe asked, and I heard her voice tremble a little.

I deliberately softened my own. "No, honey, not at all."

"You're mad at him, then. At my father."

How many times had I warned clients to be honest with their kids but to keep the emotion and the bitterness out of it? I started to deny it, but the words stuck in my throat. And every time she said "my father," it sounded to me like fingernails running over a blackboard. I wanted to dismember *her father*.

I finally just turned away and went to the kitchen. I called Sam's office. He'd picked a hell of a night to work late.

His recording came on the line, prompting me to leave a message. As I've said, Sam is a one-man show, and I finally realized that his single secretary would be long gone for the day. It was possible he was still there, working on a brief or something, letting the machine pick up rather than be disturbed. But I happened to know that Sam did his best writing propped up in bed with law books spread all around him.

McGlinchey's? Would he have gone out to happy hour without me? My head was starting to hurt as I thought about it. Two weeks ago, yes, of course he would have—especially if he'd had a hot date. But he wasn't doing hot dates anymore. Since our arrangement had started, I just couldn't see him going out without tagging me first to find out if I was available.

Then again, nothing else made much sense. It was either that, or he was lying in a hospital somewhere. Since my heart thudded uncomfortably hard at that possibility, I decided not to entertain it. I focused on the first scenario instead.

He'd made a rule about this, I remembered. One of his rules had specifically dealt with just this eventuality. He'd said that if it ever happened that there was something else he wanted to do besides get together with me, I couldn't whine or feel threatened. He'd also put something in there about not having to check in with each other every day. And come to think of it, I hadn't spoken to him that afternoon, although we had touched base in the morning.

So, I deduced, he probably *was* at McGlinchey's.

My stomach was churning. I knew I was about to do a very stupid thing. But damn it, I wanted to talk to him about what Mill had done. The hell with our arrangement bylaws, I thought. Sam was my lawyer. This wasn't personal. It was business.

Like I said before, I can rationalize almost anything.

I went back to Chloe's room. She was sitting on her bed with the teal-blue dress on her lap now. She was dressed in jeans and sneakers again, and her favorite T-shirt, a red one that Sam had given her. The letters on the front demanded "ASK ME IF I CARE."

She looked unhappy. "It doesn't fit, anyway, does it?" she asked me.

The dress, I thought. She was still on the dress. "No, honey. It's way too small. I'll take it to the Salvation Army this weekend."

"Will you buy me a new one?"

"Of course." Then I frowned. "What for?"

"For dinners with my father."

Things were pounding in my head now. "Chloe, you never wear dresses. And there's no need to wear one if we all have dinner together. You should just be yourself."

"Mom, I want him to like me."

Dear God, I thought, her lip was trembling. This was serious.

I couldn't take serious. I didn't *want* to deal with serious just then. I didn't even really think I could do it without screaming. But I'm a mother, so I went to sit beside her on the bed. Chloe snuggled into my arms.

"He does," I said. "He likes you very much, even after what you pulled with the hair and the knee brace. He invited us for dinner, didn't he?"

"I figure he's just trying to check me out, to decide if he really wants me after all. You know, to make sure I'm not really crippled. He'd want to watch me walk some more just to be on the safe side."

"He's not *that* bad, Chloe." I wanted to press a hand to the pain in my heart, but I couldn't do it without letting go of her. "He laughed about the brace, baby. He thought it was really funny." So funny, I thought, that I'd never seen him laugh like that before.

Chloe looked up at me. "He did?"

"He definitely did."

"I was thinking about it, Mom. Sometimes I used to think about it before, too, when I was little."

And now, of course, she'd reached the ripe old age of seven. I almost smiled. "What did you think about?"

"That I wished I had a dad."

"Well," I said faintly. "Now you have one."

I felt her nod against my chest. "I only did what I did last night because I got scared at first," she admitted.

"Change is a scary thing."

I really, really needed to talk to Sam, I thought again. As my attorney, and as my best friend. I gave Chloe a little squeeze. "Would you mind hanging with Grace and Jenny for about an hour?" I asked her.

"So we're not going to his house for dinner?"

"Not tonight. I'm sorry." But I really wasn't.

She sagged a little in my arms, dejected.

"Chloe, the thing is, he really needs to come to me first about things like this. I'm not saying that you—we—can't spend time with him, but there are certain rules he has to follow. He should check with me first."

"Yeah," she said. "I guess."

"Come on," I said. "I'll walk you upstairs."

By the time we got there, Jenny was home, too. She and Grace were debating whether to call out for pizza or to try to scrounge together a salad from what was in the refrigerator. I saved the day for them by turning over the chicken and the mashed potatoes.

When you're in love with someone—and starting to hurt because of it—the silliest little things can pluck at your emotions. I looked at those potatoes while I handed them over to Jenny and I thought, Three servings, one each for Sam, Chloe and me. I had assumed he would be joining us for dinner, but the way it had turned out, I didn't even have the vaguest idea where he was. And that made my heart squirm.

Actually, I *did* have an idea of where he'd gotten to, and it turned out to be right. I drove to McGlinchey's and my night went down the proverbial tube hard enough and fast enough that for a moment I wondered if I would ever be able to pull it out again.

Sam was there, all right. He was at the bar, talking to Tammy, his old semiflame.

I never got past the door. The way the place is structured, the entrance is in shadows and there's a big, fake fern between it and the bar. I stood behind the plant, staring at them. And the longer I stared, the faster my heart beat.

She wasn't Ms. Right. I knew that. She wasn't the blind-side quotient I'd predicted to Jenny. In fact, even if I hadn't already known their history, I'd still have guessed that Sam wanted to be anywhere else in that moment except engaged in meaningless conversation with her. I know his body language, and he wasn't leaning toward her to hear her speak over the noise. He looked stiff and unhappy.

I didn't think I was losing him to Tammy, but I knew I was losing him. Because he'd come here without me for the first time since our arrangement had begun. I'd done the unforgivable last night. I'd pushed. *That* was why he had cut me out, why he'd come here alone. He didn't want scenes. He didn't want complications. He wanted his rules and his bylaws and the good old Mandy who'd always toed the line before.

I couldn't breathe.

By the time I got back to the parking lot, I was shaking. I didn't entirely trust myself to drive, but I made it home in one piece and without inflicting damage on anyone else, either. I went straight to my apartment to call upstairs.

I got Jenny on the phone. "I'm back," I said. "You can send Chloe down now."

"You're not coming up?" she asked. "There's chicken left."

The thought of eating made me want to throw up. "No, thanks," I said briefly. "Long day."

The thing is, I just couldn't face them. Jenny and Grace knew me too well. They'd take one look at my face and know that I'd blown it. They'd cluck over me and they'd fuss and they'd try to comfort me—even Grace would, though to a much smaller extent than Jenny. And that would undo me the rest of the way.

I had one chance and one chance only to hold myself together, and that involved throwing myself into my mother routine, getting Chloe showered and into bed, checking her book bag for the homework situation. If I didn't let myself think too much, I might be okay.

Jenny sent Chloe downstairs and, of course, there was unfinished homework in her book bag. Her afternoon routine had been fractured, first by Mill, then by my own sudden departure to McGlinchey's, and she wasn't all that diligent about completing it without complications. We did it at the kitchen table with a little bit of ice cream I found in the freezer. My throat worked when I tried to swallow it, but I didn't get sick.

I kept her up until nine-thirty, and that was purely selfishness on my part. As long as I was busy with her, not only did I not have to sit down quietly and face myself, but neither could I glue one ear to the hallway and listen for sounds of Sam coming home.

Unfortunately, I eventually had to part with Chloe because even a desperate mother can't cattle-prod her child into wakefulness until the wee hours of the morning on a school night just to save her own sorry heart. I tucked her in, and when I was sure she was asleep I went to the kitchen to call Mill.

According to my caller ID, he'd phoned us six times while Chloe had been upstairs with Grace and Jenny and I had been seeing things I didn't want to see at McGlinchey's. I punched his number into the phone and started thinking about how this was the first night Sam hadn't been around since we'd started our arrangement. There actually seemed to be a hollowness to the air in the apartment. I was wallowing in that when Mill answered, and it took me a moment to remember why I had called him in the first place.

"You were way out of line," I said as soon as it came back to me.

"Ah, I was right then," Mill said. "It occurred to me that my approach made you angry. That's why you stood me up."

"Your approach made me *furious*," I corrected him. "Until a judge changes the status quo, Mill, you're not *permitted* to contact her at school, not without my approval. And I sure as hell don't appreciate you sneaking around behind me."

He ignored that last part. "Would you have approved?" he asked.

"Of course I would have." Then I scrambled. "Not of you calling her during school hours, but you can certainly call her here. I mean, I would have approved dinner."

"I'll keep that in mind," he said.

I was gritting my teeth so hard my jaw hurt. I didn't answer.

"Is your attorney present?" he asked suddenly.

"Now? No."

"He's not actually living with you, then."

Actually, Sam was in the process of moving on from me, I thought, but I'd be damned if I'd let Mill know that. "Of course not," I said. "What would that teach Chloe about marital relationships?"

"She was born outside of one," he pointed out. "She'll figure that out eventually unless we manage to get back together."

My stomach literally clenched at the thought. I think I groaned aloud.

"Do you feel like company, then?" he asked. "Since you're alone tonight?"

No! "Chloe is already asleep, Mill. There's no sense in you coming over now."

"I still want to talk to you. Without your attorney present."

My skin crawled, but I kept up the facade of letting him think he had a chance. "I'm exhausted tonight. Some other time."

I don't know what he said next, because I heard that single rap on my front door, then it opened and closed. I hung up on Mill without saying goodbye. I didn't hurry to the living room. In fact, I almost tiptoed. I was afraid of what I was going to find.

Sam was standing inside my door. I could tell by his eyes that he'd had more than a couple of scotches. I could also tell that he was angry.

"Hi," I said. "I guess you went out tonight." I forced my tone into calm indifference.

"Yeah." He glared at me.

"You didn't mention that you had plans." I started picking up Barbie paraphernalia from the floor as I spoke.

"I don't tell you everything," he said obstinately.

I straightened and somehow I managed to grin at him. "Obviously. Are you in a bad mood?"

He seemed to have to think about it, then he nodded.

"Want a nightcap?" I asked.

"I don't need one."

I tended to agree with that, but I only shrugged. In the end, he came into the living room, crossed to the entertainment center, and snagged his bottle of Glenlivet himself. My heart stuttered a bit as I waited to find out if he was going to pour from it or take it back upstairs to his own apartment.

He took it into the kitchen. I let my breath out. It was tremulous and that ticked me off. I didn't like this. I didn't like my heart being at the mercy of a man. But it was, so I went after him. I dug out my own precious Chambord bottle. My life was just chock full of Chambord moments lately.

Sam knocked back a shot of Scotch, glared at me for another moment, then he poured himself another one. "I was jealous," he said suddenly. "I *am* jealous."

My heart kicked.

"And I damned well don't like it," he continued. "How the hell did jealousy get into this? It wasn't supposed to."

I decided that reticence was the best way to go here. "I don't know," I said, and left it at that.

"When I saw him kissing you, I wanted to flatten him."

My heart kicked harder. I only shrugged. "Like I said, if I wanted to go back to him, I would. But I haven't, so I don't."

"Right," he said. He still sounded surly.

"Maybe you need to get some sleep, Sam."

"Don't tell me what I need."

I held my hands up in a truce sign. He was as foul as I had ever seen him. "Okay, then, *I* need to get some sleep."

I stepped around him. He talked after me. "I hate being jealous and I hate not even being able to accept a couple of damned baseball tickets from a client because I don't know if you want to go to the game or not! We were supposed to be avoiding all that!"

I turned around to stare at him, a little lost now. "What?"

"Ed Hensel offered me Phillies tickets!" he shouted.

"Good," I said carefully. "Great. You love baseball. Who's Ed Hensel?"

"A client! But I couldn't find you to find out if you wanted to go!"

I was starting to catch on. "Did you call my office?"

"At five o'clock. Some guy said you never came back from court. You weren't home, either. And you didn't answer your cell phone."

It had been in my briefcase. I had either been in the deli and the phone had been in the car, or I hadn't heard its muffled summons because I was so preoccupied with looking for Chloe and Mrs. C. "So did you take the tickets?" I asked.

"Didn't you hear what I just said? I couldn't track you down!"

I was starting to get the gist of all this, and I didn't know if I wanted to shout for joy or sob my heart out. It sort of depended on which way he went with it.

He went the route that I didn't want him to take. "Mandy," he said quietly. Apparently he was finished shouting at me now. "I never wanted this."

I decided to play dumb. "Sharing baseball tickets? Are they like toothbrushes?"

He wasn't going to be sidetracked. "You don't even like baseball," he said.

"I don't—"

He interrupted me. "I know, I know, you never sat down and watched a game and tried to figure it out."

"Right," I said.

"That's my point. Why would I want to take you in the first place?"

"I'm not sure," I said evasively.

"Because I just like being with you!" His voice was starting to rise again. "Because it would be more fun trying to explain things to you than to invite some guy to come along with me."

I was going to cry. The lump in my throat was so hard and full it hurt. "Thanks." It was the only word I could get out.

"But that's not the way this was supposed to be," he said. "So I thought, hell, it's just an arrangement, and we have our bylaws. I could go out tonight by myself if I wanted to."

So he had done it just to make the point, I realized. If not to me, then to himself. I nodded.

"Maybe we need to take a break from this arrangement thing," he said.

The words crashed over me. I felt my bottom lip trembling and I bit down on it hard. "Okay."

"I'll still help you out with this Mill thing, but…"

He trailed off. I waited. I wanted him to leave so I could fall apart. I didn't want him to leave, because I knew once he did even our friendship would be over. We wouldn't survive this. We'd be embarrassed with each other now, postarrangement.

I had been telling myself all along that it was inevitable this would end. They'd turned out to be brave words with no substance. Now I knew that I couldn't let it happen. I couldn't step back and let go of him now that I'd found him. I couldn't do it because I didn't think I could live without him.

My knees were a little wobbly as I crossed the room toward him. I snaked my arms around his waist and rested my head against his chest. At the very least, I told myself, I was one step up from an arrangement-lover now. He didn't want that. He wanted to run instead. But if he was going to run, then he was going to have to literally push me out of his arms to do it.

"Sam." I sighed. "You're making this a lot more complicated than it has to be."

His arms came around me. Not tightly, but they were there. "We woke up together," he said. "In Atlantic City."

"People do that all the time. It doesn't have to mean

anything. If they're real casual about such things, they might not ever even see each other again.''

"True," he said. I could feel him relaxing. A little, just a little. Then he stiffened again. "But they're not us. They weren't best friends to start with.''

I stepped back from him. "Call your client, Sam. Accept the baseball tickets. Take a guy pal. I don't want to go.'' Then I paused because it took everything I had to say the next words, to put myself on the line, to crawl. "Then come to bed," I added.

He watched my face. "Arrangement sex?''

"Well, technically I guess it could qualify as more make-up sex. Was this a fight?''

"It was a scene.''

"Well, there you have it. Close enough.''

"That make-up sex last night was pretty damned good,'' he said.

I managed to smile. "It was, wasn't it?'' I started backing off toward the door.

"Mandy, wait.''

I cringed inside. "What?''

"I don't want to fall in love with you.''

"Good. Then get your act together, pal, because this is just an arrangement.'' To this day, I'm not sure how I managed to get those words out.

I turned my back to him and went to my bedroom. Then I stood just inside the door, in the dark, waiting for him. If he just left, if he walked out on me, I didn't know how I was going to accept it. I would have to, of course, but I realized in that moment that Mill had been right about me to some extent. All my life I'd left relationships first. True, I'd done it when there was absolutely no other recourse, but I'd done it all the same. This was the first time I was on the verge of being dumped, that my heart was in danger of being shattered.

I was straining so hard for the sound of his footsteps in the hallway—or for the alternative, the sound of the front door opening and closing—that my ears started to ring. I couldn't hear anything. If he left, then I'd know he really did want to end this. If he stayed, I had another chance to toe the line.

Then he was there in the bedroom door. He kissed me and I breathed again.

For now, for that moment, that night, I was still safe.

Chapter Twelve

There's an old movie—I think it came out in the seventies—called *About Last Night*. And there's a song on the soundtrack of that movie about two people trying to hold it together while their love goes to hell in a handbasket. The one line that has always stuck in my mind goes something like: "If we can just make it through the night…"

Well, Sam and I made it through the night.

It's true that he got out of bed at one-thirty in the morning, dressed again and went to his own apartment. I walked him to the door and watched him trudge up the stairs until his legs disappeared around the landing. I felt as if I had dodged a bullet, but I wasn't such an idiot that I didn't know there was still a loaded gun out there somewhere and its ammunition had my name on it.

I hadn't thought I'd be able to sleep, but somehow I did. And the next morning was another one of those that started out all off-kilter. This time, instead of Chloe leaning over me, peering down into my face, I woke to find her curled up next to me.

It had been at least three years since she'd climbed into bed with me in the middle of the night, so I knew she was stressed by everything that was going on. Maybe she didn't even know she was stressed—she might be a genius, but she was still only seven, after all. But somewhere inside her heart she was reaching out for security. She was reaching out for what had always been there. She was reaching for me.

So I didn't get up when the alarm went off. I snuggled into her, and held her and she made some groggy sounds in her sleep. And that was the moment when I stopped thinking of Mill as a threat to myself. I stopped thinking of the whole thing as a court battle, and I started considering it in terms of how I was going to get Chloe through it with her heart in one piece.

Of course, to some extent that had been on my mind from the beginning, from the first night I stood in my kitchen and read Mill's moving papers—that I couldn't let this hurt her. But a lot of other things had been tangled up in there, too: pride, selfishness, a lot of old wounds Mill had inflicted on me long ago. Lying there with Chloe in my arms, it finally dawned on me that none of those things mattered anymore. The only thing that was important was what Chloe had said to me last night. She wanted a dad.

She should have a dad, I thought. That's one of those given entitlements of childhood. We don't all get them. I hadn't. Maybe on some level I'd thought that because I had gotten through without one, Chloe could, too. But why should she have to?

I took in a deep breath and when I released it again, it shuddered out of me. I was going to have to bury pieces of myself now and let Mill win this to some extent. I was

going to have to share Chloe with him. Not for his sake,
or for the sake of his political career, but for our daughter.

I'd talk to Sam about it first, I thought, but before I did
that, before I faced him again after last night, I was going
to have to talk to Jenny about Sam.

It's my opinion that the luckiest people are the ones who
have friends for all occasions. Some friends are best to
confide in when you need to be strong. For me, that's
Grace—she'll kick me in the backside every time. But then
there are those friends you lean on when you've made up
your mind that you're going to be weak. In my case that's
Jenny. Underneath all the weird analogies and the bright
waitress smile, Jenny has a keen mind. After all, this is the
woman who conceived the art museum approach to available sperm. If she was a little off base with her destination,
at least her concept was on target.

I finally slipped out of bed, careful not to disturb Chloe,
and I went to take a shower. As my workday mornings go,
this one was pretty uneventful. There were no cantaloupe
emergencies. It had been a few days since I had done laundry, but fate smiled on me and Chloe's pink jeans were
still clean and folded in her bottom dresser drawer. I stuck
her in the cab at eight o'clock with the other car-pool kids,
and I had the temerity to think that maybe I was an okay
mom after all.

I spent a lot of the day dictating motions for various
clients and researching points of law. I had at least one big
divorce trial coming up, and I like those the best. Sam is
gifted with the ability to think on his feet and he does well
with single-hearing motions. I, on the other hand, like to
plot and plan long-term, and trials are my forte. I was in
our office's law library, thinking about that, when it occurred to me that it was the same approach I needed to use
now, both with my Sam problem and with Mill.

I needed long-term plans in each quarter, I realized. I had to figure out how to keep Sam around indefinitely, even while he battled with jealousy he didn't want to feel. As for Mill, the premise took me right back to the fact that his motion had to be withdrawn come hell or high water—because *that* could have long-term consequences which I did not want.

This is why I put work behind me at a reasonable hour for the third day in a row. If I didn't watch it, my pending partnership was going to be tossed up for grabs by some other deserving soul, I thought. Then I realized that I honestly didn't care, and at five o'clock I left the office to go to McGlinchey's.

I arrived just before Jenny got off duty. She was collecting tabs and turning her tables over to the waitress who was coming on, and when she saw me she looked surprised. She glanced over my shoulder to search for Sam—who, of course, was not with me. A tiny frown etched her forehead.

I went to the bar to wait for her. There were no tables available, and even if there had been, I wouldn't rob one of the waitresses of a good-tipping party of five just so Jenny and I could sit down. As I slid onto a stool, I heard my cell phone buzz inside my briefcase—tonight, this time, I heard it.

I pulled it out to check the incoming number. Sam. Something in my heart keened a little. I wanted to answer it. The Mandy who had existed before our arrangement certainly would have. Even two days ago the Mandy who was in love with him would have done it, as well. But I couldn't. Part of it was sheer female spitefulness. If he could blow off a couple of hours at McGlinchey's by himself, then so could I. The other part was just sensible caution. Grace's advice had been to keep the terms of our arrangement without letting him know how I felt. I'd failed at that miserably, and it had had nearly dire consequences. I rarely make the same mistake twice. It was time to put a little distance back into the situation, at least until I figured out what to do about it.

Jenny finally finished with her shift and came to the bar to join me. The guy sitting next to me gladly gave up his stool to her. She inspected him with brief interest before she obviously decided that his sperm had no real potential. She dropped onto the stool with a sigh, her back to him. He seemed disappointed.

"What's up?" she asked. "Where's Sam?"

I shrugged. "I don't know. He just called me and I didn't answer. I need your advice."

She looked alarmed. "Did you guys have a fight? That wasn't supposed to happen. You have rules!"

I hesitated. "Well, the rules haven't really worked out all that well."

"Maybe you need Grace for this," she cautioned.

"Do you want Sam and me to…to…break up?" Was that what it was called when you ended something that was just an arrangement? I wondered.

Jenny looked horrified. "No, of course not!"

My order came. I took a sip of wine and looked at her dead-on. "Then I need you to tell me how to keep him, because Grace would probably tell me to just suck it up and walk away if she knew he was causing me this much heartache."

She cocked her head to the side. Her blond hair spilled over her shoulder—she'd taken it down from her ponytail when she'd come off shift. She looked a little misty-eyed. Sympathetic. Tonight it was exactly what I needed.

"You really do love him," she said softly. The word *heartache* must have tipped her off. I hesitated then I nodded. Okay, I thought, now it's official. I LOVE HIM. I imagined the words blazing in neon.

"He loves you, too," Jenny decided.

I thought about the things he'd said last night. "It's remotely possible," I said, "but he's really not happy about it."

"No, he wouldn't be."

"Why not?" I had my own theories on that, of course, but I wanted to hear hers.

"You said his ex-wife really hurt him. And he didn't even tell *you* the truth about her, about what she did to him, and you're his best friend. So it must really be a sore spot."

She turned back to the bar and ordered a rum and cola, then she peeled off some of her hard-won tips to pay for it. I felt as if I should do it for her since I had instigated this meeting, but I knew she would get prickly about it. Jenny is pretty touchy about paying her own way through her Philadelphia odyssey.

"Right now Sam is like a worm caught in quicksand," she said finally, sipping from her drink.

A *worm?* It was weird, I thought, but give her credit. The analogy brought a certain image to mind. I got it.

"Wriggling like mad," she continued, "just trying to get back to the surface. The poor little thing is doomed, of course."

"He's going under." I liked the sound of that.

Jenny nodded sagely. "Absolutely. There's no hope for him. In fact, he's already smothered. He just needs to take a few more mouthfuls of quicksand into his throat before he accepts it."

"So what do I do about it?" I asked her, then I put it more precisely. "If you were me, what would *you* do?"

"I'd kill for a guy like Sam," she said promptly.

"Well, you can't have him," I snapped. "I'm not done with him yet."

She grinned. "Oh, you do have it bad."

I had it so bad I was afraid to talk about it, as though if I tried to describe the full scope of what I felt for him, I'd jinx myself. I'd lose him and then I'd die. So I only shrugged.

Jenny sipped more rum and cola. "Okay, if I were you, I'd make myself scarce for a while. I'd take a step back."

It was exactly the same advice I'd gotten from Grace *before* I'd screwed up. I'd expected something different from Jenny's corner now. But the fact that they'd both said pretty much the same thing turned it into gospel.

"Okay," I said. "How?"

"Go on with your own life as though he doesn't matter a lick," she said.

"He *is* my life, Jen. Well, him and Chloe."

"But you can't let him know that right now."

They were *both* advocating that I play games with him, so there must be something to the theory, I thought again.

"Sam is going to need some time to come to terms with what he's feeling," Jenny said. "You need to be there for him, but not be there, you know? And you can't lose yourself in him."

I jolted. Had I been doing that?

"You can't get obsessed here," she continued. "Where most people go wrong with marriage and relationships is that they make the other person entirely responsible for their happiness. You were happy as a clam before you and Sam set up your deal, right?"

I thought about it. "Yeah. I was pretty happy."

"Go back to what made you tick then, and what's going on with Sam should be just icing on the cake of your life."

Wow, I thought. She was good.

"You and Chloe used to drive out to Lancaster on some weekends to antique hunt, remember?"

It had been a while, but of course I remembered. I never actually bought anything because I didn't possess the knowledge to figure out what was real and what was a sham. But Chloe and I enjoyed driving through the Amish farmlands and visiting the museums and chowing down on good back-country food. I nodded.

"Just live your life, Mandy," she said gently. "Do what makes you happy. And wait for Sam to catch up. If you don't threaten him, he won't run away. Then someday he'll just wake up and *poof!* realize he's in love with you. You said that yourself. Someone is going to blindside him. But it's not going to be someone new. It's going to be you."

I could only pray.

"Can I have a ride home now and save the cab fare?" she asked.

I gave her a lift and we parted ways in our apartment lobby. She promised to stop by Mrs. C.'s on her way up and send Chloe down.

I wondered where Sam was; if he was home. Then I followed Jenny's very good advice and I went into my apartment to do what made me happy, with or without him.

I made asparagus omelets for dinner, though Chloe hates them and if Sam turned up to join us, he would be displeased, too. I made them for me. To atone for that, I found a box of cake mix in the cupboard and baked cupcakes after dinner. After Chloe went to bed, I dug out my sewing kit and repaired a rip in her favorite jeans—there was no sense in replacing them because it was May. If I bought her new ones now, she'd wear them for a week or two before it grew hot enough to make shorts mandatory. Then they'd go into a drawer and by September, she would have outgrown them.

It's not that mending makes me happy, mind you. It's more that it stops me from feeling guilty for putting it off.

I was working hard to convince myself that I was enjoying myself when there came the double-action of Sam's knock on the door. It flew open immediately afterward.

"Are you alone?" he asked, striding into my living room.

"Of course I'm alone." Then I amended that. "Well, not technically. Chloe's in bed."

He frowned. "You know what I mean."

He actually believed Mill might be here, I realized. Was that good or bad? "Then I'm alone," I said.

He loosened his tie. "What a day."

I made a sympathetic sound in my throat, then I got up and went for his scotch bottle. I'd keep things normal and relaxed between us if it killed me. "I guess you don't need any more legal problems today, then," I said.

He looked at me sharply and followed me into the kitchen. "Has something come up with Mill? I tried to call you but I couldn't get you on your cell phone. Again."

I caught the jibe, but I only waved a negligent hand. "I stopped by McGlinchey's after I left the office," I said. I poured scotch, added water and handed him the glass.

"With Grace?" he asked. Translation: or with Mill?

"Actually, with Jenny."

He took a mouthful of his drink. "I needed this."

I lofted a brow. "So you dropped by here because I have your scotch?"

He frowned at me. "No. I keep a bottle upstairs, too."

That was good, I thought. "Want a back rub?"

His eyes went cunning. "You give back rubs?"

I let out breath. That was when I knew that our problems of last night—and Monday night—were forgotten. At least by him, at least for now.

Relief can be a palpable thing. It filled my limbs with an airy feeling. We were pretty much back to normal, I decided. So I lifted my hands and flexed my fingers. ''The best back rubs,'' I promised him.

''You're on.''

Instead of going to my bedroom, we went to the sofa, and that was good, too. He took his shirt off and I straddled him, working on his muscles, enjoying myself immensely. It was like our night at the Tropicana, where even time spent without sex was good.

''What happened today to make it so miserable?'' I asked finally.

''I got approached to take on a criminal case, and I'm not sure I want to.''

''Why?''

''I've got negligible experience in that area.''

His eyes were closed now, but I nodded anyway, even though he couldn't see me. ''Why did the client come to you, then?''

''Can't afford the specialists.''

I understood that, too. ''Did he do it? Whatever he's been charged with?''

''Probably.''

''Can you handle that?''

He thought about it and opened his eyes again. ''No.''

I had kind of figured that. ''There's your answer. You're not a criminal defense attorney, Sam. A prosecutor-type maybe. But you couldn't live with setting bad guys free.''

''Yeah.'' He smiled. ''You're good for me, Mandy.''

Music to my ears, I thought.

A long while later he sat up, flexing his shoulders. ''Something happened with Mill,'' he reminded me. ''We were going off in that direction before your magic fingers got the better of me.''

I got up and took our glasses to the kitchen. "I want to settle out of court."

He followed me. "You're not going to give up custody, Mandy." I heard the sudden edge in his voice.

"Of course not. I just want to offer him weekends with her."

He stared at me. "Why?"

"Because Chloe needs a father, and I can see where this arrangement would ace everybody's needs." Except mine, I thought. "It gives Mill a good complexion for the election, and she gets the attention of a dad for as long as it lasts."

Something flexed in his jaw. "The biological act does *not* make a father."

"Well, we both know that," I agreed. "But he's what Chloe's got."

"I don't like it."

"I'm your client, and I'm telling you this is the route I want to take."

"Giving up without a fight?"

"Compromise," I said. "For my daughter's sake." He hadn't seen her face last night, I thought. She hadn't crawled into bed with him this morning, vulnerable and needy for the first time in three years. "Just do up an agreement with a visitation schedule, and see if he bites. Please?"

He still didn't look happy about it, but he shrugged. "It's your kid, your call."

I wondered what it was about my idea that so clearly bothered him. I knew he loved Chloe and that he wanted the best for her, so he should have understood—even agreed with—my decision. It couldn't still be jealousy, I thought, not in this respect. I knew that daddyhood was not something Sam had on his wish list right now, if only because it sort of went part-and-parcel with the Ms. Right thing.

"I was thinking about taking her to the ball game on Saturday," he said suddenly, surprising me.

"The tickets we were arguing about last night?"

"That wasn't an argument. It was a heartfelt discussion."

"A scene," I said, remembering what he had called it last night.

"Right."

"What happened with the guy pal you were going to take?" I asked.

"I couldn't find anyone. And you—"

"Don't understand sports," I finished for him.

"Well, I figure for you sports is out there in the same category with aliens."

I shook my head. "No. Aliens are far worse."

He grinned that great Sam grin, a little bit crooked, a little bit rakish. "So do I have a date then?"

"With my daughter? Sure, if she wants to go. I'll ask her in the morning."

It seemed as if that about settled it. But he kept looking at me and his expression was a little odd.

"What?" I asked.

"I'm spent," he said finally. "I just...I don't know, I feel like turning in early tonight."

I really wasn't following him. "So go do it." Then my mouth framed into an *O* as understanding hit me. "Sam," I said gently, "you don't have to jump on top of me tonight just to prove that everything's okay between us."

He let his air out. I recognized relief when I saw it. "I didn't want you to think I was lacking in the amorous department."

I almost grinned. "You? Never."

But still he hesitated. "Want to just crash on the sofa for a while with the TV?"

He wanted to stay anyway, I realized. His idea was tempting. It was so tempting it almost hurt. But I remembered what Jenny had said about giving him time to come to terms with whatever he was feeling, time to catch up with me, so I drew in a breath and shook my head. "Sam, you'd just fall asleep there and be all cranky when I woke you up to chase you upstairs."

He finally shrugged, but I could tell he wasn't happy. "Okay, then. As long as you're not disappointed."

"I'm devastated, but I have my pride."

He looked at me sharply.

"Just kidding," I said.

"Oh." Then he gave a short, insincere bark of laughter. "Good. I guess I'll go, then."

"I'll talk to Chloe in the morning," I promised.

"I'll call Mill's lawyer in the morning and sound him out about a deal," he said.

"Call me and let me know what he says."

"Are you going to answer your cell phone this time?"

"Sam, I won't have to. I'll be at the office. You can get me there."

I was actually pretty proud of myself. I was being ultra-cool, toeing all our arrangement lines left and right. But the truth is, the strain of it was starting to make me feel as fragile as glass.

I walked out into the hallway with him, and this time when he kissed me good-night, he put it on my forehead. I wondered what that meant, but I didn't put too much thought into it. I was getting worn-out from all the wondering and the worrying. If he moved an eyebrow up instead of down, what did that mean? If he turned left instead of right, was that good or bad? I was torturing myself…and I was running out of energy for it.

I finally went back into my apartment and made my way toward my bedroom in the usual fashion. Two steps, then I dived for a toy. Another step, then I dived for a juice box on the coffee table. One more step, then I went down for the sweater Chloe had dropped on the floor earlier. By the time I crossed the living room, my arms were laden. Then I reversed the process. A few steps into the kitchen, and I unload the juice box. A few steps into the bathroom and the sweater went into the laundry hamper. I finally arrived in my bedroom with empty arms.

Empty arms, indeed. I craved Sam.

I solved that dilemma by reading until two o'clock in the morning, another old passion of mine pre-Sam, per Jenny's instructions. It was a decent book—a mystery novel—so I was able to keep at it until my eyes crossed. When utter exhaustion overtook me, I put it down and dropped off to sleep. I didn't dream.

Sam didn't call me as promised the next morning. He turned up in my office again instead. This time I wasn't kissing Mill. In fact, Mill was nowhere to be found.

"Hey," I said, looking up from my desk when he strode in.

"I've got good news and bad news," he said, lounging on the sofa.

"So this is one of those which-do-I-want-first questions, right?"

Sam nodded.

"Do the upside and the downside both concern Mill?" I asked.

"You're a brilliant woman, Amanda Hillman."

I flashed him a grin that felt wobbly. "With Mill, I've

always found that it's best to get the worst out of the way first. So go ahead. Hit me.''

"He won't withdraw the motion.''

I swore. And in that moment, I hated him as much as I ever have, before or since. He needed that motion in place on election day—and that came first. Not the daughter he pretended to want so much, but the election. That was why I knew the good news before Sam even told me—it just followed. ''But he'll agree to an adjournment until after voting day,'' I guessed.

"You've got it. *If* he gets visitation in the meantime.''

I saw what he was up to. I smiled slowly. ''He can have all the visitation he wants,'' I said, ''but I want to put it in the agreement that Chloe must never, ever be photographed with him. I have great concerns about landing her in the public eye.''

Sam grinned, too. ''Good move. That sort of picks Mill up by the back of his shorts.''

"Doesn't it, though?'' I leaned back in my chair, still smiling. I could limit the mileage he would get out of this.

"He wants Saturdays and Sundays with her. For now.''

I sat up straight again. ''No overnights,'' I said. ''Sam, I can't do that. She might think she wants a dad, but she's never spent the night away from me with anyone except Grace and Jenny.''

"I know. I thought of that. So I finagled all day Saturday, home to you for the evening, then all day Sunday.''

I know I wilted a little. I still had some painfully long weekends in my future. ''Thanks.''

"I don't know how long that will hold, though,'' Sam cautioned.

"It's good enough for now. If we can just get past the election…'' I let that trail off.

"Yeah,'' Sam said. ''But I'm ticked.''

I frowned. "Why?"

"Saturday was the Phillies game."

I remembered now. "I asked her about that this morning and she said she wanted to go, too. Mill wants to start the visitation this weekend?"

"Yeah." He paused. "Want to fill in for her?"

"With Mill or with you?"

I think he growled a little at the idea of me spending the day with Mill. At least, I wanted to believe that was the reason.

Now what was I supposed to do? I decided that distance could be damned. I *wanted* to go to the game with him. "Sure," I said.

He stood up. "What are you doing for lunch?" he asked.

"Chewing with my senior partner about the promotion." Reaffirming my chances for it, I thought.

"I guess that takes precedence over Julio's hot dogs."

"It sort of has to."

When he left, I let out a deep, shaky breath. I'd been cool—again.

I could do this.

Chapter Thirteen

I blame Chloe for what happened next. Well, okay, I don't *blame* her—but she did set things in motion.

I found her sitting on her bedroom floor in jeans at nine o'clock on Saturday morning, her arms crossed over her chest. I glanced around her bedroom quickly. Nowhere did I see the blue denim jumper I'd bought her to assuage her desire for a dress to wear when she visited Mill.

"What's going on?" I asked warily. I realized that I was asking that question far too often lately.

Out came her chin. "I'm not going."

I felt tension starting to rise inside me again. I fisted my hands. "Of course you're going. I signed an agreement. It's what you said you wanted. You've got to go." Then I realized I was taking the wrong approach and I willed myself to calm down. "How come you changed your mind?" I asked.

"I'll go tomorrow," she said. "But today I want to go to the ball game with Sam."

My head started to hurt. "Sam gets baseball tickets a lot." Well, with some frequency, anyway, I amended silently. "There will be other times when you can go with him."

"But I want to go today. I don't want to go to a stupid museum." She wrinkled her nose. "I could just go to school an extra day if I wanted to do stuff like *that* on a weekend."

I was startled. "Mill is taking you to a museum today?" He'd been calling her every night, so they'd had a few conversations between them lately of which I didn't know the context.

"He said he has *planned activities* for my time with him," Chloe informed me.

It occurred to me that Jenny hadn't been all that far off with her museum mission—if she wanted a guy like Mill. I groaned a little and went to sit on Chloe's bed.

"Now what am I supposed to do?" I muttered aloud.

"Just call him and tell him I'll come see him tomorrow," Chloe suggested.

"You do it."

"No, you."

I guess she felt a little guilty about throwing him over for Sam. I dragged my hands through my hair. "Damn it." I'd been trying to keep my contact with Mill to a minimum since he'd decided that he wanted me back. Humoring him was just too hard.

I finally stood again and went to the kitchen phone to call him. I was unhappy about this. I'd gone to the wall for Chloe because she'd said she wanted a father. I'd buried my own misgivings and hard feelings to give her what she needed. That's what mothers do. But they also reserve the right to be a little ticked off when their child suddenly decides she doesn't want what she thought she wanted after all.

She's *seven,* I told myself. Why had I done something so binding as signing that agreement on the whim of a seven-year-old? I should have stalled. I should have waited her out a little. But I hadn't done that because…well, because I felt guilty. I felt responsible for the fact that she'd lived seven years with only one parent. I felt like maybe I hadn't danced the double jig fast enough because she'd obviously been missing something after all. I had made the decision to leave Mill all those years ago for me, so I made the decision to let him back into our lives for her.

But what do kids know, anyway? They're famous for changing their minds—at least mine is.

I blew out my breath, but nerves were still gripping my stomach. I turned away from the phone, and Chloe was standing right behind me. I was scrambling for the best way to handle this and I jumped a little in surprise when I found her there.

"I'm going upstairs for a minute," I decided.

"Did you call my father?"

"No. I told him I'd drop you off at ten so…I think I'll just go there without you and explain." The truth was that Mill was probably going to blow a gasket. Well, a Mill-type gasket, which is to say he'd turn mildly red and inform me in precise tones of why he was upset. In any event, I didn't want Chloe within earshot of the conversation.

She was frowning as though weighing the feasibility of my plan, then her face cleared. "Okay."

"Coward," I muttered under my breath as I turned for the door.

"So where are you going now?" she asked me.

"To tell Sam I'm not his date this afternoon, after all.

You are. And to ask him if you can hang with him while I go deal with your...with Mill.'' I still couldn't say it. I still couldn't bring myself to call him her father.

I left the apartment and jogged up the stairs. Unlike Sam, after I knocked I waited for him to come answer the door. Maybe deep down I was afraid he'd had more second thoughts about our arrangement. Maybe he had Tammy in there with him and I wanted to give him time to hide her in the closet.

The door swung inward. He stood there bare-chested in gym shorts, and my knees went a little wobbly again. I wished helplessly that I was going to be spending the afternoon with him instead of the morning with Mill.

''What's up?'' he asked.

He looked and sounded surprised—with good cause. I don't often go to his apartment. This is largely because, as I mentioned previously, he doesn't have much in the way of furniture. He also doesn't often have food, and when he does, it's usually the kind that comes in cardboard boxes and containers. Plus, even before our arrangement, there was the woman issue for me. Even back then I hadn't ever wanted to interrupt him with anyone.

''Change of plans,'' I said, leaning one shoulder against his doorjamb.

''You're dumping me to go with Chloe and Mill,'' he said immediately, and if he had been a dog, the fur down his spine would have been bristling again.

''Yes and no,'' I said. ''Yes, I'm dumping you, because Chloe wants to go with you today rather than with him. And no, although I am going to see Mill, I'm not taking her with me.''

He opened his mouth a little and closed it again. Then he grinned. He was obviously pleased with Chloe's decision. "Great," he said. Then his eyes went narrow. "Why are you going to Mill's then?"

"To tell him about this change in his planned activities."

"Why don't you just use the phone?"

The obvious question. I told him about not wanting Chloe to overhear.

"You could call from here."

"Could she just hang with you for a little while?" I asked. "I really feel like I need to do this in person."

Coming up the stairs, I'd started thinking that I really had to confront Mill face-to-face on this issue. It was the first weekend of his visitation, and Chloe would still be seeing him tomorrow. There were a few things I had to say for this inaugural event, things that had no place in any written agreement.

I was going to start putting my life back in order, I'd decided. I'd been on an emotional roller-coaster ride for weeks now, but that was about to end. I was tired of letting Mill call all the shots. I had pretty much been operating on his every whim and decision since he'd filed suit. Now it was my turn, and the consequences could be damned.

Sam shrugged one shoulder. "Let me grab a shirt and I'll come downstairs."

"Don't dress on my account." I wagged my brows at him.

"If I run into Mrs. C. in the hallway like this, the sight might be too much for her."

"Ha!" I laughed, then I wrinkled my nose the way Chloe had earlier. "The thought of that woman swept away by passion could put me off sex for a week."

He pressed up close to me, chest to chest. "I could change your mind about that," he said in an intimate undertone, bending over a bit so his mouth could find the little hollow behind my ear. I didn't mean to—I had lines to toe, after all—but I shivered in sheer pleasure.

"Do you *really* want to go see Mill?" he murmured.

"No."

He started reeling me into his apartment.

"But Chloe is downstairs alone," I continued.

"Send her to Jenny's. I have plans for you. I'll wait."

"Mill's expecting Chloe in half an hour. I have to go tell him she's not coming."

Sam let go of me abruptly. He wasn't happy with my decision, and I felt sorry for that. But I also felt pretty good about finally taking charge of things instead of...well, flopping around like a fish on the lakeshore. I was developing a certain understanding of Jenny's weird analogies recently.

So I left Sam, and he slammed the door a little too hard behind me. But that wasn't necessarily a bad thing, I told myself. I was toeing lines. I was following *his* rules. I had something else I needed to do this morning, and he wasn't allowed to complain or pout. But he wanted to, and that made me smile a little.

Chalk this one up on the side of "good things," I decided.

"Well?" Chloe asked when I got back to our apartment.

"Sam will be downstairs to stay with you in a minute," I told her.

"He's going to be mad."

"Sam?" I frowned. "No, he's not."

"My father."

"Oh, well, yes. He's going to kick up his heels a little. But I can handle him." Right out of the starting gate, I thought again, he had to understand that what Chloe wanted in all this was inviolate. And Chloe wanted to go to the ball game.

I grabbed a jacket out of the hall closet. It was dreary

and drizzling outside. That should have been my first warning that by the time the day was over, my life was going to be a mess. If the sun always shines on the bad moments of my life—like Sam upstaging me in Larson's courtroom during the Woodsen motion—then just think what rain can do to me.

Sam came downstairs a few minutes later. I left him and Chloe fighting for dibs on the remote control. She was giggling so explosively at his antics that I was afraid she might actually wet her pants for the first time since she was three. I noticed that Sam didn't have a lot to say to me.

I took a cab to Mill's place. He lives in a beautiful brownstone in Elfreth's Alley where no parking is allowed. It was easier and faster for me to be dropped off at the corner and walk the half block to his door than to try to find a parking spot six blocks away. Besides, I was already late.

I left the cab and started up the alley on foot, hugging my jacket more tightly around me against the cool misty air. Then I found myself pausing in front of Betsy Ross's house regardless of the fact that Mill had expected Chloe five minutes ago. I laid my palm against the wet brick for a moment and I stared at the American flag laid out in the window.

One of the things I'd always hated about Mill's place was its proximity to this building. It had too many poignant memories. Sometime back before I'd turned six, before my father had flown the coop, he'd brought me here once or twice. Those afternoons were still dazzling, brilliant memories tucked into the back of my mind. I'd loved our visits to the historic area, sneaking a touch with a single fingertip to the Liberty Bell, wandering through the steeped history of Independence Hall. I'd often thought that maybe those days were part of the reason I'd grown up to become a lawyer. I'd felt a lot of reverence back then for our fore-bears setting up a democracy, a country of freedom and inalienable rights. Or maybe I had become a lawyer be-cause I thought my dad had liked those afternoons, too, that he felt the same way I did, and maybe he would be proud of my decision. Wherever he was. If he was even still alive.

I finally pulled my hand away from the brick, but instead of moving on to Mill's address, I merely sat down on the tiny step in front of the door. I felt the dampness seeping into the seat of my jeans but I didn't care. The place was open, and I thought about going in. Maybe I would after I finished with Mill. Maybe not. Maybe I didn't want to see the inside again without my father.

A tourist would come by shortly, I thought, and then I would have to get up and make way for them to get inside. I would have to move on. But for the moment I just kept thinking about my dad.

Because of him and what he'd done to me, I'd decided that Chloe didn't need a father, either—though she did. I knew too well that it was better not to learn to love some-one only to have him disappear. And that was another rea-son I wanted to see Mill today, another thing I had to say to him. I wanted to make damned sure that he didn't drop Chloe like yesterday's garbage after the election was over. Because if he did, if he hurt her like I had been hurt, I would have to kill him.

Because of my dad, I was terrified of losing Sam, too, I realized. Because Sam was the second man in my life that I'd ever loved.

"Amanda? What are you doing over there?"

I literally jerked at the sound of Mill's voice. The shat-tering crystal of memories and deep thoughts rained down inside me. I pushed to my feet to see him standing on his stoop, five doors down and on the opposite side of the alley.

I couldn't answer him. I had never told him about my father—and he had never asked.

"Where's Chloe?" he called as I started toward him.

"Home," I called back.

"You came here without her?"

I drew still closer. "I need to talk to you."

"If you're going to try to back out of this deal, Mandy, I feel compelled to tell you that the law is on my side."

Suddenly I was so very tired. I was tired of all of it, the strain of Mill's antics and Sam's skittishness of what he felt—or didn't feel—for me. As I took my last steps toward Mill's address, I felt like my feet were made of stone. It was hard to keep moving.

"I need to talk to you," I said again when I reached him.

He was very unhappy. As I'd predicted, his face had gone mildly red. "All right," he said shortly, stepping back from the door.

I went inside. Nothing had changed in the seven or so years since I had last been to his home. Guys like Mill really don't change much. Their security is in routine. Their bliss is in ennui. As I've said, his family is Old Philadelphia. I think he is actually distantly related to one of the signers of the Declaration of Independence, though maybe it wouldn't hold up to DNA testing. And Mill tends to do things just the way his ancestors did. That adds up to a couple hundred years or so of boring repetition.

He was making the requisite dabble in politics. He tends to acquaint himself only with acceptable women—his family never particularly liked me because I fell somewhat short of that mark. My own ancestors weren't the best.

Then again, I'd passed the commonwealth bar, had been accepted by a pretty good law firm, so that was something.

In any event, this explains why Mill's same Matisse was in the same position on the same wall as it had been all those years ago, and the same rich blue Indian rug was on the same parquet floor in the entry. The same doddering housekeeper came to take my jacket from me, though she did look worse for the intervening years.

"Coffee, miss?" she asked, though I was sure she recognized me. That was the same, too. I had always been an outsider to her, a stranger, and she treated me accordingly. She had never called me by name.

"Please," I said, as though I were in a restaurant. "Black, no sugar." Miss Mildred's coffee didn't need sugar, either.

"Come along, then," Mill said stiffly, leading the way to the parlor. Yes, the man actually has a parlor. Not only does he have a parlor, but he uses it with some regularity. At least he used to, and it didn't appear that that had changed, either.

I followed him and sat on a burgundy velvet chaise across from his favorite chair—a Queen Anne in a blue-and-burgundy brocade. Sounds awful, doesn't it? But the hell of it is, the decor all ties together—if you like stuffy.

I really couldn't see Chloe's Barbies cluttering the floor here. Then again, they probably wouldn't. Miss Mildred would swoop down on them the moment each of them left Chloe's hands.

I sighed and plunged right in. "Chloe wanted to go to a ball game today instead. I wasn't going to force her to spend the day with you at the museum."

His jaw tightened. "You are obligated to force her," he said.

"No. I. Am. Not." I let each word out like a bullet. It

was why I was here. This was what we were going to get straight.

"You signed the agreement. Ah, thank you, Mildred," he said when the woman brought the coffee.

She set the service on a tea table and I got up to pour my own cup. "Screw the agreement," I said mildly.

"I beg your pardon?" He stepped up beside me to get coffee as well.

"You heard me. I don't give a damn about the agreement. This isn't about points of law. It isn't about which of us wins." I suddenly put my cup down and turned to face him. We were very close, virtually nose to nose. "Why do you think I approached you with this visitation deal in the first place?"

"To get me to withdraw the motion."

"No. *This is about my daughter.*"

Mill took a startled step backward at my vehemence. I realized then in all the time I'd known him, we'd never fought. He'd never heard me raise my voice before. For one thing, displays of temper were something Mill simply didn't give in to. But I'd never cared enough to get really stoked about anything with him, either.

What a far cry from my relationship with Sam, I thought.

Suddenly I felt galvanized by that realization. I decided there was something to be said for honesty of emotion, no matter how loud or painfully blunt it got. I poked a finger into Mill's chest, and he made an alarmed sound and jumped back even farther.

"I signed that agreement because Chloe wants to know you," I said, my volume rising still, "and I won't deprive her of that. But damn it, Mill, she's going to know you on her terms. Not yours. Not mine. *Hers.*"

"I had plans for us today," he said, almost—but not quite—whining.

"Well, you're going to have to stuff them until tomorrow. She still wants to see you tomorrow. She just wants to do something else today."

"She's a child! You can't let her dictate what's best for her!"

"In this situation, I absolutely can. I will let her get to know you at her own pace and in her own way and I will fight for that right."

"You gave that right away," Mill said.

"Are you the U.S. Constitution?" I demanded. "Or are you a man? Are you a lawyer or a father?"

"I'm all of those things," he said, then he added, "except the Constitution."

"If you're a father, then act like one. Put Chloe's well-being and her happiness first."

Then his gaze went thoughtful. "Are you willing to do that?"

I frowned. More anger twitched inside me, bright and alive. But it was mingling with wariness now, too. "I do that every day of my life, especially lately," I said finally.

"The first night you received my motion papers, when you called me, you said you'd marry me."

I wasn't sure what that had to do with putting Chloe first, but my heart gave a hard, sick thump. And I was really caught up in my honesty-of-emotion campaign so I barreled ahead.

"You know why I did that," I said.

"Because the idea holds some appeal for you," he said smugly. "You could give Chloe both a mother *and* a father, a real, traditional family, if you *really* wanted to put her first."

I had just picked my coffee cup up again, and some of the hot liquid sloshed over the rim, burning my hand. I swore and put it down. "You were taping that conversation!'' I said. ''I wanted to sound like I was willing to work with you if you ever produced that tape in court!''

Mill scowled. ''No, I wasn't. Such a thing never occurred to me.''

Panic started to beat wings in my gut. ''Well, I would have taped it if I were you.''

''Mandy, you're good at this type of law. It's what you do. I never thought to try to trap you on such an emotional issue.''

The hell of it is, I believed him. Then I gaped at him as what he had just said really started to sink in. ''You honestly thought I said that because I really did want to marry you?''

''Of course.''

Ego is right up there with ennui with this man. ''I've been over you half my life!''

''Amanda, with all due respect, you're not that young anymore.'' Ouch, I thought. ''I believe we parted ways more along the lines of a fifth of your lifetime ago.''

''Fifth, half, my point's the same!'' I protested.

''And what is that?''

All that honesty of emotion was charging through my blood now like galloping horses. That's my only explanation for what I said next.

''I don't want you!'' I yelled. ''I've just been humoring you these last weeks! I was trying to placate you so you'd agree to push the hearing back until after the election! I love Sam!''

I think my voice actually ricocheted through the room. Well, I thought, that certainly made it official. First I'd given Jenny that little nod when she'd said it aloud, and now I was shouting it from the rafters. The only one who didn't know about it was Sam, and he would run like hell if he heard it. Mill's mild color went pale, and poor Miss

Mildred began to step into the parlor only to turn tail and run for her rigid Kramer-controlled life.

"I'm sorry," I said more quietly.

"Is it true?"

"Yes." I gulped a little. "I love Sam. There is not the smallest chance whatsoever that I will reconcile with you, Mill."

"But you kept my Cloisonne."

"I really did feel sacrilegious about dumping it out on top of the garbage."

His air went out of him. He sat hard in his Queen Anne chair again. I almost felt sorry for him.

"Well," he said after a moment. "This certainly skews things."

I stared at him before I understood. "I wasn't your back-up plan?" I asked to be sure I was on the right track. "I was your *whole* plan?"

"More or less."

"The Chloe thing was just to get back in my life again?" I couldn't believe it.

He gave a weak smile. "It worked, didn't it?"

"*That's* why you wouldn't drop the motion after I gave you visitation!" It made sense now, I realized. Visitation would have looked almost as good in the eyes of the public as custody. Going for the whole enchilada was really unnecessary. But if he had just dropped the suit, if we weren't wrangling about it anymore, then he would lose many of his chances for contact with me.

"*Why?*" I demanded. "You never loved me." It was blunt, but it was a blunt kind of moment. Emotional honesty was really the name of the game now.

"The election was part of it," he admitted.

"A sort of you-me-and-daughter image for the voters?"

"In the beginning. You are, after all, the mother of my child. It was tidy, neat."

I dropped onto the chaise again, my head spinning.

"But…I must admit that things changed after I met Chloe. She won my heart with her antics with that leg brace. Now I'm in a position that I really don't want to let her go. I want all three of us to be together."

The air went out of me. "I'm not asking you to let her go, Mill. I'm just not part of the package. And when you do this visitation thing, you've got to take Chloe's plans into consideration first. Sam had already invited her to go to this ball game before we signed the agreement."

And just like that, Mill starting sprouting bristling fur, too. I was really getting tired of all these testosterone flares. "She's going with Sam?" he said sharply. "You didn't mention that part."

"What difference does it make?" I waved a hand. "It's not germane."

"I think it is."

I stood again. "Chill out, Mill. This is the way it's going to be. Sam is a part of her life, too." And I prayed he would be for a long time to come.

I was finished. I couldn't think of one more thing to say to him. I'd done everything—hell, I'd done *more*—than I'd set out to do.

I went to the door. Mill trailed after me like a confused puppy. "She doesn't want to go to the museum *at all?*" he asked. "Or was that just for today?"

"She said it would be like going to school for an extra day," I reported. When I looked back at him, he seemed genuinely upset.

"What do I do with her, then?" he asked. "What activities should I plan?"

"Try bumper cars. A fast-food restaurant. The zoo." I

thought of mentioning the park business, but I really couldn't envision him throwing a Frisbee. I glanced up Elfreth's Alley again. "You could also go to Betsy Ross's house."

"That's like a museum, too."

"Yeah, but it has a way with little girls. Trust me on this one." I went outside. "I'll have her here by ten o'clock tomorrow morning," I added. "Oh, and Mill."

He was watching me with an expression that was part amazement, part dawning potential for emotional honesty and part alarm. "What?" he said.

"It's the millennium. Voters don't care if you have custody of Chloe just as long as you clearly love her. Think about it. Think of some of the politicians this country has seen lately. If Chloe and I are the only skeletons in your closet, that makes you a political saint."

I finally turned away from him again. This time I didn't look back. It was time to go clear the air with Sam, too, I decided suddenly.

Chapter Fourteen

This is my way of saying that I just snapped that day. I didn't plan what I did next. I didn't wake up that morning and suddenly determine that I was going to come clean with both Mill and Sam. I just got up a good head of steam. It had felt so good to stop pretending with Mill, and pretending with Sam was killing me by small degrees every day, so I decided to confront him, too.

If I had stopped to think about it at all, I might have remembered Jenny's advice, and Grace's. But the strain of toeing the line with both men had pushed me to the edge. If Chloe ever behaved the way I did that morning, I would call it a tantrum.

The cab dropped me off in front of my building and I jogged inside. I tried to burst into my own apartment and rammed facefirst into a locked door.

"Sam!" I called through the wood.

Nothing. No answer.

"Chloe?"

More silence.

I turned at the sound of footsteps on the stairs, and they were just coming from Sam's apartment. Chloe had on a Phillies cap that was way too large for her, and she wore a baseball mitt on her hand. The mitt almost sidetracked me.

"What's that?" I asked.

"To catch fly balls with," my daughter told me.

It looked new. "Did you buy her that?" I asked Sam.

"Yeah, the other day. It was a surprise."

It was definitely a morning for surprises, I thought. I'd figured that I would have time to talk to him before they took off for the ball park. "You're leaving already?" I asked dumbly.

He was obviously still grumpy about my decision to see Mill that morning. Sam shrugged and gave me no answer.

"Isn't it early?" I persisted. His mood was just getting me more stirred up.

"I thought we could catch warm-ups and maybe get an autograph or two," he said finally. "Give me that," he said, holding his hand out to Chloe for the mitt. "I told you we needed to break it in. You'll never catch anything otherwise. You've got to keep working with it." He started to flex it in his hands.

"Don't talk to her like that." To this day, I have no idea where those words came from or why I said them.

"Like what?" Chloe and Sam asked me in unison.

"Telling her what to do," I said, answering Sam specifically.

Sam frowned. "I always do that."

"You're not her father," I said. "And with these arrangement circumstances we've got going on, you're barely a mentor."

He slid a gaze in Chloe's direction, then back to me. "What does our arrangement have to do with any of this?"

"A lot," I said obstinately. "When you made all these rules, you distanced yourself from our life."

His frown got darker. "I did not."

I mimicked his voice. "Don't cuddle, don't call everyday, you stay on your side of the line and I'll stay on mine."

His eyes went to slits. "Do you really want to talk about this now?"

I thought about it. "Yeah. Yeah, I mostly definitely do."

"Chloe, go inside and watch TV for a few minutes," he said.

"You're doing it again!" I almost shouted.

Even Chloe was starting to look alarmed. "Mom, I don't care. It's no big deal." She went into our apartment. Actually, she fled.

"What the hell is wrong with you?" Sam demanded when she was gone.

"I want to share toothbrushes," I blurted. Now I was near tears. "Well, you know, not as a matter of course, but if an emergency came up, I'd like to know there was that option."

He looked at me as though I had lost my mind. With good cause, I thought. I could admit that, but it didn't stop me. While toothbrushes weren't the issue, they had become symbolic of all his rules, and those rules had really been eating at me.

"Okay," he said slowly. "I would definitely share my toothbrush with you in an emergency."

"That's not the point," I muttered, crossing my arms over my chest.

"So what is?"

My jaw came forward. "I want you to spend the night

instead of tiptoeing out of my apartment at two o'clock in the morning. I want to check in with you every day. I liked it when you called me honey. And I don't want you to go to McGlinchey's and talk to Tammy without me!''

He stiffened visibly. ''How do you know I was talking to Tammy that night?''

''I was there!''

''Where?''

''At McGlinchey's! In the fern!''

''You were *spying* on me?''

I shook my head hard and fast. ''Of course not. I just changed my mind and decided not to go in.''

His jaw was dropping open a little more with every sentence I whipped out.

''Don't you get it?'' I almost shouted.

''I'm not sure.''

''I don't want to be your arrangement-lover! I want to be your…your…'' What? I hadn't planned this out at all, so words failed me for a moment. ''I love you,'' I finally blurted.

When I'm ninety, I will still remember the look on his face right then. It was pure, sheer shock. There is no other way to describe it. Then he simply stepped around me and opened my apartment door.

''Come on, Chloe,'' he called to her. ''We need to leave now.''

My heart slugged my ribs. As responses went, that was pretty bad. ''I'm trying to be emotionally honest,'' I said, and my voice was going a little feeble now.

''Well, thanks for that,'' he said. Then he frowned at me. ''I mean it. I'm big on honesty.''

''I know.'' I was almost whimpering now. ''It matters to me, too. That's why I couldn't keep…pretending.''

"You shouldn't have to," he said, then both he and my daughter were gone, escaping out the lobby doors.

The silence in the lobby was deafening. It was huge. But underneath it, I thought I heard something tympanic. My heart.

What had I just done?

I was shaking. My throat hurt because I was trying hard not to cry. I backed up toward my apartment, my gaze fast on the outer lobby door that they'd disappeared through. Then, suddenly, he was back. He pulled open the lobby door and looked in at me.

"Love is against the rules," he said.

This time when he disappeared, I knew he would keep going.

I turned around, fumbled with my door and stumbled inside. When I'd come clean with Mill, letting my true feelings fly, it had been exhilarating. Now I only felt terrified. He wasn't coming back, I thought. Then I shook my head. Of course Sam was coming back. He had to come back. He had my daughter. And he lived one floor up.

But he wouldn't be coming back to *me*.

My answer to this was to clean. I despise household chores. I loathe them. I basically get itchy when I'm not doing something that involves my mind, and I consider manual labor to be a waste of time, though I greatly appreciate the result. This is probably why I like *Bewitched* so much. I yearn to be able to take care of the dull necessities in life with a little magic.

All the same, there comes a time in every woman's life when a needy apartment starts looking like manna from heaven. This was one of those times for me because my mind wouldn't work. Its processes had come to a screaming, sudden halt the moment Sam had stepped around me to open my door and call Chloe, when he'd said, "Love is

against the rules.'' Cleaning requires no thought whatsoever, and when you reach the condition I was in that day,
you basically have only two choices: you can stare dazedly
at a wall, in which case snippets of the conversation or
event that is tormenting you will zing through your head
now and again, making your heart seize up and your eyes
well up with tears. Or you can dive into some chore. You
can wipe and scrub mechanically, putting your full focus
on the repetitive rhythm of something that does not require
concentration.

This is why I decided to wash the kitchen floor I'd never
gotten around to last weekend. When that was done, I
scrubbed the tub. I stripped the sheets off both my bed and
Chloe's, and I washed them. When it seemed like I was in
danger of running out of things to do, I yanked down all
the curtains, too. I washed them, then I ironed both them
and the pillow cases.

I had never ironed a pillowcase before in my entire life.
When I started to do the same thing to Chloe's underwear,
I knew I was losing it. By the time I got to the last pair of
Barbie panties, I was crying silently. My tears kept plop-
ping down on them, but the iron dried the spots right up.

I had lost Sam and I was dying inside and cleaning
wasn't going to fix things, I realized. I needed Jenny. I
needed Grace.

I looked at my watch. It was just past three o'clock. The
game should have started at one. I knew from Sam's focus
on sports that baseball games lasted approximately three to
three and a half hours. So they wouldn't be home much
before five-thirty, I decided, maybe even six. And I had
just about run out of things to clean.

I went upstairs. Remember when I said that if you love
someone and are hurting over it, the craziest, littlest things
remind you of it? They become like blades to the chest.

Last week it had been the mashed potatoes. Today it was the stairs. I hesitated on the landing to the second floor and remembered how Sam had started out standing right here the night we'd decided to have an arrangement.

Oh, God, I thought, covering my face with my hands, who was I kidding? *He* had decided to have an arrangement. I had gone along with it, I had leaped at it, torturing myself over rules of my own, because that was the only way I could have him. I knew that now.

Grace found me like that, standing there on the landing, my palms pressed to my cheeks. She came trotting down the steps looking drop-dead gorgeous in flame-red shorts—this in spite of the weather—and a white windbreaker. I don't know where she was headed, but one look at my face told us both that she wasn't going to get there.

She stared at me for a good thirty seconds, then she grabbed my shoulders and literally shook me until my teeth snicked together. "Damn it, damn it, damn it!" She kept saying that, over and over.

"You're hurting me," I said, trying to wriggle away from her.

"What did you do?"

"I think I need Jenny. You're going to kill me."

She finally let go of my shoulders and grabbed my hand instead. She began dragging me back upstairs. When we got to her apartment, she threw the door open hard enough that it cracked against the wall with a sound that made me wince.

"Put on coffee," Grace snarled at Jenny. "Mandy blew it."

Now it was Jenny's turn to stare at me. "Oh, no. What did you *do?*"

I had defied the advice of both of them, and now I was going to pay for it. I started crying again.

Grace shoved me until I sat down hard on the sofa. She ended up going to the kitchen herself to make the coffee while Jenny ran for the tissues.

"Where's Chloe?" Jenny asked when she came back and shoved the box in my hands.

"With Sam." I was making gulping sounds now, and if I had been in any company other than theirs, it would have been utterly degrading.

Jenny frowned. "That's a good thing, not a bad thing."

"Not when I just told him I loved him and he grabbed her and ran."

Something crashed in the kitchen—it sounded like a coffee mug hitting the floor and shattering. "You *what?*" Grace shouted.

"His response to that was to kidnap your daughter?" Jenny yelped, flabbergasted. I don't know if I also mentioned that she also has a tendency to take things verbatim.

"No!" I said. "He was taking her to a ball game *before* all this came up."

"And he still did it?"

I frowned at her. "Of course he did. He wouldn't disappoint her, no matter what."

Jenny sat down, relaxing. "That's sweet."

I started crying harder.

Over the course of the next hour, I told them everything. I told them about my meeting with Mill and how I had gotten all worked up on that emotional-honesty theme. About how I knew I couldn't play Sam's game anymore— or Mill's, either—and how, if I was ever going to have another sane day in this lifetime, if I wasn't going to rattle apart and land myself in an asylum, then I was going to have to come clean with both of them. I had to be true to myself. Grace swore in words that I honestly have never heard before or since, and Jenny started crying right along with me.

We drank coffee and when I couldn't stop shivering, Jenny went to the hall closet and got me an afghan. She wrapped it around my shoulders. She really was going to make someone a great mother someday.

"We need a plan," she said, sitting down next to me on the sofa again.

"No!" I said, alarmed. "Plans are what got me into this mess in the first place!"

"They wouldn't have if you had just followed them," Grace said darkly from where she was sitting on the floor.

"Following them was driving me crazy!"

"You can save this," Jenny said. "He loves you."

My throat twisted into a knot all over again. "Jenny, if he loved me, he would have responded somehow when I told him I loved him." But that wasn't entirely fair, I thought. He had responded. "He would have said something other than love being against the rules," I amended.

"No," she said, "that's exactly what he *wouldn't* do. He's a man. Men absolutely refuse to get coerced in situations like this. He could love you so much he can't see straight, but he would never admit it under adversarial circumstances."

Grace and I exchanged glances. We needed to get Jenny off the baby kick and back into college, I thought. She'd make a great family law attorney. Or a psychologist.

Grace got up for more coffee. "I think this might be Jenny's area of expertise," she admitted. "Men tell me they love me all the time, but they never mean it, so I wouldn't know the real thing if it was labeled with a neon sign."

Later—if I ever survived my own life—I would have to

think about that. For the moment I looked at Jenny. "Now what do I do?" I asked.

"The same thing I told you to do before, which you *didn't* do."

"Let him catch up?"

She nodded. "Before you would have been able to do it while you enjoyed his company. Now I guess you're going to have to do it alone."

Hearing her say it aloud—something I already knew—made my throat constrict all over again. "He's going to dump me," I whispered.

"Honey," Jenny said gently, "he already has."

I nodded, and they let me cry a little more before they kicked me out. Tough love, and all that. No one really thought Sam would get over this in a hurry, so I had to start standing on my own two feet, and the sooner I managed it, the better. Besides, they both had dates.

I would have given my life in that moment to know that the worst had already happened to me. But it hadn't. It was yet to come.

I dragged myself to my feet again and went downstairs to my own apartment. I waited for Sam and Chloe by sitting on the sofa. I was doing the wall-staring routine. Finally, at six o'clock, I started worrying that something had happened to them.

I turned the television on to the local news for word that there had been a horrible accident outside Veteran's Stadium involving a great-looking man with a heart of gold and a little girl. Instead, I found out that the baseball game had suffered some sort of rain delay. It hadn't even *started* until three o'clock.

I was in agony. I needed *something* to happen, good or bad, important or indifferent—just *something*. I wanted to look into Sam's eyes so I could gauge just how bad this

really was. I wanted a chance to say something that might
fix it. The phrase for this involves grasping for straws. And
I was trapped in time, so I knew nothing was going to
happen for some while yet. I finally got up off the sofa and
cleaned some more.

I pulled the kitchen pantry apart, found a box of Pop
Tarts that probably should have been retired in 1999, and
scrubbed the shelves with pine cleaner. Just before seven-
thirty, I remembered that emotional honesty was only good
as far as it went. Sure, I'd enjoyed a moment of clear
breathing when I'd been letting things rip earlier—and look
where that had gotten me. The fact of the matter is that
guile and cunning are not entirely bad things, either. At
least not when your life is on the line. I'd already gone to
one extreme, blurting out that I hated our rules and that I
loved him. Now I had to make sure that if Sam was really
leaving me, he knew what he was walking away from.

He might find it less than difficult to walk away from a
woman wearing pine cleaner-splashed jeans and one of his
T-shirts. Maybe, just maybe, I still had time to change into
something more provocative before he brought Chloe back.
Maybe I had time to clean up.

I bolted for the hallway. I decided not to risk a shower—
I didn't want to be lathered up and out of hearing range
when they got home. I settled for splashing hot water over
my face and slapping on a little foundation and blush to
cover the evidence that I had spent some significant time
since they'd left crying my heart out. Then I hurried into
my bedroom.

The black sweatpants and my kangaroo top were clean
and folded in my bottom drawer. Serendipity. I shed the
pungent-smelling jeans and changed. I'd just finished when
I heard the front door open.

I flew back to the living room. Chloe was standing in the middle of the room. Alone. My heart dove.

"Where's Sam?" I asked.

"Upstairs. Mom, we had a *great* time."

He'd just shooed her through the door, I realized. He hadn't even come in with her. The last of my hope dissolved and the truth was unbearable: it really was over.

This is the deal with motherhood. You are not permitted to melt down in the presence of your child. It's a rule not unlike Sam's arrangement rules, but this one must have some merit because it has survived generations of good mothers. You might be screaming inside. You might be as terrified of your future as you have ever been in your life. You might not even be able to take in air without feeling it in your chest like blades. But you can not—*must* not—melt down and scare the holy hell out of your daughter because she has no clue yet about the kind of grown-up things that can make women come apart. So you hold it together even while you pray halfheartedly that she never *has* to have a clue. But you know someday she will. Because she's human, and I'm pretty sure broken hearts are one of those lifetime milestones that happen to everyone.

So when Chloe screeched, "I caught a ball!" and threw it at me, I caught it.

"It's a ball, all right," I said.

"We had seats right on the first-base line. Sam says that's the best place to sit for pop-ups and fouls and tips."

My heart stopped, unwilling to move past Sam's name. "Well, he would know about such things," I said after a moment. "I think baseball is his favorite sport."

"He played it in college," Chloe said.

I hadn't known that. Something else I hadn't known about him. How could I love someone this much without knowing he'd played baseball in college? How could someone rip my heart out when I hadn't even known until recently that he had a cowboy brother who liked his beer? Because, I answered myself, we'd spent six months finding out all the things about each other that really mattered. Like the fact that he never told a lie, and I always stood up for my friends. Asparagus was something he thought I'd once tried to poison him with, and I felt pretty much the same way about aliens.

My eyes were starting to fill for the thousandth time that day. I knew I really wasn't rallying to the occasion. I got my voice back again. "Did you eat a hot dog?" I asked hoarsely.

"Sure. Sam says you can't *not* eat hot dogs at a ball game. So I had three of them."

Stop saying his name! "Do you feel okay?" I was clinging to mother mode with everything I had. I happened to know that Chloe's stomach wasn't quite experienced enough to handle three ballpark franks.

"Yeah," she said, heading down the hall. "I had the first one *real* early, while we were waiting through the rain delay. But all those peanuts kind of have me thinking about throwing up now."

Peanuts *and* three hot dogs? Two weeks ago, seven days ago, five hours ago, I would have demanded to know what Sam had been thinking. I couldn't do that anymore. I couldn't run upstairs and smack him upside the head. I'd lost my best pal.

I have a vague memory of getting Chloe in and out of the tub, and a somewhat clearer one of holding her head when her stomach revolted at the onslaught of all that ballpark food. Somewhere during the process, I learned that Sam had also fed her cotton candy and that she'd shared his nachos. If I hadn't loved him so much, I would have been tempted to kill him.

I finally measured the Pepto-Bismal into a fifty-nine-pound child dosage and tucked her in. Chloe slept through the night. I didn't.

I'll be honest—I never even got out of the black sweat-pants. I never even *tried* to go to bed. There are times in life when you know even the basics are beyond you, and this was one of mine. I just stared vacantly at old movies on the television for most of the night.

Once or twice—okay, maybe three or four times—I thought about going upstairs to Sam's apartment just to finalize things. I wanted to say, "Okay, we both know it's over, so let's bury it." But in the end I just couldn't bear to hear him say, "Okay." So I didn't do it.

I didn't end up going upstairs until Tuesday, and I lived through the intervening days in a numb haze. Prearrangement, and in midarrangement, we had never gone this long without speaking to each other, not since the first day I stumbled across him standing in our apartment building lobby. I found myself remembering that a lot, the way he'd looked tired and miserable as he moved his stuff into that second-floor unit. I'd wondered what made his eyes so sad. Now I knew, of course. It had been Shelly, the ex.

That had happened on a Sunday, and the very next day I encountered Sam in court. I found out later that he'd actually been in Philadelphia for four weeks by then, setting up his practice here, living in a hotel. Something about his grin had delighted me—a far cry from his lost frown in the lobby—so I invited him to dinner that very night.

For the most part, he'd never really left after that. He hadn't missed many meals with us—until now. So when I realized I was going to go upstairs to see him, that there was very little I could do to stop myself, I told myself I was just worried that he wasn't eating.

I made lasagna on Tuesday night—I was still burying

myself in domestic issues—and I took some upstairs to
him. It was time to say, "Okay, we both know it's over so
let's bury it." It was time to hear him say, "Okay."

I waited until Chloe was in bed. Then I attacked the last
of the lasagna with a spatula and severed off half the block
for Sam. I dropped it onto a plate, covered it with tin foil
and headed up the stairs. My knees were knocking together.

I rapped on his door three, four, then five times before I
accepted that he wasn't home. Which made utter, absolute
sense, I realized. Our arrangement was over, so I figured
he had thrown himself headfirst back into the dating pool.
I was turning away from his door, still clutching my lasagna, when the one behind me opened up.

Sylvie Casamento—just what I needed at the moment.

"He's not there," she said. "He's not home."

"I got that," I said, and headed for the stairs.

"He hasn't been there since Sunday."

That stopped me. I looked back at her. "What?"

"Any time I hear commotion in my residence, I like to
know what's up."

"What happened to him?" I asked, suddenly alarmed.

"It's what happened to the hallway here."

I waited. Sometimes that is the only way to deal with
her.

"Sam was throwing suitcases around the hallway," she
said finally. "One hit my door."

"He was throwing things? On Sunday night?"

"He was unpleasant." Mrs. C. sniffed, clearly injured by
that.

It stood to reason. I had just tossed his rules in his face
and broken the biggest one in the book. *No falling in love.*

"I bet you told him so," I offered shakily.

"I certainly did."

"What did he say?"

"That he'd had enough of the female persuasion to last him a lifetime, and I ought to shut my mouth."

My eyes widened. It sounded like Sam—yet it didn't. He generally schmoozed better than that. And he was never rude to anyone of the...well, the female persuasion. Which could only mean that I had upset him deeply.

I withered inside. I think I nodded. "Did he say where he was going?" I asked.

"Mars. Men live there."

I frowned. "Come again?"

"He says men are from Mars and women are from Venus. And pink planets and angels with wings shooting arrows have damned well ruined his life." She sucked air in through her nose. "He swore. I don't lower myself to that, mind you. I'm just repeating his word."

"Damned?" I asked dazedly.

She nodded. "That's it."

Did he mind losing me, after all? I ran what she had just said through my head one more time and my heart trembled. What Sylvie Casamento had just described was a man who was *really* angry, panicked...maybe even catching up. After all, blowing me off wouldn't have been this upsetting for him if he hadn't started missing me right away.

Then again, that was in woman-speak. In man-speak, his temper tantrum could just mean, Damn it, the sex was great and she had to go and ruin everything.

"So he went away for a few days," Mrs. C. said again.

I finally went back downstairs. Sam was gone—*really* gone. Out of town. He'd run.

That was when it occurred to me to do the exact same thing.

Chapter Fifteen

The next morning I tangled with Mill again, expecting the worst when I explained to him that I wanted to keep Chloe myself the next weekend. But I didn't get it. Maybe because—no matter that I had never had to do it before—I was learning to share my daughter with aplomb.

I called him from my office. "I'll give you tonight and tomorrow night instead of Saturday and Sunday," I said when he came on the line.

"You're negotiating," he said, his voice neither hot nor cold.

What was the point in denying it? "I'm desperate," I admitted.

"Why is that?"

I couldn't tell him about Sam. And yet I almost had to. "I need to take Chloe out of town this weekend. For me."

"Is it the pizza guy?" he asked.

Have you ever noticed how one single word can grow

thorns and just lodge in your throat? You can neither swallow it nor spit it out. I was supposed to say yes at this juncture, but I couldn't do it.

"My next question," Mill said to my silence, "is if he's gone, do I have a chance after all?"

Suddenly, I didn't hate him anymore. Mill was just... Mill. Deal with him on his own terms and he can be practically palatable. "I would make a horrible politician's wife," I said. "Just remember what I did to you Saturday morning."

"You came at me with both guns blazing." I think he chuckled.

"An accurate assessment," I agreed. "The first lady can't do that. I got all emotional. I do that sometimes."

"I gave up my time with Chloe last Saturday," he pointed out, getting back to business. I guess that meant he agreed I wouldn't make a good politician's wife. "I did it for Sam Case," he said.

"Yes," I agreed. "You did that. But you didn't do it for Sam. You did it for Chloe."

He was quiet for a long time. "All right. This time I'll do it for you. In the interest of...potential."

There was no potential to be had. Not with Mill. And I knew suddenly that no matter what hell my honesty-of-emotion campaign had wrought, I would be seriously cheating myself if I didn't stick with it. So I just came right out and said it.

"Mill, Sam was the best thing that ever happened to me. I won't ever settle for anything less."

"Ouch," he murmured.

"I'm sorry." I was so well acquainted with misery that I really couldn't bear to hurt anyone else.

"It doesn't matter," he said finally. "I more or less knew

that on Saturday. So I withdrew my motion. You were on to me, anyway.''

It was the first and only good news I'd had in a long time. It made me cry again. I kept sniffing, dragging back on the tears. The weekend was over, I was back at work, and I couldn't keep falling apart.

''Thank you,'' I managed.

''Are you going to vote for me?'' he asked.

I laughed, soggily, but almost as hard as he had done over Chloe's knee brace.

After I hung up, I went to ask Gina, my secretary, to pull off a miracle. I had two motions scheduled for Friday, but I needed to adjourn them. If I had my way, Chloe and I would be on the highway, heading for parts unknown at just about the time I was scheduled to appear in court. I needed two sets of lawyers and judges to agree to post-ponements for my ''personal reasons.'' Somehow Gina pulled it off.

I've always awarded Chloe one or two mental-health days per school year—days when she's not sick but she can play hooky with my full knowledge. I take a day, too, and we do things together. I believe wholeheartedly that when you have a single, working mom, these times are as im-portant as perfect attendance and anything that reading, writing and arithmetic can dish out.

We hadn't done it at all yet this school year, and I got to wondering why. The answer quelled me. Sam had turned up in our lives in October, one month into the school year, and he'd monopolized my life after that. Realizing that con-vinced me I was doing the right thing now.

Over dinner that night I told Chloe what we were going to do. ''Want to skip school on Friday?'' I asked her.

Instead of looking elated, she seemed momentarily con-fused. ''We haven't done that all year.''

"So we're overdue."

"Is Sam coming with us?"

I had another one of those moments when the pain went so deep I felt dizzy. "No," I said finally when my head cleared. "It will just be you and me."

"He hasn't come to dinner in *ages*," Chloe said.

I was well aware of that fact. In fact, I didn't even know if he was back in town again yet or not. I had thought briefly of calling his office to find out, but I didn't trust myself to successfully disguise my voice. I'd talked to his secretary so many times over the months that she would certainly know it was me. And I had come around to the point where I didn't want Sam to know I cared that much, that I was finding it very hard to go on without him. My pride was starting to kick in.

"Are you guys mad at each other?" Chloe asked suddenly.

"Something like that," I agreed. If we were in second grade, that would accurately describe this state of affairs, I thought.

"I was kind of thinking of *him*," she said out of the blue, "not my real father. You know, when I said about wanting a dad."

It was like a slap in the face out of the blue. I reeled. I couldn't answer.

Chloe pushed her plate away. "It was just, you know, that I wished Sam could live with us. That's what I was thinking about all those times I wanted a dad. I mean, I like my real father okay. But he's not Sam. He doesn't know diddly about baseball."

I was dying. I was literally dying. I shot to my feet. "Well, I think it's just going to keep on being you and me, anyway," I said, "no matter who you were thinking of. And you'll see your real father twice a week or so."

"Even if I'd rather have a different one?"

"Give him a chance, Chloe. He's really not all that bad." I still had my voice. I wasn't sure how. I was sure I was strangling.

"Being with him is like wearing a dress," she said. "You know, I gotta sit just right, make sure my knees are together."

I choked. Chloe is a very good judge of character.

"And he likes *museums,*" she went on.

"So does Jenny," I pointed out.

"Maybe *they* could get married. And then you could marry Sam."

I couldn't do it. I couldn't keep up with this conversation. It was killing me. So I just bailed on her. I fled. I went to the bathroom—my hiding place when the chips were down—because as I've said, you can't melt down in front of your kid. Then I remembered that Sam had been the first person in my whole life to figure out why and when I ran to bathrooms, and I had another crying jag.

Somehow I managed to hold it together through one more day. I saw clients on Thursday. Jenny and Grace showed up at dinner time with take-out fried chicken so I wouldn't have to stretch my last emotional resources and cook. I knew they couldn't afford that, and it broke my heart that they cared that much.

I didn't set my alarm on Friday morning. I slept in just a little, and at eight-thirty I called Chloe's school to tell them that she wouldn't be in. We set off at nine o'clock.

Sometime during the course of the last week, I had come to the conclusion that Jenny was moderately more wise than Grace. Grace went through life with her dukes up. Jenny tended to observe and absorb. In any event, the memory of what she had said in McGlinchey's that night gave me the only semblance of comfort I'd had since I'd stood in our lobby and blasted Sam with my emotional honesty. She'd reminded me of doing all those things that I used to enjoy BS—Before Sam.

So I made a beeline for Lancaster County. Chloe and I hit the first flea market just after noon. I bought a chamber pot for sixty-seven dollars. It was supposed to be honest-to-God three-generations old. Who knew? I told Chloe what it had once been used for, and she peered inside it so suspiciously—as though suspecting its mummified contents were still intact—that I laughed for the second time in a week. I think the sound came out more like a gargle because Chloe clapped me on the back as though to restart my breathing.

Then we spent the rest of the day wandering from town to town. I admire the Amish, not only for their quaintness, but for their integrity. They stick to their principles even while the rest of the world presses in on them. They hang in there with their horses and their buggies while the rest of us bemoan rising oil prices. They light their kerosene lanterns while the rest of us curse utility companies. Most importantly, they are home with their loved ones in the evenings, eating cholesterol-laden food without a care in the world, while those of us in mainstream America are in places like McGlinchey's, telling their best friends that all they need in life are the three Cs—companionship, comfort and conversation. They plow their fields while we choke on our own words several weeks later.

Chloe and I moseyed through their world that whole day. Then we finally checked in at our hotel and went to our favorite place for dinner.

By the time we got there, I was feeling bits and pieces of my old self twitching and coming to life inside me again. I was never going to be the same as I had been before Sam. I knew that. All I wanted out of life was a way to go on.

I just wanted to get through days without crying. I needed to learn how to exist all over again, I thought, how to go back to being the way I'd been without him. Harried, overworked sometimes, but loving my child. If I could get back to that place, all my basics would be intact, and I wouldn't have to hurt unless I found myself in rare, quiet moments alone.

The restaurant Chloe and I favor is actually an inn that was built somewhere in the late 1800s. You can get far more succulent food in Philadelphia. What you *can't* get in Philly—at least as far as I know—is your cholesterol cooked over an open flame in a fireplace that is original to colonial Pennsylvania. Chloe loves the way they do hamburgers, in a cast-iron skillet over the fire.

We had just ordered and she was waiting for her soft drink. I was looking forward to a glass of wine. Then I looked up and saw Sam at the bar.

Time stopped. I am pretty sure the earth quit rotating for a second or two. Someday scientists will admit to it, though they will be at a loss to explain why. At first I kept trying to chug in breath. My next instinct was that this couldn't be happening.

It wasn't fair, I thought. I was just starting to remember the old Mandy again. I knew I was still months—maybe even years—away from reclaiming her, but at least I had realized that she still existed and she was out there somewhere for the reclaiming.

And now…here was Sam. And he still looked like all I had ever needed.

What was he doing here? This was insane. Then I pegged it, and I felt a little shaky. I vaguely remembered mentioning that Chloe and I came here sometimes when I needed a break. Which could either mean that the way I'd described it appealed to him too…or he had come here on the chance of running into us. Maybe he was having a hard time letting go, too.

Chloe saw him, too. She squealed and the sound caught his attention. Sam turned around; she waved at him wildly.

He got up from the bar and came to our table. He reached out to ruffle her hair, and he sat down on the bench seat on her side of the table. Nowhere near me.

"Hey, rug rat," he said.

She dove against his chest so hard and suddenly that he had no choice but to hug her. "Where have you been?" she asked immediately.

Her volume covered up my own voice. "You came *here?*" I breathed. "When you left Philly, you came *here?*"

He heard my question over Chloe's anyway. Or at least he answered it first. "'I like that hotel with the ship in the parking lot. Great deals.' Plus, the area has great antiques."

"You don't even have a living room set," I blurted. "What do you want with antiques?"

"Someday I'll have one," he said.

"Did you buy anything?" I asked.

"Not yet. Mostly I've been sleeping in a lot since I got here."

That sounded like a man who was…well, depressed. Loving someone and missing them.

"Mom bought this big jar people used to poop in," Chloe announced suddenly.

Out of the mouths of babes, I thought. I shrunk a little on my bench seat as we caught the attention of other diners. Sam just laughed. Then his words about the hotel he was staying at finally registered with me. Chloe and I always stayed at the place with a ship in the parking lot. He was even using the same hotel.

"What is it *doing* there?" I asked suddenly.

And he knew exactly what I was talking about. "Mental negotiation," Sam said.

I nodded. "If you want to be a vacation place and draw vacation crowds, you need to have a vacation-place type theme," I agreed.

"I could have done without the piped-in sound of sea-gulls, though," Sam said.

"Isn't that weird?" I asked. "In landlocked Pennsylvania?"

Then something happened that had never happened to us before. We ran out of conversation.

We stared at each other. Actually, there was too *much* to say, and too much had already been said. I prayed that my eyes wouldn't brim, that I wouldn't start crying again and embarrass myself.

"Sam," I said.

"Mandy—" Then he broke off when the waitress brought our food.

Sam had ended up ordering a burger to match Chloe's. They chowed down and I pushed food around on my plate. If things were strained between him and me, I think we kept it from Chloe. More than once she chirped up, "This is so cool!"

"I need to go," Sam said finally, when the meal was finished.

My heart stalled. I ground down to the core of me and tried to look at what was in my heart. What was more important? My pride—or Sam?

Here's what I realized in that moment: if something matters, if it *really* matters, you have to give it your all. You have to give even when it hurts. Later I'd wonder if this is one of the reasons that marriages lasted longer a hundred years ago than they do today—because we've forgotten this. Sometimes you have to swallow your pride and sometimes you have to put your whole heart on the line to save something. Sometimes you have to risk hurting more than you already do in order to have the only stab at real love that this life is ever going to give you.

So I opened my mouth and the words tumbled out of me. "Come by our room later," I said. "It's 316. Let's talk."

I could live without him, I thought. I could even excel without him—in my chosen career, as a mother. But I would never be *whole* without him.

Sam never really answered. He got up from our table and left us, and I didn't know if he was heading out for a night on the town in rollicking old Lancaster County, Pennsylvania, or if he was going back to his seagull-sound room at our hotel to dwell on what I'd suggested. I really couldn't form a coherent opinion either way. My stomach was rolling.

I paid the tab. He'd left it for me again. Did that mean anything?

We went back to our room and I tucked Chloe in. She wanted to wait up for Sam.

"He'll be around all day tomorrow," I assured her.

She scowled at me. "Are you sure?"

Actually, I wasn't. For all I knew, he had already checked out and was running for his emotional life again. "No," I said honestly. "But waiting up for him isn't going to make him come here any faster."

Too bad I couldn't heed my own advice. Chloe finally fell asleep at half past ten. At midnight, I broke down and called the front desk, despising myself for the weakness.

"Do you have a Sam Case registered?" I asked. I knew she was going to tell me he had checked out tonight.

"Room 412," she said instead. "Would you like me to connect you?"

I hung up on her. There was no way on God's green earth that I was going to call his room. I'd just wanted to know if he was still in residence.

Now I knew that he was. Theoretically, anyway—unless he had bolted without checking out. And Sam was way too money-conscious to do that. But he hadn't come by, hadn't taken me up on my offer. I was letting the meaning of that seep in on me when I heard his knock at the door.

I shot up from the bed where I'd been sitting. I knew it had to be him. Who else would be knocking on the door to my room after midnight? And that was the second time since I had known him that I was terrified. The first had come in the Tropicana's bathroom. What was it with me and hotel rooms?

If he had come here to say goodbye, then the rest of my life was a yawning chasm.

I opened the door. He was standing there with that lock of dark hair falling over his forehead. He had one shoulder tucked nonchalantly against the doorjamb. But I noticed that his hands were fisted inside his jeans pockets.

Okay, I thought, okay. So we were both swallowing our pride and putting our whole hearts on the line here.

Was that good...or bad?

"Got scotch?" Sam asked. Like we had never parted. Like we had never loved. Like he might have said months and months ago before we entered into our arrangement.

"We're in Amish Country," I replied, like he had never run from me. "Think about it."

"They call one of their towns Intercourse. Intercourse and scotch can go together," he observed.

I gulped in air and went for more emotional honesty. In for a penny, I thought, in for a pound. It's always been one of my favorite sayings. "You can have one," I said. "Not the other."

His eyes flared. I was very sure they flared.

"Arrangement sex?" he asked quickly.

"*And* make-up sex," I said. "This is a two-for-one special." I couldn't live without him, I thought, so I would have to live with him on his terms if I had to. If I had no other choice and if he let me.

But then he said, "We need to talk."

I nodded jerkily. I backed off from the door and he came inside.

I don't know what I expected him to say, but his next words floored me. They were almost exactly the same ones I had used that morning when I had told Jenny that he would never voluntarily wander down a primrose path again.

"You blindsided me that day," he said.

I shrugged and it felt brittle. "I was past the point of blasting."

He nodded as though my words made all the sense in the world.

"If it helps," I said, "I did it to Mill first."

He studied my face. "What are the odds that it was all just a case of female hormones?"

I had to be honest. I could crawl, but damn it, I would crawl honestly. "Slim to none. The rules were really bothering me."

"Then I guess now I need to know just what loving me entails."

This had to go on record as being one of the oddest conversations I'd ever had—but then, when were arrangements ever par for the course romantically speaking? It occurred to me that Sam and I just weren't normal. Then again, we're lawyers. At least, *I'm* a lawyer. He's more like a world-class actor with a law degree. And he certainly has schmoozing down to an art.

Given all that, I decided to stick with the basics. "I hated your rules from the first time I heard them," I admitted.

"They were good rules," he said indignantly.

"For keeping the love out, and the distance in," I pointed out.

"They helped us avoid all those relationship complications."

"Sam, we never *had* relationship complications until we had rules." Sometimes, when you least expect you're going to, you find all the words. Sometimes letting your heart speak is the only way to go. And that said it all. I knew it and, watching his face, I knew he knew it, too.

"Would it help any if I told you that I'll never take up with another man and leave you?" I finally asked to his silence. "Would you believe me?"

"You're Mandy," he said. "So, yeah, I would." Then he fell deep into thought. "If I say this all back to you, then I'm going to have to marry you," he said suddenly. "This I-love-you business."

I'd lied to Grace when I told her that I never wanted to marry him. Because in that moment I realized that I could never be happy with anything else. I needed him beside me when I woke up in the morning. I needed him with me when I drifted off to sleep at night. And when you have a child, there's only one way to do all that properly. You have to commit. You have to show that child the meaning and the scope of true love. So I risked losing him for a second time.

"It's the only way I can love you the way I want to," I said. Then my heart skipped, because emotional honesty is really very hard on the heart.

"Can I think about it?" Sam asked.

"Not if you want to stay here tonight."

"I want that a lot."

Everything inside me expanded. Air filled all those places in my chest that it hadn't quite been able to reach before. But I waited because I sensed there was more.

"What are the odds that we can find a justice-of-the-peace tonight in Intercourse, Pennsylvania?" he asked.

I breathed again. Deeper. "Slim to none. They go to sleep early around these parts."

"Would it cut it if I got down on my knees and proposed?"

I lost my air again. "It might."

And he did it. He did it right then. By the side of the bed I was sitting on, with Chloe curled up snoring behind me.

"I've always loved you," he said. "It was why I held off so long on suggesting our arrangement. I knew if we went there, I was done. And that scared the hell out of me."

"Is that a compliment?" I honestly wasn't sure.

"I loved you so much I never even minded when you turned the channel away from *Star Trek.*"

"Sam, you never let me do that."

"But I watched *Bewitched* with you."

"Under duress."

"Still. That's love."

Well, I thought, it was certainly close. And the bottom line was that I couldn't go on without him. "Good answer," I said.

"So can I stay here tonight?" he asked.

"Not with my daughter in the same room."

"I'll share my toothbrush," he offered.

"I brought my own."

"What if there's an emergency? Don't you want to know that mine is available?"

I grinned. "Yeah. I might even kiss you before I use it."

"Now *that's* commitment."

"Okay," I said. "You can marry me." I leaned forward and kissed him to seal it. My best friend, my everything.

Then we woke Chloe up to tell her. It was a win-win deal. She got Mill...and Sam. And Sam and I got each other.

* * * * *

*Watch for Beverly Bird's next
exciting Silhouette Intimate Moments
title in Fall 2003.*